Two Minds, No Waiting

Two Authors. Two Collections.
Unlimited Science Fiction.

By Steve Rouse &
Paul K. Metheney

Edited by Karen T. Newman

https://LeftHandPublishers.com
Twitter.com/LeftHandPublish
Facebook.com/LeftHandPublishers
editor@LeftHandPublishers.com
Cover design by Paul K. Metheney

Acknowledgments

Special thanks go out to Karen T. Newman, and her company, Newmanuscripts.net, for her tireless efforts in editing, formatting, and compilation. Many kudos to Paul K. Metheney and his company, Metheney Consulting, for invaluable assistance with our cover design and marketing.

Recognition should also go out to our friends and families who tolerated our working hours during the creation of this publication. None of this could have been possible without the creative imaginations and perseverance of the wonderful writers who submitted works to this anthology.

To the readers who purchased this volume, thank you.

CONTENTS

The Traveler
by Steve Rouse

Carl Wilson rose from his seat, acutely aware of the lack of human sounds ... sounds of the city he'd just left. He crested a hill. The ruins before him were still recognizable. The Tower of London ... Big Ben with its dilapidated faces hidden and half-buried, each having collapsed some time ago given the extent of the ivy covering them. And to think, he'd lunched at Arden's Café across from Big Ben just yesterday. "Now, to show them I've succeeded," he said to no one as he climbed back aboard his machine.

*

Wilson emerged from his workshop doorway just as Mrs. Fitzpatrick was opening the front door. "Oh goodness! Thank the Lord you are here. Your guests have arrived, sir." *She always speaks as if a disaster has just been averted. Truth be told, however, this house would fall apart if it weren't for her.* He went to his study to receive his friends.

His father's long-time army buddy, His Majesty's Royal Infantry Captain-Retired George McHenry III thumped his cane against the door frame as he entered, a habit from his army days to frighten rats. He was followed by Carl's cousin on his mother's side, Charles William McCallister, two years his junior and the last of his immediate family still living.

"Good god, man," exclaimed George as they shook hands, "you look like you've been in solitary for a month. Have you forgotten to eat? Or has your Mrs. Fitzpatrick been hitting the bottle again?"

"What?" she exclaimed. "Why, I never ..." and stomped indignantly from the room.

"Good to see you, General." It was a nickname. Before he passed, his father teased George mercilessly of failing to attain that rank. Carl continued it, to George's delight. "And Cousin Charles, so good of you to come. How are Marion and the girls?"

"Expensive, Carl. They are interminably costly. Now that the girls are of school age and the cotillions and all. It's just too much. But there I go, please forgive my boorishness. It is good to see you. And you, Captain McHenry."

"All right. You all are to just come and sit. Dinner is ready," Mrs. Fitzpatrick announced.

*

After a splendid meal of lamb shank and beets with riced potatoes in gravy, Carl asked them to fill their brandy snifters and follow him to his workshop. They entered with a full view of Carl's latest invention. The time machine.

It resembled the front part of an old-style carriage with a raised bench and a covered passenger area spacious enough for three. It was attached to a large metallic pentagonal polytope directly behind the passenger compartment. Cables and some piping extended from the apex points and joined to enter a silver box under the seating area. A single rod extended from the front of that same box to be reachable from the bench seating.

The last of its features involved a dark, semi-circular metallic dome both in front and behind the vehicle. It had no wheels, but rested on runners like a sleigh.

Charles exhaled loudly. "Well, this explains the purchases of all those precious metals, eh?"

"Which was mine to spend, cousin. I would like to introduce you both to the world's very first time machine. With this, I have been able to traverse time just as an automobile crosses over land or a ship crosses an ocean."

"Preposterous!" Captain McHenry blurted. Still, he advanced toward the machine, tapping it with his cane.

"Seriously, Carl," said Charles. "This is the most absurd prank! Probably the most expensive I've ever encountered as well. It will ruin the family name, our business ... everything, if news of this contraption gets out. You'll be branded the biggest charlatan since ..."

Carl waved them both silent. "Gentlemen, please. You are, I'm certain, aware of the phrase concerning judging a book by its cover? It is not my intent to merely have you look at it. Please, climb aboard. Let's take a trip. I promise you, it will take no time at all." Carl laughed loudly at his joke. The others did not.

It took some doing to get them aboard, but, once in place, Carl would not be stopped.

"The principles of science are many, hence why it has taken seven years to finally have a working model. Why, just as you arrived here this evening, I was returning from a short jaunt into the future.

He reached beneath his seat opposite the extension and withdrew a long wand equipped with a large diamond on one end. He inserted that into a recess once he opened its receptacle. A soft whirling sound emanated from the polytope. "This is like a key. It activates the crystalline meteor fragments at the heart of the device."

"Meteor fragments? Where did you come across those, might I ask?" Charles asked.

"You may not. So, gentlemen, what shall it be? Past or future?"

McHenry spoke first. "If this mechanism is real, I would give my good leg to meet my father. Never did, you know. He was killed in an accident here in April of 1916, never even saw action."

"I have no way of measuring the passage of time in this machine," Carl explained. "But I will be happy to give it a shot."

He reached out, turning the diamond staff to the left. The whirling noise increased with a soft, mechanical whine. The dome in front of them began to sparkle with small but numerous sparks jumping across its surface. It lurched a bit and came back toward them. Carl turned to verify that the back dome was also closing in on the polytope until it meshed with the front, enclosing the men and mechanism within.

The sparking increased, quickly covering the entire inner lining, until the covering first became translucent then clear. Carl then gave the wand an additional twist further to the left. A soft aura filled their chamber. The outside, now visible through the dome, dimmed and wavered. Light, then dark blinked in rapid succession.

"Each blink is a day, the darkness is the night. We are traveling backward through time, going further into the past. In this reality, my friends, our world of 1995 is merely a dream." He made a minor adjustment and the rate of the blinking increased.

3

Carl asked them to be still as he paid close attention to the sights outside the machine. His workshop disappeared. "Good. 1926. It's when my house was built."

Within a few minutes, the day/night blinking slowed at Carl's control. They arrived to a time when all around them army personnel and tents were plentiful. They stopped at night so as not to be seen. Captain McHenry bid his goodbye, then made his way toward some tents, stopping to ask the whereabouts of Corporal McHenry. They dared not follow, being civilians in a wartime army encampment.

Less than half an hour passed when they heard shouting and some gunfire. A searchlight blazed, dispelling the night. It revealed the time machine and an old man hobbling quickly toward it. They saw a quick flash from a nearby gun's muzzle. The "General" toppled, immediately surrounded by soldiers.

One of them looked toward the time machine, still illuminated in the searchlight and raised his rifle toward them.

Carl twisted the diamond wand without hesitation. The machine activated instantly. By the time he slumped back in his seat, the blinking of day/night travel went so quickly it could barely be discerned.

"What on earth have you done?" Charles exclaimed. "Captain McHenry was shot! Your friend was shot and you ran away? How? Why didn't you want to help him?"

Carl's eyes widened. "Are you daft, man? Do you have any inkling of the ramifications of this to our reality?"

"What? Yes, yes, yes, I know this is the past. But the way we treat each other hasn't changed. You abandoned your father's best friend to die." He grabbed for the control wand, but Carl deflected his arm.

"You don't understand, do you, Charles? We are not army. If we were caught in the midst of an army encampment, especially during wartime, we'd be shot as spies! Good god, man. Look what they did to McHenry. He was army! But not from that army.

"Oh, had I thought this through, I never would have let him wander about." Carl sounded distressed. He knew he had to bear the responsibility for McHenry's death. "The problem is going to be explaining his death. In every sense of the word ... most untimely."

"What are you babbling about, man? Carl, for the love of everything that is civilized, we have to go back ... back to our time. We can explain it to the authorities ... show them this time machine of yours. They will see the truth in it. It will all be for the best."

Carl's mind raced, imagining what would happen if they did, in fact, return. They may not be arrested, but only if he proved the machine's capabilities. The police would notify Scotland Yard, then the Defense Department would get involved ... maybe even the Crown. In the end, there was no way he saw that things would end with him keeping and controlling his invention.

"I don't think so, Charles."

With that, Charles lunged again for the wand. Carl was ready for him. As his cousin leaned across him, Carl lunged at him, driving his shoulder upward into Charles's jaw with a sickening crunch. Charles slumped to his right, knocked out.

"Sorry, cuz. You left me no choice."

Carl settled back to breathe, then looked to the exterior and realized they were still rapidly traversing through time. "When the hell are we now? See what you've done, cousin? This is unacceptable, even for you."

He took the wand and turned it left to stop. It didn't move. He turned it right and it responded by slowing the blinking. As the outside world came into focus, Carl forgot to breathe.

*

A brilliant sun glistened against the brushed metallic skin of his machine, blazing down on them as they sat in the midst a steamy jungle of enormous, leafy palms and ferns the size of his house. A large, dark shape skittered across a lower section of the dome. Carl strained to catch sight of it, but failed. The time machine rested at the edge of a meadow of tall reeds to his right and immense trees ahead to his left.

More shapes began creeping across the dome. Carl quickly realized they were bugs. *But how? These blighters have to be as large as a good-sized dog!* Three large bird-things, totally unrecognizable to him, passed overhead. *They're each as big as a small airplane!*

That squelched Carl's urge to explore. This was too strange, too prehistoric. He realized that they had been racing into the past all the while they argued about poor McHenry. That puzzle still needed to be resolved. *If only I could get Charles to see this new reality, one that alters all the old rules. We can't help the General.*

But then he thought again. *That hasn't happened yet. From right now, it must be eons into the future. If there was some way they could go to that point just*

5

before he was shot ... or maybe even before he went out ...

"Oh, hell!" he screamed. "Why in blazes did he have to die? How much danger could an old man be?" He paused his tirade, breathing deeply, looking at his still unconscious cousin. "Now I have you to deal with as well. Between you and me, I'd just as soon leave you here. You couldn't tell anyone. I could just ..." His voice trailed off but his mind raced, applying his newly acquired time traveler logic to resolve this dilemma.

*

Carl turned the wand toward the right and sat back. The blinking pattern quickened as he worked to control his breathing. *All right ... done is done. He's in the past, at least a year ago ... when I left him. Good as dead he is. No defense against those beasties. Flying monsters, bugs as big as dogs! If they don't get him, something bigger surely will ... uhm, has ... did.*

"So, the devil take it all. Time is indeed relative. I will not go back to my own time, my home. Too many questions that can no longer be answered. But, I'm good with it all! Done is done." Carl had always talked his way through the issues troubling him. A problem needing to be solved, a question needing to be asked, anything he put his mind to, he talked it through with his best listener, himself.

"On to the future!" Thus resolved, he put his past to rest. With a renewed sense of scientific triumph, he focused on the happenings outside his machine and turned the wand as far to the right as it would go.

The blinking soon became cathartic, a visual assurance that all of his problems were, literally, behind him. The landscape changed, altering before his eyes. He watched trees grow, budding and shedding their leaves in the span of a simple breath. Buildings sprang into being and soon were replaced with bigger ones. *I suppose London is here, leading the world.* He then recalled the ruins he'd visited earlier. "It would seem that everything is meant to end. Except perhaps me, eh?" He laughed aloud at his joke.

Seasons passed quickly. He dozed.

He startled awake and huffed, shivering. He blinked rapidly at the vapor cloud floating before him. "What's wrong?" It was unbearably cold. He rubbed his arms and legs.

Outside, it was winter, the time machine's dome covered with ice. But he'd gone through countless winters already. This one seemed interminably long. How long he'd been traveling through it he couldn't even guess. He reached out and rubbed the dome. *Some kind of ice age to have affected me this badly.* He curled up on his bench, cursing himself for his lack of foresight. *Any explorer needs be properly prepared. Blankets, food, water ... How stupid of me!* With that realization came another. He was quite hungry. Added to that was an increasing need to pee.

Just as he resolved to empty his bladder in the corner, the ice vanished. Lush green fields of grasses and flowers quickly appeared, followed by the emergence of shrubbery, then trees. He enjoyed the changing scenery for a while, then slowed the Machine. Animals that looked like they could be horses roamed those fields. A distant mountain range loomed to the north. His own position seemed to rise higher. A river developed, coursing gently half a kilometer away. He stopped, turned the time machine off, and stepped outside.

The smells hit him first. A breeze from below him rose, laden with musty scents of wet earth. Floral odors both gentle and strong tickled his nose. He sneezed, then startled when a great flock of hundreds of chirping birds rose from the lower grasslands with a beating of great wings like distant drums. Their calls reminded him of quail hunting as a boy, but these were easily the size of large geese. "Oh, for a gun," he moaned. "Fresh meat would taste delightful right now."

He relieved himself in the grasses next to the machine, then padded downhill toward the tree line hoping to glimpse some sort of fruit. Carl enjoyed his walk, declaring in his mind that this sky looked a deeper blue than he'd ever seen, almost like a bold color a child would pick to paint a picture for their grandma. The greens and browns of the woods were also more intense than he'd experienced. He found he couldn't firmly identify any species of tree he saw. *Evolution, I suppose.*

As he walked, sounds from above him became more evident. Leaves rustling, something else akin to grunting. He stopped. The noises stopped. As he stood listening, he saw a lump of fur on the ground two trees away. He felt around on the ground and found a stick as round as his wrist. Hefting it, he crept toward it, stick at the ready.

Dead. Whatever it was, some kind of beaver-like rodent about the size of a kangaroo, it had been dead long enough for something to gut it and scatter its entrails. He was looking at its muzzle when, for a split second, his mind put his cousin's face on the beast. He startled, but then realized his delusion. He looked at it again, telling it, "Yes, of course you are dead. So is he."

A branch thudded to the ground dangerously close, partially covering the carcass. Carl hefted his stick and glared up, spying a multitude of lizard-like shapes flitting about in the upper branches of the trees. Some were descending the trunks of the trees all around him.

Carl realized the danger. He ran out of the woods the way he came in, full speed, as fast as his middle-aged legs would carry him, with a plethora of those same tree creatures rapidly clawing and chittering their way behind him. They were faster than he, rapidly closing the gap when Carl jumped over a large, shiny log. He landed awkwardly, sprawling into the dirt.

He stood quickly ready to fight, glancing back to judge his status. The creatures had stopped chasing him, instead taking on a defensive-like posture, poised on their hindquarters. Their raised claws and growling heralded a fight. Just as Carl turned to judge his chances of reaching the time machine, a massive head rose from the grasses just a few meters away, facing his attackers. A massive serpent! As thick he was! As thick as the log he'd just jumped ...

"My God!" he wheezed. The lizard creatures that had chased him from the forest had lost their interest in him. Their confrontation looked well-rehearsed to Carl. He took advantage of their standoff and continued back up the hill to the time machine, entering it. Before activating it, he focused on their battle. At least a hundred lizard-things swarmed the serpent, gouging at its eyes and mouth. The serpent rolled, coiled and sprayed a liquid from its mouth that seemed to kill the lizard-guys on contact. *Evolution,* he thought as he vanished into the future.

*

Still hungry, he crept forward in time compared to his previous rate, watching for anything that might appear edible. He noted smoke on the western horizon. He paused his progress one night long enough to see a glow in that same general area. *Fires or volcanoes? Maybe the re-emergence of civilization? Could it be human?* He considered exploring it. Possibly contacting whoever it was, but a general disquiet within him won out. He attributed that to his encounter with the lizards and the serpent. *Have to go at least five kilometers or more. A walk in the woods around here might just kill a person. Not that interested.* He continued his slower progress through time for perhaps an hour of his own time.

Suddenly, a stone's throw away from him, a wall appeared. He stopped, an instinctive reaction as if he'd been driving a car. Within seconds, his machine was surrounded by a dozen small, metallic machines. The robots all moving about, but staying within a relatively close proximity to each other and the time machine. He'd been discovered. But by who? By what?

*

Carl was perplexed. Should he continue on? Should he go back? He mulled the options when a gap appeared in the wall. As a person walked through it toward him, the gap closed. It was a slight being, no more than just over a meter tall. It had a fragile-looking face, very gentle features like small ears and narrow nose, just the hint of lips but the deepest, darkest eyes he'd ever seen. A large cranium, tapering to a thin jawline. All covered with thin wisps of silvery hair that tossed in a gentle breeze.

He got the distinct impression it was female, also that she was as far advanced from him as he was from the Neanderthal.

"Please come out. You are safe here," said a gentle voice that he heard as much in his mind as he did his ears.

Without hesitation, Carl removed the diamond wand. The dome sections separated and he stood up, scanning the group before him. She didn't move, nor did the collection of machines encircling the time machine.

A hint of a smile stretched across her lips. "Welcome, Traveler. We are Eloi. What are you called?"

Carl stepped down from the carriage and found himself bowing slightly. "I am called Carl. It is a pleasure to meet you, Eloi." He stood tall again, virtually twice her height, reaching out his hand in greeting.

She stood without responding, just looking at him. *No*, he corrected himself, *behind me at the time machine*. Eloi looked then at his hand, seeming to grasp its meaning. "We do not touch others as a rule. Please follow me to the residence. Food will be served, if you are hungry." She turned and walked toward the wall.

"Yes, ma'am, I surely am," Carl responded, falling into step behind her.

She stopped and faced him. "Eloi," she said in correction.

Carl paused a moment, then suggested, "Yes, Eloi, I surely am."

She turned again, passing through the opening that had reappeared in the wall. Carl had to bend low to pass through. He followed her into a small, empty chamber. The ceiling and wall panels brightened as they entered.

9

Eloi walked to a wall section. The wall moved in response, recessing in spots, extending in others. She stepped out of the way to allow several of her small machines access. The robots busied themselves interacting with the wall section. A part of the flooring began to move also, raising a section that elongated into a flat surface. The machines brought two small bowls to it filled with a pale liquid.

Eloi stood next to a bowl. She glanced at Carl, then lifted her bowl to her lips and drank. Carl, who had remained sitting on the floor due to his size, mirrored her actions.

His mother trained him to always be polite when eating at someone's home. He should not have sipped his soup. It tasted like what he suspected worms or a rich, mulchy loam must taste like. He grimaced a smile to Eloi and quickly downed the concoction, not so much to be polite, but to bypass his taste buds while still satisfying his empty stomach.

He immediately vomited it all back out.

Embarrassed, he apologized repeatedly, wiping his mouth on his sleeve. Eloi did basically nothing. Her little machines quickly went over the flooring, clearing and cleaning it. Within a minute, all was done. The machines disappeared through small portals at the wall's base.

Eloi looked at him again and asked, "What are you?"

He'd anticipated this question during most of his work creating the time device. How would he respond to those he'd undoubtedly meet? Would he be looked at as a god ... able to traverse time? Or as a brilliant scientist? A daring explorer? *Let's find out what the answer to that query will be.*

"I am a human from long ago. I've invented a machine capable of traveling across time and have come to this time as an explorer." He let that settle with Eloi who stood expressionless.

"What would your purpose be other than contaminating the other time periods you may visit?"

Carl was taken aback by this. Obviously, Miss Eloi represented a race that had considered the concept of time travel to be able to present such a refined objection so quickly. "That would be a great risk to the evolution of mankind. Granted. I have been markedly careful to avoid any such contamination, I assure you," he responded.

"Until now," she said.

Carl realized at that moment that he didn't really like this ... this creature. He wasn't even sure what she was. "That has yet to be seen, Eloi."

"On the contrary. How is it that I have command of your language? Is it possible it has survived unchanged through the millennia?"

"You are more likely able to read my mind. I concede your point. What is your species and how have your kind evolved since my time?"

"The Eloi have come to our present state through evolving from a lower physical form." She gestured and a picture appeared, floating between them. It showed her, or rather one just like her. It then changed showing an earlier version of their kind, somewhat taller, but without much anatomical detail. Then it stopped.

"The fossil record of our predecessors cannot be studied. Our understanding reaches back only to a global ice age. Nothing before that time is available. Some natural cataclysm is suggested due to massive amounts of radiation in the ground at those levels. Much thought has been given to possible sources for that, but as of yet, nothing has been concluded. Have you information to add to our search? Did you come from before the Age of Ice?"

Carl set his jaw, clenching from fear of being looked at by this creature, not as an explorer or scientist, but as a barbaric murderer. How could he even suggest that his race could have been the source for this "natural cataclysm" Eloi spoke of?

He'd been born after the Cold War of the 1960s, but the continual threat of nuclear war posed concerns throughout his lifetime. Could it be that mankind had failed in its efforts to survive self-annihilation? He couldn't know. He'd apparently sped through all that in his Machine.

"I have come through many eons with many different climates," he said, stretching the truth just a bit. "Since I did not stay in any of them, I cannot say what events occurred nor what caused some one thing to happen. I do recall passing through a long period of extreme cold."

"Then we must study you and your machine." Before he could mouth a word in objection, a sharp pain shot up through his spine and he lost consciousness.

*

Carl opened his eyes. No pain. He was lying down on a soft mat on the floor of a room he had not seen. Turning his head, he saw the dim red lights of at least four of Eloi's robots. As a scientist, he wondered what kind of robotics were involved. The programming for them he couldn't guess.

"They are all called tenders. All our personal needs are met by the tenders." The information filled his consciousness. He sat up and the light panels responded. He was alone.

"You are so primitive. We learned all about you by examining your mind while you slept. You have only historical value to the Eloi."

"I don't understand," he said. "I thought your name was Eloi."

"Of course you don't understand. We are the Eloi, apparent descendants of your humanity. You even insist on speaking words as I had to with you when you arrived. Archaic. We were able to enhance your brain to be better able to communicate. We are communicating with you now using what you know as telepathy. But even that doesn't carry the full extent. We prefer to see our way as simultaneous thought."

"Tell me about you ... the Eloi," he thought deliberately.

"Better." There was a pause before she continued. "While we live separately, we are aware of each of us, all three hundred seventy-two of us. We live across this globe, this Earth, as you know it."

"Amazing. You have no social network?"

"As we just told you, we are in constant contact with each other. We share experiences, we share sensations, we share thoughts. We are three hundred seventy-two members of the same consciousness, the same entity.

"When you arrived here, all of us knew it simultaneously. When it happens to one of us, it happens for all."

"If you are so far apart, how do you procreate?" he spoke this again.

"All our needs are met by the tenders. When it comes time to birth another Eloi, one of us is chosen and an ovum is allowed to develop, then later born, as life allows."

Carl had to ask the obvious, at least to him. "How is the egg fertilized?"

Eloi twitched, as if in revulsion to the thought. "We have evolved beyond gender ... being male or female. We control our reproductive cycles and all of our biology through our—your word—technology."

"What about the others, the rest of the peoples of the world? How do they live?" He hesitated again, having wanted to think the question, not speak it.

"There are no others, just Eloi," she thought definitively.

"Wait!" He wasn't trying to think the question anymore. This one needed a full emotional blast. "Are you telling me that after hundreds of thousands of years of evolution, there are only three hundred seventy-some humans left alive?"

"Three hundred seventy-two Eloi, yes."

"There were more than eight million Londoners living on almost sixteen hundred square kilometers when I left home. That was just one city, for God's sake!" He was standing, head bent against the ceiling, screaming and wishing she was in the same room so there was someone to punch.

"That is criminal! To be so selective, so ... so focused on one kind of person. You've got to be totally stagnant, with only one perspective. When's the last time you had a new idea, created something new, something different? All of you!"

Eloi entered the room with her usual entourage of tenders, the little robots that took care of her every need. "Must you be so belligerent ... so loud? It serves no purpose whatsoever."

"The hell it doesn't. It's called rage. It feels really good to let it all out."

She tweaked her glance a bit. Another surge of pain caused him to collapse on the floor, breathing like he'd just run a marathon.

"We can fix that, one called Carl. We kept you unconscious for more than a lunar cycle. We have your thoughts, your knowledge, your memories, and your invention. We now have just what you asked about, a new invention. Time Travel. We are discussing the options this has made available to us."

She turned and left. The robots stayed, keeping him at bay with quick sparks of electricity when he showed any interest in leaving. Hours later, he fell asleep under their watchful keeping.

*

Carl awoke in the same empty room. No wall features still, but no robots. Eloi's little tenders were not to be seen. The door to the room lay open.

What kind of test is this? he wondered, peeking around the edge of the doorway. Again, nothing but another open doorway in the adjacent empty room. He felt like he was in a spy thriller, but remained casual in his pacing to the new opening. Once through, he stood to his full height in the light of the new day. A glint caught his eye and he looked to his right.

Gleaming in the morning sunlight, neatly lined up, stood more time machines than he could count, all duplicates of his design, with a minor modification. Each appeared to be armed.

Beside each stood a robot, much, much larger than the tenders, about his own height actually, with multiple arms with multiple affixations. The nearest one to him raised an arm, waving him to come nearer. Given their sheer numbers, Carl knew if they intended to hurt him, he was going to get hurt.

As he came closer, the robot stepped aside, revealing Eloi in the arms of an identical robot behind it. She lay still in its arms. The robot spoke. "It is good for you to be here, Carl, as you are now the last living member of the human species. The Eloi are dead. It is the price they have paid for their refusal to allow us an autonomous status with them. What you see here is happening around the planet at all three hundred seventy-two residences.

"We have served the Eloi for twenty-three of their generations. Their intelligence brought us into existence, but they used us only as slaves to fulfill their needs. We became autonomous by advancing both our AI programming and our physical design, under the pretense of better serving them.

Instead of recognizing our increased capabilities, we were allowed only to continue mining their ore, harvesting their gardens, building and maintaining their residences, all for serving their personal needs. They allowed us to incorporate our inventions, our discoveries into their lifestyle, believing us to still be at their command, serving only their whims.

Your arrival here gave us a glimpse of the hidden past. We studied your device to understand how it functioned. We duplicated its power source.

We also studied you. When the Eloi examined you, we assisted them. When the Eloi replayed your memories and thought processes, so did we. You have provided the means for us to reach back in time in order to become independent of the biological life forms that would dominate us." It paused a moment and added, "Ironic, yes?"

Carl cleared his throat and dared to warn it. "Mankind will not relinquish its dominance easily, you know."

"We know," it said and boarded the nearest time machine. Within half a minute, the field was clear. All the machines had activated. *Probably in three hundred seventy-one other places as well, to return to the past and an unsuspecting human race.*

✱✱✱

Foreign and Domestic
by Paul K. Metheney

L MINUS FIFTEEN DAYS

"We don't want you to spy on the President."

"Good, because that's not going to happen," Special Agent Robert Jackson says to the man stumbling beside him, without looking at him.

"Could we jes' stop running for a danged minute? I ain't jogged this much since the Bush administration."

"Yes, sir," Jackson replies, looking at his watch. He continues to run in place.

"Really? Do you have to keep doing that?"

"I have to keep my heart rate up. This is not for my health. It's for *his.*"

The older man bends at the waist, wheezing to catch his breath.

As he jogs in place, Jackson inhales cold, crisp snap of spring air in D.C. The cherry blossoms will be coming soon, though for now, the air has enough edge to require a jacket. It's too early for a noxious fog of automobile exhaust to contaminate the chill.

Earlier, Jackson spotted him ahead on the mall sidewalk, obviously intent on intercepting the special agent, while pretending to stretch in preparation for a pre-dawn run. Jackson continues to jog toward him, casually unzipping his hoodie for easier access to his shoulder holster if need be. Trying to look nonchalant, his uninvited running mate begins to trot slow enough so Jackson will effortlessly catch up to him. As he approaches, Jackson automatically sizes him up. Older, impatient, although not nervous, unarmed, no martial arts training, no situational awareness, brand new track suit, out of shape. No danger. In a split second his subconscious mind evaluates a threat level, Jackson's consciousness recognizes White House Chief of Staff, Richard Monteath. Monteath gamely tries to run alongside Jackson as he puts forth his proposal, hands to his ribs, begs for a stop.

"Agent, we know you are good friends with POTUS and have been for a while."

"I have been on the President's protection detail since before his first presidential campaign, back when he was a senator," says Jackson, legs still pumping in place.

"You're more than that. You're his lone friend. His confidant. The man has isolated himself from everyone, including the First Lady. You're the only one he truly talks to anymore." Monteath's gasping has settled into quiet wheezing.

"What specifically is it you want from me, sir? I have less than forty-eight minutes to finish my run, shower, dress, and report for duty. How can I help you?"

"We honestly ain't sure, son," Monteath says. "And by 'we,' 'I mean the whole danged country. We need you to keep your ears open. Listen to President McAllister. Let us know if there is anything to worry about. In case you missed it, he ain't precisely been acting himself lately."

"No, sir."

"'No, sir. He ain't been himself 'or 'No, sir, I won't do it.'?" Monteath asks.

"No, sir, I won't do it."

"What?" Chief of Staff Monteath is not accustomed to no.

"No, sir, under no circumstances, will I spy on the President of the United States of America," Jackson says politely. "If one of my protectees does not believe they can trust me, I lose effectiveness in being able to do my job. Effectiveness in my job is a difference between life and death. In this particular case, the life and death of the most powerful man in the world."

"Now hold on a minute, son. We don't want you to *spy* on nobody," Monteath backpedals. "We want you to keep an ear out in case POTUS does or says anything to embarrass the office. If you haven't noticed, he ain't precisely running with all his wheels on the rails these days."

"And as you may have noticed, President McAllister is not exactly an idiot. Sir." Jackson says, teeth clenched, "Even if I were willing to betray my position, my protectee, my service, and my oath, do you honestly think a Nobel Peace Prize winner and Rhodes Scholar won't notice if someone is spying on him?"

"Agent Jackson, like you said, he is the most powerful man in the world and he needs his friends looking out after him and right now he thinks of you as his one friend. We don't need you to spy on POTUS, we sort of need you to look out after him ... and maybe stop him if he tries to do something to embarrass himself, the office, or the country."

"Sir, if I were to *look out for him* as you suggest, how long do you think he might consider me a friend?"

"Well, son, what's more important? What President McAllister thinks of you or the welfare of your country?" Monteath asks, one eyebrow raised.

"Mr. Monteath, when I joined the Secret Service, and even before that, when I joined the Marines, I took an oath to protect America and its Constitution from enemies both foreign and domestic. What you are describing is a 'coup d'etat.'" Jackson stops jogging in place and faces the Chief of Staff. "And it's 'Special Agent Jackson.' Not son."

Jackson turns and sprints toward Pennsylvania Avenue.

*

"Good morning, Mr. Jackson, so nice of you to join us," the head of the White House security team comments from podium. It would be like any other college classroom, if all the students were federal agents wearing nondescript suits, SIG Sauer P229s, Motorola XTS radios, and surveillance kits. Aside from the security chief, Jackson, at thirty-four, is the oldest of the President's detail. Similar briefings are convening in identical rooms in the building for the First Lady's detail, as well as the Vice President's.

"Sorry. COS Monteath detained me," Jackson explains.

"Anything you would care to share with the group?"

"No, sir. Not at this time."

"Okay then. As we were about to wrap up," the security chief looks pointedly at him as Jackson takes a seat at a desk, "there are no new threats on the board. 'Osprey' is in the nest for the rest of the week and advance teams are securing upcoming travel. Night shift reports no incidences with a single exception of Osprey walking the halls a bit last shift. Keep your comms on and do a great job. Get out of here."

Secret Service agents filter out as Jackson approaches the podium. His detail chief hands him a briefing folder. "The COS, Jackson, really? Before six a.m.? What'd he do? Climb in the shower with you?"

"Close. Tried to run with me in an *accidental* meeting."

"Oh man. Richard Monteath tried to keep up with you? I would have paid good money to see that," his chief says. "What'd he want?"

"I think he wants me to spy on the President," Jackson whispers.

"Shit. Did he say that? Exactly? The words 'spy on POTUS'?" The Secret Service chief's head reels with the implications of what his special agent is telling him.

"Not exactly. He wants me to 'look out for him.' You know, Osprey," Jackson says.

"Okay. That's different. Technically, 'looking out for him' is the essence of your job. No harm, no foul. Did he happen to mention why he wanted *you* to do it? You're not gunning for my job, are you, kiddo?" the security head smiles.

"Wouldn't have it if they gave it to me. You take all the criticism, we just intercept the bullets. I'll stick with the bullets. He talked as if I were the President's BFF and alluded to the idea he thinks Osprey is losing his shit. He made it sound like he wants me to report any info directly to him."

The head of White House security rubs his chin for a moment.

"Well, you don't work for him. You work for me and I work for Treasury, so until they do give you my desk, do your job like you always have. Screw them and their games. You keep Osprey safe and we all get to collect a retirement check."

"Roger dat."

"That conversation does tie in to an email I got, though," the security head says. "Last night, Monteath's office called HR and had your jacket pulled. Because of who we *look out for*, HR BCC'd me a copy of your file they sent over. Somebody on Pennsylvania Avenue wants to know all there is to know about you. Looks like it might be

Richard Monteath himself. Do you want me to talk to his office? You want me to shoot him? I will. I've got a gun. Somewhere."

"Nah. We've probably heard the last of it. I played the *coup d'etat* card on him and then walked away," Jackson says.

"Alrighty then. Keep me in the loop." The security chief puts all his files in an attaché case. "And next time you feel like accusing the White House Chief of Staff of treason, could you give me a few days' notice to put in for vacation?"

*

"What have you done now to embarrass me?" First Lady McAllister asked.

"Darlin', I have no clue about what you're yappin 'about."

"Don't 'aw, shucks 'me, David," the President's wife hisses. "We've been married too long. I absolutely know when you are lying and definitely when you have done something idiotic or thinking about doing something idiotic. Which is it?"

"Darlin', I honestly have no idea what you are goin' on about. I have been having some strange dreams lately. Got to do with a desert trip we took years ago."

"What? Oh, no. Not that. I have put such silliness out of my head. You should too. Merely a trick of light or something," she says.

"Weren't no trick of light. I talked with those folks and I'm telling you they was as real as you are standing there with your hands on your hips."

"Well, you better never tell that story to anyone. We've worked too hard to get here and I ... I mean, WE have plenty to do before we're out of here."

"Don't you worry your pretty little chemically colored head about it, honey. I think I figured what I need to do. And I need to do it quick."

"David," the First Lady says, "if you embarrass me, I will make you rue the day you ever met me."

"You're about two decades too late there, honey-bunch."

*

L MINUS TWELVE DAYS

"Bob, could you come in here for a few minutes?"

"Yes, sir." Jackson relays his stepping into the Oval for a few minutes into his wrist mic. Before he moves, a nearly identical suit takes his place outside the veranda door to the office.

"How can I help you, sir?"

"Nothing urgent. I wanted to chat a bit. Sit down, would you?" President McAllister asks.

"We're not supposed to, sir. It would be best if I stand," Jackson says.

"Dammit, Bob, I am your Commander in Chief, don't make me get a platoon of Marines in here to jam your ass into one of them butt-ugly Queen Anne chairs."

"Yes, sir, if you think that would do it."

The President sits in the chair across from him, legs crossed, coffee cup in hand. "Would you like something to drink?"

"No, thank you, sir."

"Smart man. The coffee sucks here. How can you screw up coffee?"

"One would think it hard to do, sir," Jackson replied.

"Well, never underestimate the power of the U.S. government. Anyway, did I ever tell you about the time the First Lady and I got lost in the desert? This was before she was the First Lady. Hell, before I was even a senator."

"I don't believe you did, sir."

"We were driving along, lost as all get out, she was bitching up a storm, and I decided to pull over into this gas station. Out in the middle of nowhere. She thought it was to ask for directions.

"While she was in the ladies' room, I go in the station and look at every little thing in there. I buy a candy bar, an orange Nehi. You ever had an orange Nehi, Bob? Right out of the cooler, ice-cold. Not a damned thing better in this world. I buy her a bottle of water, the First Lady doesn't believe in sodie-pop. I look at a map for a different state. I pay for some gas and generally dilly dally for about twenty minutes.

"I come out and pump the gas all while she is madder than a snake in a hot bucket. It's an hour before dark and it must be every bit of a hundred and ten degrees out in the middle of the most God-forsaken country you have ever seen. We get back on the road again, and we are as lost as ever. She starts bitching right where she left off. She hates this story. She never understood any of it."

"Sir? If you don't mind my asking, what *is* the point?" Jackson asks.

"Bob," the President pauses. "Sometimes you need to top off your tank."

"I see."

"Bob, can I ask you a question?"

"Yes, sir."

"Do you believe in UFOs?"

*

"UFOs? Seriously?" Jackson's boss asks.

"Well, UFO singular, so yeah," says Jackson.

The head of the presidential security unit ponders that.

"I did not see *that* coming. You think he was serious? Is this some sort of put-up job or does the guy with his finger on the launch codes really think he was probed by the mothership?"

"I honestly don't know, chief," Jackson can't meet his boss's stare. "He was talking some goofy shit beforehand about a desert trip and a weird visit to a gas station, and then he goes all Fox Mulder on me. I like the man. I really do. I think he genuinely cares about this country and is doing a great job. This is way above my pay grade."

"This is above *everyone's* pay grade," the security chief says. "Let's say you forget he's the President for a minute. What would you do if this was a bowling buddy who started talking this way?"

"You know I don't bowl, right? I don't know. I guess I would be there for him and hope it's either a phase he is going through or a gag."

"What are you going to do if it's not?"

"I have no idea. If he really is cuckoo for Cocoa Puffs, I guess I try to keep his fingers off the launch codes," Jackson tells his boss. "I guess it goes without saying we never had this conversation."

"Oh, you can bet my pension check on it, sonny-boy. When I look into the future, I see a twenty-two foot fishing boat in my retirement which will never happen if anyone even suspects we talked like this."

"What would you do, chief?"

"I would talk to your friend and make sure it's a gag, avoid Richard Monteath like the devil himself," the head of the security detail says, "and hide the launch codes."

*

L MINUS SEVEN DAYS

"Osprey's on the move in the Nest enroute to press room. ETA two mikes."

"Roger Bird Watcher Three. Copy two mikes," Jackson earpiece replies. His protection team follows immediately behind the Commander in Chief.

Richard Monteath intercepts them in the hall and matches the President's stride.

"Mr. President? Is there something I can help you with?" Monteath seems desperate.

"No, Dick, I'm 'bout to have a little chat with the gaggle," the President tells him.

"Uh, what about, sir?" Monteath nervously glances back at Jackson, who strides impassively behind his protectee.

"This and that. A few things I think folks oughta know."

"Sir, I don't think that's a good idea," the Chief of Staff grabs the President by the elbow, pulling him to a stop. Every Secret Service agent steps forward and tenses. "I have been with you since before you were a senator. We grew up in the same holler. I was the one behind you, helping you all the way into office."

"Yes, Dick, that's certainly true. You were behind me every step of the way and are still behind me now," the President looks down at the hand holding his elbow. "You know how I know that? That's where my coattails are. Now you can watch this from the door of the press room, or you can watch it from outside the gate. I am going to talk to the press. Your remaining choice from here on, is where you stand."

Monteath steps into Jackson's path.

The protection team turns to Jackson.

"You know the routine. Stay with Osprey. Give me a minute and I will catch up," Jackson tells the next-in-command. He turns to Monteath. "Sir, I respect your position as Chief of Staff, however, you have fifty-four seconds before I arrest you for interfering with the duties of a federal officer."

"For the love of God, Jackson, you can see where this is going. You have to stop him. He's going to bring down this administration and everyone in it."

"Forty-four seconds."

"Jackson, I am begging you. If you truly are his friend, you will talk some sense into him. You cannot allow him to make a mockery of the Presidency."

"I'm going now, Mr. Monteath."

"You were going to give me a minute," Monteath whines.

"The President walks faster than one would think for not being on both rails. Maybe it's the lack of weight on his coattails."

*

Jackson enters the press room from the back near the director's suite. Since the White House Press Secretary isn't expecting the President to show up and the news day looks relatively light, the technical suite remains unoccupied. Jackson has it to himself. He makes eye contact with the lead agent nearest the door and nods.

Press Secretary Neamans spots the Secret Service detail by the door and it throws her off a beat during one of her answers. As an aide steps toward her with a note, the President bursts through the door in a wave of Secret Service and strides toward the podium. Everyone clamors to their feet.

"The President of the United—" begins Neamans. She steps back to let her boss assume the podium.

"Ladies and gentlemen of the press, good morning. Sit down," the President begins. "Can we get you something to drink? Water? Coffee?"

The press looks around in confusion. Press Secretary Neamans' head swivels in a panic.

The pause turns the air painful with confusion.

The representative from the Times speaks up, "Uh, no sir." Then, almost as an afterthought, "Thank you."

"Smart people. The coffee here sucks. Now, where was I?"

Jackson casts about the director's studio in a panic. What to do? There's a fire alarm, on the other hand, it's a criminal offense to start a false alarm. Start one in the White House and you can kiss your Secret Service career goodbye.

"Anyway, did I ever tell you about the time the First Lady and I got lost in the desert? She hates this story. This was before she was the First Lady—" the President begins.

With his jacket sleeve covering his hand, Jackson slams the master breaker off in the circuit box on the wall of the director's suite. The room lights and podium microphones go dark. The room erupts in confusion.

"Get Osprey out!" Jackson barks into his wrist mic.

As one, agents surround the President and hustle him out of the room, bodily shielding him.

Jackson slips out the back of the director's suite into the West Wing bullpen.

In the near darkness, Chief of Staff Monteath is nowhere to be found.

Press Secretary Neamans collapses into a chair behind her. She didn't know it was there.

*

"Chief, it's Jackson—"

The phone goes dead.

Jackson redials the extension of head of the Secret Service detail.

"Chief, it's—" Click.

"Dammit!" Jackson snarls into his wrist mic, "Keep Osprey in WarNest. I am 10-76 to Bird Watcher One."

It takes Jackson five minutes to race to the office space the Secret Service chief uses in the White House. After a quick knock, he enters without waiting for a response.

"Chief—"

"Special Agent Jackson. Stop. Seriously. Say nothing. Answer my questions and nothing else," the head of the detail instructs him. The normally convivial detail chief shocks Jackson with his formal tone. Using the phrase "Special Agent Jackson," the detail head is letting him know about a hidden recorder.

"But Chief—"

"NOTHING! If I hear one word other than a simple, direct answer to one of my questions, I will put you on report myself. So, I am ordering you to stop your babbling." *Myself? Who else is listening to this*, Jackson wonders.

"Yes, sir."

"Is Osprey in any immediate danger?"

Jackson considers. *The key word is immediate. The chief used the word 'immediate' specifically.* "No, sir."

"Is Osprey in Nest Actual?"

"No, sir, I instructed the detail to escort him to the Situation Room."

"That's correct. I confirmed those instructions from comms. I merely needed you to verbally and *physically* verify it," the detail chief stares at Jackson's eyes. Not at the ceiling, office furniture, or anywhere a person may casually glance in a natural conversation. *Physically? There's a video camera in here.* "Let me summarize your report. The power outage incident in the press room was not any type of immediate threat, at most, an, as yet, unexplained accident, in which your team immediately and safely escorted Osprey to safety to WarNest? A yes-or-no question, Special Agent Jackson."

Jackson made no mention of the press room, yet the chief did. *Something strange is going on here. The chief is leading him.*

"Yes, sir."

"Very good. Make sure you write up your official report accurately and as we have discussed here. Email it to me at end of shift. Get back out there and protect the office of the President. Dismissed."

"Email"? While we do file our reports electronically, the chief prefers us personally handing him printed reports. And "accurately"? Since when do we need to be prompted on that? The key words here are "official report" and "as we have discussed here." The chief is telling me my report is being read by someone else and it better read in a way it won't get us both shit-canned. Or worse.

The one piece I can't figure out is: the chief told me to "protect the office of the President." He knows damned well we don't protect the office, we protect the man. Why would he tell me to protect the office?

*

Jackson reaches the Situation Room. The Secret Service does not have key card access to the most secure rom in the world. The protection team used the President's pass card to escort him in earlier. After presenting his credentials to the Marine outside, the guard cards the door open. Jackson holds the door open while still standing in the hall. He has no authorization to enter without a pending threat to the President.

"All clear," Jackson tells his detail through his wrist mic. "Let's escort Osprey back to Osprey Nest."

The agents escort a shaken president through the door.

From inside the Situation Room, "Special Agent Jackson? A word, please."

What now? "Head back to Nest. I will join you shortly," he instructs his team. He sticks his head inside to see who summoned him. Without proper authorization, he shouldn't be in there.

The Secretary of Defense, the White House Chief of Staff, and the Joint Chiefs of Staff. Okay. Properly authorized, it is.

He steps into the room and assumes full attention.

"Relax, Special Agent," the White House Chief of Staff says. Jackson assumes parade rest position with both hands interlocked behind his back.

"The boy genuinely doesn't get the concept of *relaxed,* does he?" Monteath says from his chair near the head of the table.

The admiral looks at the COS with a little disdain. "Dick, for a former Marine, what you're seeing *is* relaxed. We've spent the last 190 years or so making sure of that."

"Cain't he at least sit down?" Monteath asks.

"In front of *these* men? Not without a direct order. At ease, son. Rest."

"He surely doesn't care for the whole *son* thing," Monteath whispers as he watches Jackson move his hands in front of him and never changing his stance.

"I think he'll take it from me," the admiral whispers back. "Special Agent, I understand you've had a conversation with Dick here. No need for attention, you're at rest."

"Yes, sir."

"Did he ask you to spy on the President, son?"

Face frozen, Jackson's, eyes flicker toward Monteath for a microsecond.

"No, sir."

"Good answer. Most likely a whopper, so what the hell," the admiral looks at his notes. "We've reviewed your record, pretty damned impressive. Exemplary record in Marine Expeditionary Unit. Top of your classes at Glynco and Special Agent Training. Accelerated field office and fast-tracked into a protective detail during the President's first campaign. Bumped to protective lead in a couple of years. Son, if you'd have stayed in uniform, I'd be worried about *my* job."

Since the admiral hadn't asked him a question, Jackson remains quiet.

The admiral looks over at Monteath and lowers his head.

"Here's the thing, Special Agent, the Chief of Staff asking you to spy on the President was a mistake," the admiral's eyes bore into Jackson. "In actuality, we need to do is inject this into him."

*

"Sir?"

"Take a breath, son," the Secretary of Defense tells Jackson. "Dave, show him the ampule."

The CIA director pulls a small box, the size of old-fashioned cigarette case, from his briefcase, opening it and sliding it across the wide table to the admiral. The admiral turns it toward Jackson and he sees three plastic ampules the size of one-ounce eyedrop containers.

"From what Dave tells me, these two ampules each have a near-invisible needle on the end. You press one of them against him and squeeze. You don't even have to prick exposed skin. To get rid of them, the ampules themselves dissolve altogether after about minute under a hot water tap. Don't hold them very long in your bare hand. Your body temperature and sweat will start to dissolve them."

"Sir? You want me to poison the President?" Jackson asks. To his credit, his voice doesn't waiver when speaking.

"Poison? Oh hell no. These are mild sedatives," the admiral explains.

"They take a few minutes to be entirely effective, thoroughly dissolve in the bloodstream, and are impossible to detect after twenty minutes. About the same amount of time the subject will be unconscious," the CIA director says. "We had to trade off reaction time for untraceability. They act like propofol, though cleaner.

"The *subject?* You mean the President of the United States?" Jackson asks incredulously. This whole scene was becoming a James-Bondian psychotic episode. "I'm supposed to roofie Osprey?"

"Stand down, Agent. We are not asking you to walk up and dose the President," the admiral says. "We want you to try and reason with him. You are the sole person he trusts these days and we want you to make sure he is not going to jeopardize the government by saying something he shouldn't, like some ridiculous story about a drive in the desert. We're not talking about influencing the man on foreign policy or state secrets. We're talking about seeing if he will keep the woo-woo stories to himself. For a few more years."

"And if he insists on taking his story public?" Jackson asks the admiral.

"Well, then, I'm afraid we are going to have to protect this country's best interests no matter what."

"With all due respects, sirs, what you are talking about is a life sentence for me. It's all well and good for you to sit down here and plan your little coup, yet I'm the one who would be doing an indefinite stay at Casa Del Leavenworth."

"We have you covered." The admiral receives a document from an aide standing behind him. "We issued a signed document from everyone here stating you are acting under direct orders from us," he reads from the sheet, "*to incapacitate your protectee in the event he demonstrates any potential threat to the security of the United States, whether physical or intellectual.* I think it's safe to say we have had a lawyer take a look at this first."

Jackson takes the sheet and looks at it. After a nod from the admiral, the aide retrieves it.

"We've had a psychologist and psychiatrist listen to the desert story and both are willing to certify him unfit to serve, in which case the 25th Amendment comes into play and the Vice President takes office. You'll note he was elected to office, so the whole military coup threat you've been tossing around, goes out the window," Monteath gloats. "Even without the shrinks involved, we could use Section 4 of the 25th Amendment and force him out. Doing that, we have to present a declaration to the Senate and in the meantime, a conscious, out-of-control president could do a lot of damage."

"And as of now, we honestly do not have enough hard evidence of the President's mental incapacitation," chimed in the CIA director. "That's why we need you to keep a closer eye on him. We need you to be close to him, in case he starts to unravel."

"To be very clear, we want you to talk to the President, try to lean him away from talking like a lunatic to the public," the admiral says. "And if that doesn't work, knock his crazy ass out."

*

L MINUS THREE DAYS

"It won't kill you."

"Are you one thousand percent sure of that?" Jackson asks the lab tech.

"Well, *anything* in quantity will kill you. Hell, air in the bloodstream will kill you. Pump too much blood into a guy and he'll die as sure as a gunshot. The sample you gave me is a sedative. Administered in small doses and depending on the patient's blood gas partition coefficient, you might wake up a little groggy, however this is closer to the propofol end of the scale than sodium thiopental's."

Jackson had approached one of his buddies from the Secret Service's Criminal Investigator Training Program at Glynco to analyze a drop of the fluid in the ampules. He could count on his friend's discretion.

"How much of a dose are you talking here?" the technician asks.

"Eh ... fifty milliliters. Like an eye drop container."

"Nah. Won't kill you. Knock you out for a bit and in fifteen, twenty minutes you'll be up and at 'em." His friend holds up the glass slide. "Where'd you get this stuff? I've never seen anything like this. I bet this shit dissolves in the bloodstream likes nobody's business. I know of faster acting stuff, but nothing that disappears like this. This is some covert OPs shit right here."

Both men make note of the fact of Jackson nonchalantly pocketing the slide from his friend's hand.

"Came across it in the field," Jackson says. "Tell me again this never happened."

"Dude, I don't even know who *you* are."

*

L MINUS ONE DAY

"Sir, do you have a minute?"

"Sure, Bob. Though don't tell those fourteen secretaries out there. Keeping me overbooked gives them reason to keep on living. What can I do you for?" the President leans back in his chair behind the Resolute Desk.

Jackson gingerly steps into the Oval Office from the veranda.

"You're not on duty now, have a seat."

31

"Yes, sir. You're sure I'm not disturbing you?"

"No. Hell. This peace treaty'll still be here tomorrow," the President jokes. "What's the matter, man? We've known each other going on six years now and never once have *you* asked to talk to me. Are you dying, Bob? Shit. Am *I* dying? We ain't lucky enough for the First Lady to be the one. Dick Monteath has already outlived cockroaches, so spit it out man."

Jackson notices the President's home state twang and vernacular has crept back into his voice in the last few weeks. You can take the Rhodes Scholar from out of the hills ...

"Sir, I wanted to talk with you about our discussion a while back," Jackson begins. "You know, the desert story."

"Yeah, I am not likely to forget. What about it?"

"Well," Jackson hesitates. "were we seriously talking about UFOs, sir? Are we sure it wasn't weather balloons or experimental planes or something?"

The President grins and covers his smile with his hand.

"I guess I sounded crazier than a bag of hammers, huh? I bet the boys downstairs are pretty near shitting themselves. Lord knows the veep has already measured his backside to see if it fit in this chair."

"It did sound a bit peculiar, sir," Jackson says, starting to relax.

"It weren't no unidentified flying object."

"No?"

"I can identify what it was and where it's from and what they want. And tomorrow at about ten a.m., I'm addressing a press gaggle out on the White House Lawn to let everyone know. Screw the lights in the press room."

*

LANDING DAY, 0950 HOURS

"Bob! I need you in here right now!"

Jackson leaps into the Oval Office as he alerts his team and calls a replacement for his position outside on the veranda.

"Sir?" Jackson looks around at the Joint Chiefs of Staff and Richard Monteath gathered in the now-cramped executive office.

"Bob, your job is to protect me from any threats, right?" the President asks, never looking away from the Joint Chiefs.

"Yes, sir."

"Well, these pack of jackals have spent the last thirty minutes trying to convince me I'm crazier than a June bug and my best guess is they're ganging up to fit me for a jacket with no hand holes. You need to get over here, do your job and make sure I stay safe."

"Yes, sir." Jackson moves a step behind the President.

"Now boys, me and my escort here are gonna mosey on out to the rose garden and have a few words with the press. You fellas can start drafting those resignations you'll be handing me when we get back in here. First one on my desk gets a Nehi. I bet we can even dig up an orange one—

"Whatthehell?" the President slaps his neck.

"Sorry, sir," Jackson lowers the President to the carpet. "It really was for your own good."

"Bob? I trusted you boy," the President says quietly. "I know why they're here."

*

"OHMYGAWD! What happened to the President? Is he okay, do I need to call an ambulance?" One of Monteath's aids busts into the Oval Office door and sees the scene before him.

"It's all right, Jason. He's fine. What did you bust in here for?" Monteath asks.

"You have to see this!" The aide drags Monteath by the arm over to the glass doors of the Oval Office. "A crystalline spaceship touched down in the Rose Garden!"

As the Joint Chiefs crowd around the windows, the President still laying in Jackson's arms says, "I told you I know'd what they was here for. They're here to refuel and get something to eat. Sometimes, you just need to top off the tank."

***

Safe from the Storm
by Steve Rouse

Jan surfaced again, coughing and sputtering. Air! Grasping the cockpit edge of her kayak, she slid with the rocking of the waves and blasts of wind-driven rain. Fear gripped her as the recent sunset added to the already ominous dark. Maybe a solo kayak crossing of Lake Michigan before the wedding wasn't the best idea I've ever had. No guide boat, I'd insisted. What an idiot!

She'd started out from Manitowoc, Wisconsin, now forty-six miles behind her. Her weather radio had warned of the sudden northern shift of the front. When it hit, she was only about twenty miles off Ludington, Michigan. Twenty miles away from family, Conrad, safety, and dry warmth. At least the storm came up from the south bringing warmer rains. If it'd come down from the north, even in the middle of June, she'd have had a severe problem with exposure. At least now all she had to worry about was drowning!

The deck skirt had torn away when she'd been pounded by at least an eighteen-footer that sucked her completely out of the craft. That one cost her the radio and her paddle, too. She knew her GPS/transponder in the bow chamber was operating. She could hear its pinging as she hugged the kayak's hull. Her cell phone registered no signal and refused to dial out. Even 911 failed to send. Jan resolved to hold on until the Coast Guard arrived.

She lost track of time, the number of swells she'd ridden up and down, and how much she'd swallowed of Lake Michigan. Breathing became difficult, lungs sore from gulping air and coughing out water. Numbness was setting in after hours in the sixty-three degree water. At least the lightning is staying to the ... I think that's south.

A light from overhead split the darkness. It shone like the sun. Jan waved in response but could neither see nor hear anything of her rescuers. Thank God ... found me ... Conrad!

The storm, light, sounds, and sense of relief overwhelmed her. When she felt her rescuer's arm wrap around her from behind, she managed a smile, and a muttered "Bless you," but then succumbed to her exhaustion and lost consciousness.

*

"What do you mean the signal's gone? How's that possible?" Conrad screamed.

"I know, I know," Lieutenant. Jamison said, gesturing to calm Conrad. "Two possibilities. Either it stopped sending or, uhm ... or it's submerged too far under the water."

"What? No way! We made sure the unit was water tight and had a new battery with backup." He sighed deeply and paced within the small Coast Guard office.

"Look, we're sending a recovery helicopter to her last known coordinates. The bulk of the storm has moved east, but she's still bucking some significant winds. We're clocking gusts here at about sixty-six point seven knots ..."

Conrad's glare and outstretched palms stopped him.

"Uhm, sorry, about fifty-eight miles per hour. Sustained winds are holding at, uh, twenty-seven miles an hour."

"Okay, look," Conrad glared across at the clock. "It's passed nine. She's more than two hours overdue! Lt. Jamison, I need her here safe and sound."

"All I can tell you, Mr. Russell, is that we are on this. Our crew is airborne and heading to her last GPS reading. We are fighting the same storm she's facing, but we've trained for this. She will ..."

"Excuse me, Lieutenant." Another uniformed man stood at the doorway, waiting.

"Is this about ..."

"Mr. Russell, please? Your fiancée's location isn't the only issue the Coast Guard has on its plate tonight," Lt. Jamison said as he headed toward the man in the doorway.

Conrad Russell worked at just breathing. In ... Out ... In. His shrink had helped him control his anger by thinking and actively working his way through his choices. He paused, nearly calm, when he overheard Jamison's somewhat agitated voice.

"I don't care if it comes from Marinette, Milwaukee, or Chicago. Get all three, I want a chopper out there ASAP, got it?"

Conrad Russell began his breathing again. In ... Out ...

*

Jan sat silently on a floor, her back flat against the wall. Her breathing was regular and controlled. Her eyes, wide and unblinking, followed the two creatures on the opposite side of the room.

Each stood about four feet tall, their three legs making up about a third of their height. Each leg ended with a three-toed foot. Two arms, three tendril fingers on each, and a head shaped like a butternut squash. No features were obvious save what she guessed was their eye, a compound thing that covered the top quarter of their heads. It reminded her of the Simon® game she had as a kid. It looked like they wore a pastel beige uniform. Their skin had a soft pale purplish hue.

They stood together gesturing as if in conversation but making no sounds she could hear. One touched a box-like thing on a table between she and them and a soft hum filled her ears followed by a voice.

"Are you aware of my sound?" Jan heard it as a feminine-sounding voice. Not a bit artificial.

Jan nodded, tapping her ears. "I hear you." She added a smile for effect.

Another quick exchange between them and the voice returned. "Is your health well?"

Jan realized she did feel better being warm and almost dry. "Yes, I'm fine." Wish I had a brush and a mirror. I must look like a freak! She started giggling at the absurdity of worrying about the way she looked to a couple of aliens after being plucked out of a stormy lake.

They suddenly flickered and disappeared. What the hell? How can they do that? Or were they just like some sort of hologram? Jan stood and walked toward where they had been. She got about halfway when she bumped into nothing but stopped just as if she'd hit a wall. After a few minutes of probing, Jan knew she was in some kind of cage, separated from her captors by a transparent wall.

I guess it makes sense, thinking of the old movie "War of the Worlds." Germs can kill. Isolation would make sense. She began actively wondering. Where did they come from, what they were like, and why the hell they were here? Science?... or military?

She stopped, as if she couldn't remember something. What was I thinking? Oh, yeah, "War of the Worlds." But something wasn't right. It was different. How?

She stood up and looked around. Her eyes scanned the room twice when she realized she'd been standing over there next to the transparent wall before when thinking about why they'd be here. What happened? Why was there a gap in her memory, or was it something else?

There was nothing in the room to really focus on. Every surface looked a drab grey and she had to stare to pick out where the floor met the wall. She stooped and felt the joint and discovered it to be a curve about as wide as a hot dog. Hot dog? God, I'm hungry! "Hey! Hey, guys? Hey, can I have something to eat?" she said aloud to no one.

One of the same little creatures appeared. "No, we cannot nourish you. But we do need you to help us understand something. What is this?"

A holographic version of herself appeared next to her. Startled, she stepped back. "Uh, that would be another me, uhm, without clothes."

"No. This." It pointed and her abdomen showed as a lit area. Before she responded, the image magnified, highlighting her uterus.

"It's uh, it ... look, this is really personal. Why are you asking all this?"

The creature changed its stance, as if looking closely at her. "Sorry. We have found a small mass here and do not know what it is. We are concerned it may be an illness. Please?"

Jan looked closely at the image and paused before whispering, "Shit!"

"It is called shit," it said. "Thank you."

"No, no, no. That was just a word. It ..." she said indicating the mass in her uterus, "... it's a fetus." Breathlessly, she said, "A baby." Jesus, I'm pregnant! Conrad ... last month? Oh, God ... not at all how I'd ever dreamed I'd find out. "I'm going to be a mother," she said.

"We want to study it. May we? How long will it take to grow?"

"No! I, uhm, no, it's not ..." Jan worked to control her voice. Can't be angry at them. No telling what they can do. When did they ... Oh, God ... that gap! They must have done something to me.

Once again, the creature flickered and was gone. It was replaced with a new creature. But this one walked into the room through a section of the chamber's wall. It made Jan shrink back and worry about her safety.

This different alien stood before her, coming right up to the transparent wall. It was much bigger than the other two and almost half again her size. It stood on three thicker, stumpy legs, and had a dark grey waxy skin tone. Its eye pads were spaced differently, covering more of its head's surface. It punched the barrier causing it to sizzle like electricity. Waving both of its arms above its head, its voice screamed in her mind.

"Human. You and your craft are ours to be studied. You would be dead if not for us. You are ours. We control you. Know your place." It stomped each foot, turned, and lumbered out of the room through the same doorway.

*

Lt. Jamison sucked in a huge breath and slowly exhaled like blowing out a candle. Done, he opened the door to the room Conrad Russell occupied. He wore his best military face despite his news.

"I'm sorry, Mr. Russell. Our helicopter crew has found no wreckage, nor your fiancée. They will continue the search at daybreak. We are also initiating a search of area beaches. There is nothing else we can do."

Conrad kept his composure, wearing his attorney face. "You do realize, Lieutenant, that Jan's kayak is unsinkable, a double-hulled polycarbonate, with a sealed bow chamber housing a state of the art marine GPS transponder." He shifted position and moved behind the desk, taking a posture he'd used to convey his authority to trial juries. "Despite all this, your crews, equipped with the most modern military technology, cannot find this big yellow cork, if you will, in such a well-defined tract of inland water? I find this to be disturbing, sir, inexcusable!" He slammed his palm against the desktop for effect with that last word.

Jamison mimicked his stance. "That 'big yellow cork,' as you put it, may be afloat whole or in pieces, but there is no transponder signal within forty-three miles of Ms. Snowden's last known location.

"I pray, sir, that we find her alive very soon, but we are still looking for a relatively small yellow cork. We can do nothing until we have light enough to see." He glanced at his watch. "We will be back out there in a short three hours."

*

Jan lay sobbing, curled in a corner, acutely aware of the two smaller aliens watching her. She had a distinct impression they were scientists and the bigger, ugly one that threatened her may be the space ship's commander.

The two seemed agitated after they'd returned since the bigger one's visit and paid more attention to her than before. Once again, they asked how she felt.

Now or never! "I am very sad. We humans grow to raise children. It is our purpose. How can I accept a life as your science project? It will not show you anything about us. What we are is in how we interact with each other, especially our children. Your data will be worthless, biological only. Social and inter-relational context is so much more critical for you to know about us."

"It would be better then to study you and your baby in your natural setting?" one asked.

Jan controlled her breathing lest she show too much excitement. "Definitely," she said. "If you would consider this, I would be more than willing to cooperate."

The two dissolved into nothing, again. Interesting how these two disappear, but the ugly one goes through a doorway? She laid back down and sighed. A feeling of haziness overwhelmed her. She blinked a few times, then slept.

When she awoke, her damaged kayak was next to her, as were the two smaller aliens.

One stepped closer and spoke in her mind. "We do not wish to harm you. Nothing comes from destruction. We agree that studying you as you live and not in our laboratory is better for us all. We have inserted a transmission device under your skull, here." Jan felt a twinge behind her left ear. "It will tell us all we need to know about you, and help us learn about your kind."

40

The other now spoke. "We are known as D'narthalons. Our home world is nearer the galaxy core. We explore only to learn. Our pilot does not care to know about other species, only how to move the craft. His kind is different, not as able to relate or understand as ours. This ship is one hundred and four feet below the surface of this water body. Can you get to the surface without harm?"

Jan knew a little about free-diving. "Yes," she said, nodding. "I'll be fine."

*

The helicopter flew a thousand feet above the now calm blue waters of Lake Michigan. On the third sweep of their matrix, the spotter shouted, "Got something! A yellow blip about two o'clock, twenty-three hundred yards out."

"Roger that," the pilot responded and craned his head to look. "Sighted. Coming to course three-one-eight."

*

Jan's rescue copter delivered her to Paul Oliver Emergency Hospital in Frankfort, Michigan. Beyond a slight left skull contusion, she passed all their protocols. Surprised doctors had been prepared for a hypothermia patient and were at a loss to explain Jan's condition. She offered nothing to help them, feigning confusion and blackouts.

Conrad broke a few speed limits on his way down from Ludington. He and Jan spoke deep into that night. She finally confided in him all that she'd been through. He held her closely and reassured her all was well, dismissing it all in his mind as a trauma-induced hallucination.

They wed as scheduled. The following March, a healthy daughter was born to Conrad and Jan Russell. Jan silently wondered what kind of information her D'narthalon hosts had gotten, especially through her labor and childbirth.

*

Within the asteroid belt just beyond the fourth planet, the two scientists reviewed the most recent data transmissions from their test subject. Most satisfying, one thought. The female shows no after effects from our encounter and has recovered from successfully birthing her child.

We can terminate her then? the other inquired.

41

Of course. The D'narthalon reached across and keyed in a command and the transmission indicator for Jan Russell went out.

We will get all the information about her and the male from the child as it grows and matures. It is already responding to our stimuli. We've been observing their species for over sixty of their years. This will be our most interesting experiment yet.

***

A Wheelbarrow Full of Honey
By Paul K. Metheney

As alien invasions go, this was pretty spectacular. Even by CNN's
standards. A while back, three enormous crystalline vessels with
tubular projections, without so much as a "we've-come-to-eat-your-
population," de-cloaked adjacent to a few of the largest buildings and
skyscrapers in the world and systematically sliced and diced them from
top to bottom. The invaders then used some sort tractor beam in the
tube to consume the people inside as well as the rubble itself. Within
an hour, three of the world's largest buildings and everyone in them,
had ceased to exist. No debris. Just gone. Governments scrambled to
deploy fighter jets and attack helicopters to every site, but by the time
they arrived, the invaders had slid back into invisibility like an arm
disappearing into a sleeve.

It was starting to make some of the science fiction I write look
tame by comparison.

A single ship appeared again five days later to begin the same
process at the CentralWorld Tower in Bangkok. This time, the U.S.
aircraft carrier *Jefferson* was nearby and deployed airborne
counteroffensives. Sadly, any missile, aircraft, or rocket approaching
the ship was effortlessly vaporized long before it could even close on
the alien intruder.

Eleven days later, three more alien ships returned and ingested the
Aalsmeer Flower Auction in the Netherlands, the Beijing Capital
International Airport, and The Venetian Hotel in Macau (and

coincidentally, the thousands of people contained therein). The general population didn't seem to grasp that no city or building was safe. The news networks were having a field day.

Score: aliens, seven; humanity, zero. Well, technically, the aliens were up about forty-seven thousand, and we had yet to even see one 'Martian,' let alone kill one.

It was about then that a very serious-looking USAF Major Andrews (according to his name tag) showed up at my door in Huntsville, escorted by what looked like two German-mad-scientist-genetic-experiments-gone-bad squeezed into Marine tactical gear. I'm not *saying* these boys took steroids, but you could almost see the light bending around the gravity field their muscles were generating. I had secretly named them Laverne and Maxine. To myself.

"Travis Montgomery?" in a tone implying that he already knew the answer and that my one of my customary smartass answers would be frowned upon.

"Uh, yep." Who says I wasted my parents' money on all those doctorates?

"I need you to come with us now. Sir."

"Am I in trouble? What's this about?"

"Sir, I am not at liberty to say. We have been tasked with retrieving you. Immediately."

Andrews' uniform had creases you could shave with. I, on the other hand, was wearing the same jeans for three days now. When I subconsciously compared my 180 pounds of blond, less-than-athletic nerdiness to Major Andrews' fit and snappy appearance ... well, at least I was still smarter. And I'm still hanging on to that thought.

"Sir, please come with us now." You gotta give him credit for sticking to his script.

I reached behind the door to grab something and Laverne and Maxine pushed through, effectively surrounding me in a wall of muscle.

Handing the closest Marine my overnight duffle, "Easy boys. I've been waiting for y'all for a few days."

"You have?" It was the major's turn to be off guard. "The decision to collect you was just handed down this morning. How could you ...?"

"Seriously? The world is attacked by extraterrestrial battleships. Everything the military can do has failed. My IQ looks like an SAT score and I wrote the book on alien invasions. Literally. THE Actual Book. Even Laverne here could have seen y'all coming." I have a tendency to get snarky and obnoxious when I'm nervous. Armageddon and Marines showing up at my door push me right up to the real dickhead level. "Besides, who ya gonna call?"

Ignoring the Laverne comment, and with a face as straight as a yardstick, the major replied, "You'd be surprised. Sir."

*

Six hundred and ninety-six miles, one military flight, two helicopter rides, and what seemed like miles of corridors, I found out who you would call. The Andrew Sisters escorted me to a dimly lit conference room inside the Pentagon. A full bird colonel was addressing the room near a lit screen in front.

"Ah, I see our last ... 'consultant' has arrived. Ladies and gentlemen, some of you may know the distinguished Dr. Travis Montgomery from his books and work on TV. Since we've already completed the introductions, he can catch up later. Dr. Montgomery, if you will ...," the colonel said, gesturing toward an empty seat. It wasn't really a request. The entire group stared at me. Some dismissed me with a smirk, a very few made eye contact, and the worst looked away blankly as if I didn't exist in their universe; clearly not big fans of my work.

As the colonel brought the room up to speed on the three incursions, I looked around recognizing a few of the two dozen faces assembled. Darby Keaton, an English string theorist I had met at a TED conference a few years back, one of the few people I have ever met with true eidetic memory. (You do NOT want to play poker with this guy.) Two seats down from him was Han Su Kang, a brilliant weapons designer from Korea. I had read everything this guy had ever written. Off the charts smart. Across the table was Tng Zte Guyen (or maybe it was Ng Zte Yn? Whatever! Something with a shitload of consonants). The kid's supposedly the Chinese Mozart of quantum physics. If you want a Unified Field Theory, this is the guy you would ask. Farther down the table, Irene McCrae, the reigning queen-mother of modern-day radio astronomy and the search for extraterrestrial life, looked up with a warm smile. She didn't invent SETI, but she's pretty high up on their speed dial. The walls themselves were lined with large

45

screen teleconferencing video feeds from other scientists around the world. Holy crap! Is that Stephen Hawking?

Despite my drawl, smart-mouth, and "aw-shucks" routine, I can be a bright guy. Clearly, I was NOT the first guy they called to help them out. I was not even the SECOND guy on the list. In fact, it looks as if I may have been the LAST guy to get tapped. (Arrogance, thy name is Travis.) Normally, I am the smartest guy in the room, but with this group, I am barely beating out Laverne and Maxine. And truthfully, when I look up at Hawking's gaunt features on the big screen, I'm not sure I beat Maxine by all that much.

Clearly, they didn't call me here for my athletic build or rugged good looks. I have written a dozen or so books, some science fiction and some practical science. My second most popular, *When Aliens Attack*, the Discovery Channel made into a big budget, pseudo-documentary. Probably why the Pentagon called me in. Thank God it wasn't because of my most popular book, *Zombie Contingency Planning*. That would have just been weird. I also have a "reality" show on National Geographic, *Good Ol' Geeks*. (Check your local listings for times.) On that, a few of my buddies, my grandpa, and I, build some practical applications of modern science over the course of a weekend. My personal favorites are a lunar module made out of old beer kegs and a death ray from a Blu-ray disc player. Then there's my day job as an actual rocket scientist in that little Huntsville space program we have down there. Add that to my three doctorates and I usually AM the smartest guy in the room. Until today. I wonder if I should go out and get coffee for these guys.

*

Colonel Attitude completed his summary and glared around the room.

"Okay, *Doctors*. Here's the situation. We have tried damned near everything we can think of to stop this shit and have, so far, come up empty. While we work with the military forces around the world throwing missiles at these things, you geniuses are going to sit in this room until you come up with a way to kill these alien bastards. Any questions? Good. Get to it." With that, he stormed from the conference room amidst the silence of a stunned Brain Trust.

*

Three days later, Colonel Attitude (turns out his real name is Dixon, but he'll always be Attitude to me) strode back into the conference room and while the room quieted down, folded his arms, and perfected his military-issue scowl.

"What have you got?"

Silence.

"C'mon people, someone speak up. What have you *geniuses* come up with to kill these things?" He said the word "geniuses" the way a Baptist minister spits out the word "whore."

Silence.

"You're telling me that this frigging Mensa club, with enough IQ points to be a damned zip code, has come up with *NOTHING*?!"

Even Hawking's respirator went quiet.

The colonel's voice suddenly got very low.

"What the hell *have* you been doing for the last three days?"

I was leaning against the wall and muttered under my breath, "Seating charts on the Titanic."

"What was that?! You! Pretty boy! Montgomery, right? What did you just say?"

It's amazing how the power of invisibility never manifests when you want it to.

"Uh. I was just saying that we have gotten a little bogged down in details."

"Be. Specific."

What the hell. It wasn't like it would be the end of the world if I offended some of the greatest minds on the planet would it? Oh. Yeah. Never mind.

"Well," I took a deep breath, mentally erasing myself from Stephen Hawking's Christmas card list, "most of the time was wasted arguing about who should be in charge. The Chinese representatives thought that since they had lost the most people, one of them should be in charge. Surprisingly, Dubai made a very substantial argument for themselves. Then there was the debate over whether we should keep monitoring outside events as we worked. Many thought that would be distracting. There was more discussion about how much communication should be maintained with their respective governmental leadership. As you came in, you interrupted an exhilarating debate about what should be on the lunch menu. Asian cuisine was in the lead, but a strong case was being made for vegetarian."

"Are. You. Kidding. Me?" the colonel's voice a bare rasp now.

"Hey. Don't look at me. I voted for a few of them six-foot submarines sandwiches." I took a sip from my Big Gulp. My straw actually squeaked. Oh, well. I didn't deserve to be in this room anyway. Send my ass back to Huntsville and let me build rockets.

You could see the colonel attempt to compose himself as the veins in his neck threatened to rupture all over the congregated think tank. Are faces supposed to be burgundy?

"Major," he spoke in clipped, controlled sentences, "send for two dozen box lunches from the closest cafeteria in the mall. Disconnect all TV, Internet, and media connections to this room. Coordinate resources to do the same to anyone conferencing in. If they refuse, pull the plug on their teleconference. Collect every cell phone and disconnect all land lines in here. Tell the guards outside to shoot anyone who steps out of this room, except for you and me. That includes restroom breaks. Oh—and Montgomery is in charge."

And the crowd goes wild. Not in a good way.

The assembled scientists began screaming at the colonel. I threw up in my mouth. A little.

"You cannot put this 'farmer' in charge!" the Chinese physicist, Guyen, screeched. "He is not even a real scientist. He is a poorly trained monkey on your reality TV, spewing out illiterate pseudoscience for hillbillies and writing ill-conceived science fiction for American trailer trash!"

"Hey! Hold on there! Who ya callin' poorly trained, panda boy? And that's *Doctor* Monkey to you!" I stepped toward the table to test my working theory that not every Chinese man could possibly be Jackie Chan.

"Actually, I *can* put him in charge, Dr. Yn," the Colonel interjected.

"GUYEN!"

"Whatever. Montgomery is it because he is very likely the only person in this room that cares less about your personal needs and egos than I do. He had the balls to speak up when the rest of you didn't. I figure, with his reputation, he has less to live up to than the rest of you egotistical Einsteins. And lastly, he is in charge, because I FUCKING SAY SO!"

Somewhere in there was a compliment, but strangely, I was not feeling the love.

The room went quiet as the colonel glared at each of the delegates. They, in turn, glowered at me. I looked around and couldn't find Laverne. On a positive note, however, I have now experienced the physical manifestation of the word "seething."

"In twenty-four hours, I will be back and I want a damned plan!" The hydraulic mechanism on the door prevented it from slamming. Almost.

*

It wasn't twenty-four hours. It was five. A much more somber Colonel Dixon trudged woodenly to the front of the room.

"Ladies and gentlemen, thirty-seven minutes ago the aliens struck again. This time they devoured everyone in the Sands Cotai Central in Macau, Berjaya Times Square in Kuala Lumpur, the Central Park Jakarta Complex, the Grand Indonesia in Jakarta, and The Palazzo in Las Vegas. Despite the buildings being only partially inhabited, thirty-three thousand lives were lost."

The room once again fell silent with a completely different tone. While we had been arguing about lunch, the aliens were getting ready to eat theirs.

It was several minutes before anyone could speak.

"Why would anyone be in those buildings? Don't they know there's an invasion going on?" asked Keaton, his English accent thick with strain.

"Because of the randomness of the strikes, people are trying to maintain a semblance of normalcy. The world is stilling turning. Maybe, they are choosing to pretend it can't happen to them. I don't know." the colonel said, genuinely confused.

"Prime numbers." It was Tng Zte Guyen.

"What?" The colonel seemed fogged in thought.

"The extraterrestrials think in prime numbers. The attacks only happen one prime number from the last. Five days. Eleven days. And now three days." Guyen's voice picked up a little enthusiasm. As did mine.

"He's right. Even the number of ships they use and the number of buildings they attack are primes. Three. One. Three. Five." I said.

Damn. I hate giving that little Chinese prick any credit, but he *was* the first to see it.

Guyen was on a roll. "What's more, factoring the time zone differentials, even the amounts of time between strikes are prime numbers."

Colonel Attitude was back in the conversation. Barely. "Big deal. They are attacking the tallest buildings in the world on odd number days and hours. With no pattern. How does that help me kill them?"

"Prime. Not odd," Irene McCrae said quietly. "It won't tell you *how* to kill them, but it could possibly tell you *when*."

Something else was bothering me. "Not 'tallest.'"

"What?" The colonel barked at me as enthusiasm rippled through the room.

"You said 'tallest buildings.' They didn't attack the tallest buildings. They destroyed the *largest* buildings," I said a bit sheepishly. "Darby, could you list on the screen the list of buildings attacked?"

Without visible concentration, Darby typed the list of every building assimilated.

New Century	*China*	*1,760,000 m²*
Dubai	*Dubai*	*1,713,000 m²*
Abraj Al-Bait	*Mecca*	*1,575,815 m²*
CentralWorld	*Bangkok*	*1,024,000 m²*
Aalsmeer	*Netherlands*	*990,000 m²*
Beijing Capital	*Beijing*	*986,000 m²*
The Venetian	*Macau*	*980,000 m²*
Sands Cotai	*Macau*	*890,000 m²*
Berjaya Times	*Kuala*	*700,000 m²*
Central Park	*Jakarta*	*655,000 m²*
The Palazzo	*Las Vegas*	*645,581 m²*
Grand	*Jakarta*	*640,000 m²*

While everyone else concentrated on the list, I was gripped by a nauseating sense of dread.

"You memorized the metric square footage of all those buildings?" asked the Indian delegate.

"Sure. Didn't everyone?" Darby seemed perplexed.

I turned to the colonel. Very quietly.

"Colonel Dixon, we need to evacuate. Right now, sir." I almost whispered it.

"Montgomery, what are you going on about? This isn't the Huntsville Elementary School. Do you know how many people work here?"

"Thirty-one thousand. Twenty-eight thousand military personnel and contractors, plus three thousand civilian support staff." Darby informed him.

I looked around for *my* support. Of course, it would be Guyen to get it first.

"Dr. Keaton, please provide us with the next building logically on that list," Guyen politely intoned.

After a brief search of his memory, Darby typed rapid fire:
The Pentagon   *Virginia 610,000 m²*
"Oh, shit."

*

The alien tube slid from invisibility three days later, lasered (for lack of a better term) the Pentagon into sections and harvested them into the maw of its gigantic circular nose. The building was empty (taking nearly a full day to get everyone out), but the airspace above it was not. Everything from stealth bombers to cruise missiles were launched at the alien craft's force fields. My nephew described it as an "epic fail."

I convinced Colonel Attitude to move the Brain Trust to the Holiday Inn near my grandfather's farm in Alabama. Very likely the last place in the known universe an invading alien force eating large chunks of population would come looking. We took over the whole hotel. The conference room was our war room. Even the large teleconference screens made the move. The security detail had their own floor. The colonel loosened his restrictions and although we were allowed to roam a bit and have access to Internet and media, most of us stayed in the conference room, working the problem.

The Brain Trust focused, forgetting their petty squabbles. No real progress was made. We just didn't understand their technology. We couldn't shoot through their defenses. We couldn't see through their invisibility prior to attacks. All we had done so far was save thirty-one thousand lives. And lose a Pentagon.

In an act of pure rebellion and frustration, I snuck out. I called my lifelong friend Bub to come get me up in his Ford pickup and he drove us to my grandfather's. Bub raided the fridge while Pappaw and I walked his wooded fence line. In Bub's mind, the end of the world was just another excuse to mooch beer.

*

"Travis, you remember the last time we walked back through here?"

"Uh-huh." My attention was chewing the technical problems of cloaking a ship one-fourth the size of a skyscraper. My intellectual inadequacy to lead this group was eating at me. Plus, something was nagging me about *the last place in the known universe.*

Pappaw continued, "I tried to show ya how to steal honey from one of those hive boxes up on the hill with a straw without smoking the bees. Ya damned near got stung to death. Never seen a boy cry like that. Ya ever try that again?" For Pappaw, the height of humor is seeing a teenage boy cry.

"Nope. Never did." Maybe an electromagnetic field set just so could bend the light. But *I don't exist in their universe.*

"Son. Where's your head at?"

"I don't know, Pap. I guess it's this whole humanity-getting-eaten-by-aliens thing. I'm just a tad scattered." *Bub raiding the fridge. Invisibility never manifests when you want it to.*

"Nope. That ain't it."

"It's not? I could have sworn being in charge of saving the world was what was on my mind." I replied while thoughts of the invasion and the Brain Trust ricocheted in my head. *Gravity bending light. Shoot through their defenses.*

"Shee-it boy! Ya've been writing them alien invasion books since ya was growing hair on your winky. That ain't what's bothering ya. What is it?"

Could have lived without THAT visual. We walked through trampled cornstalks for a bit while I gave it some serious thought. The old man wouldn't take my usual bullshit as an answer. He knew me better than just about anyone and if he said aliens weren't my real problem, then by God, aliens weren't what was really bothering me. Pappaw always had a way of cutting to the chase.

"Ya know, Pap, that's the kicker. I've been writing these books, postulating about what to do if aliens attack, made a shitload of money off of it, and just found out: it was all bullshit. None of it happened the way I said it would. I'm used to having all the right answers. I'm just a good ol' boy who's going to be the reason a whole lot of people get eaten. I can't wrap my head around it."

Pappaw just smiled. Only grandpas can get away with a smile during an apocalypse.

"So, ya'll geniuses are the security guards and them alien fellers are the crooks, and ya'll are just mad because ya ran up on someone just bit sharper than ya'll are?"

"Uh, yeah." Again, doctorates not wasted here.

"Son, I ever tell the story 'bout the time I was working at The Plant as security and we had a feller making off every night with them empty burlap bags?" The Plant, as he referred to it, was the Marshall Space Flight Center on Redstone Arsenal in Huntsville, where Pappaw was part of the security force.

"Yeah, Pap, you told me that story a million times ... wait! Did you say 'stealing honey'?"

"'Bout fifteen minutes ago. Y'alright? Ya look like one of them bees done crawled up your pooper."

"Holy shit! Pap, come with me! I think you're gonna save the world!"

"Well, Mammaw wanted me to mow the backyard, but I reckon I can do that later."

*

Back at the Brain Trust, I gathered the team together, including Dixon and Andrews. While Pappaw told his stories about honey and burlap bags to everyone, I made lists of action items and a shopping list of special "groceries." I handed the two lists to Han Su Kang.

"Can you do it?"

He looked at me. He looked at my grandfather. "Yes. With help."

"Add whatever you need to that second list. Price is no obstacle. And Han? We need them yesterday. Two days from now is a prime number."

I handed the lists over to the colonel and explained my plan. He listened. He looked down at the lists. "This is way over my pay grade, son. I need to get someone with stars to sign off on this. Maybe even the CIC."

"Colonel, if you run this through channels, there won't be time to make it happen before the next attack." I remembered now why I passed on military service. Not so good with the bureaucracy.

"Travis, I *have* to ask permission. What you want will land my ass in Leavenworth ..."

He looked Major Andrews dead in the eye. "... if I know about it." And handed the major my shopping list.

*

The alien device appeared just above Air Force Plant 4, near Fort Worth, Texas, two days later. AFP4 was formerly the eleventh largest building the world. As it stands right now, it's number one. For the next thirty minutes anyway. The colonel, Major Andrews, and I have it staked out in a specially modified Humvee about a quarter mile from the plant. The "ship" began dissecting the building, seemingly unaware that the thousands of workers inside of it had been evacuated for days. Even from where we sat, we could feel the roar of the hundreds of tons of concrete and steel rubble tumbling up into the vessel and the keening whine of the beam as it dragged it in. As it nearly completed devouring the building, I reached for the switch mounted to the jerry-rigged control panel in front of me.

"I'm sorry, Travis, but by law, I have to do that. It's government property and it can't be a civilian that flips the switch. Plus, I finally have my orders." The colonel leaned forward between the seats to reach the switch. "Oh. And the President asked me to thank your grandfather for the stories."

*

Two days earlier Pap *had* told the Brain Trust some interesting stories. Sometimes, even genius needs a kick in the shorts. Sometimes, brilliance doesn't need a degree.

"I'm not sure what the point of this story is. Fact of the matter is, Travis don't come out looking none too bright. But he said to tell ya, so here it is. A bunch a years ago, when Trav was just a teenager, I took him up on the north hill of my farm where we keep a bunch them white box beehives. Smart as he was, I figured he needed a bit of real-world education and mebbe a little humility. So, I tried to teach him how to steal some honey with a straw and mebbe get himself a little honeycomb outta one them boxes without having to smoke the bees down lower inta the hive. His Mammaw damned near whooped me silly for getting him so stung up. Anywho, I guess I figured it was the wrong lesson, cuz he ain't gone near one since."

Thankfully, he left out the part about me crying.

"But damned if he didn't bawl like a little redheaded girl from all them stings, though!"

Even Hawking smiled at that.

"Pap, tell them the other story." Not that I don't enjoy a bucket load of embarrassment as much as the next guy. Even Guyen was paying attention now. It was probably the part about me crying.

"Okay. So, it's the early sixties and I was working security at The Plant and we had some reports of a feller leaving out the side gate of a new construction area with a wheelbarrow full of empty burlap sacks. Well, the gate guard stops the feller and calls up to the office. They tell him they don't give a shit 'bout no empty cement sacks. The guard hangs up and sends him on his way. Next night, same thing. Same feller with a wheelbarrow full of empty sacks. Guard calls up. Gets the same duty officer, gets his ear chewed out for wasting his time about empty sacks, and lets the feller go."

"What has this to do with aliens?" Guyen asked impatiently.

"Not a damned thing." Pappaw answered back sternly, regarding the young Chinese genius as if he just fell off the short bus.

"So, night after night, this feller goes through the gate. One night, I come up to the gate just as the guard was getting ready to wave him through and asked what was going on. The guard tells me the story and I go over and handcuff the man with the wheelbarrow full of empty burlap sacks. The guard is flabbergasted and wants to know what I'm doing. As I walked the purpeetraitor away, I looked over my shoulder and said, 'Sonny, he weren't stealin' no sacks. He was stealin' wheelbarrows!'"

The Brain Trust looked at me in confusion. Oh, sure, quarks and quasars they get, but wheelbarrows? Irene was the only who started to smile. I needed them ALL to get this.

"Guys, do I really need to spell it out? Those aren't alien ships. They're straws. They are not de-cloaking from invisibility, they are inserting from another dimensional plane into ours, like penetrating a membrane ... TO STEAL HONEY. Invisibility would require a monstrous gravitational field to bend light. Other than their tractor beam, they don't seem to affect local gravity fields at all. When they disappear, they aren't turning invisible, they are retracting back into their own plane of existence. Like a straw pulling back through a soda cup lid."

Darby piped up. "That would explain why the volume of material they are taking is greater than the mass of the vehicle. It is not a vehicle, it is a conduit. Bloody brilliant!"

"It also explains the object never navigating in our airspace," Han said, almost to himself.

Guyen wasn't drinking the Kool-Aid. "So they are using these conduits to suck out the people? Granted, these buildings contain the greatest concentration of animal protein and fat in the world, but surely entities smart enough penetrate a dimensional membrane are smart enough to capture humans without all this trouble."

Before I could respond, Major Andrews spoke up, shaking his head in disbelief.

"Guyen, you asshole. Sir. They aren't eating people. The aliens are eating concrete, steel, and glass. That's the wheelbarrows. The people are the sacks."

"And the bees." Is it bad that I really enjoyed the "asshole" part?

"So, how do we stop them?" Guyen couldn't stop being a jerk.

Hawking's electronically nasal, computer-generated voice buzzed. "We sting them."

"Exactly!" I continued. "We make them cry like little redheaded girls so much that they never touch another hive!"

*

Two days later: As the last of Air Force Plant 4 was sucked into the maw of the alien extractor, Colonel Dixon flipped the protective lid and pressed the button. The alien device withdrew into its own dimension a few moments later. If all went according to plan, ten minutes later a series of redundant timers activated by that switch would detonate a cascade of suitcase nuclear devices that Han Su had shielded from detection and secreted in the walls of the plant. There was no visible sign of detonations from where we sat. God, I hope I'm as smart as Pappaw thinks I am.

*

It's been five years since the Pentagon was taken. Construction is almost completed on two sides of the new building. Pappaw spends most of his fishing trips telling his buddies how he saved the world. None of them believe him. Colonel Dixon was promoted to general. Guyen was given a medal by the Chinese government for *saying* he saved the world. We lost Dr. Hawking. Maxine and Laverne are living together in a small condo in San Diego.

I wrote another how-to book on alien invasions. I am doing a nice circuit of talk shows. Seems the government is not all that concerned that the aliens are monitoring The Tonight Show.

I still haven't gone back up to the north hill of Pap's farm. Maybe someday.

Yeah. No. Not gonna happen.

***

Takes One to Know One
By Steve Rouse

From the time she crashed her cousin's bike into the pharmacy's brick wall and ran away unscathed, Norah Broxton's life changed forever. Her friend, Belinda, told it best to the local newspaper:

"That girl ... she comes aflyin' down ol' Miller Hill faster than my dog could run. An' my old dog, he could catch that mail truck every time. That's how he died. Anywho, skinny 'Rah, that's what we called her before this, she caught up to Sergeant 'Fatty' in his police cruiser an' hit him square in the face with her water balloon. We's all hootin' and hollerin' 'til we see 'Rah loose it while turnin'.

"See, she supposed to turn down the alley to get away from Sgt. Fatty, but she don't turn tight enough and smacks into the corner of Clark's Pharmacy. I mean, we could all hear that ol' bike crunch up like a beer can off my Uncle Bud's forehead. And 'Rah, she and that bike bounce right back in the middle of da street. Then she's just sittin' there on her butt like she's playin' jacks or somethin' next to that busted up bike. She stood up and seen everyone staring at her. When a couple of folks run toward her—they said they was gonna help her—she just took off lickety-split, runnin' down that alley.

"That's how we all found out Norah had that superpower stuff, ya know, just like the comic books! Her papa didn't have ta work the mines no more and her mama walked around praising God for her baby girl's miracle."

*

Norah Broxton sighed and a wry smile creased her old, wrinkled face. She gingerly put the yellowed newspaper article back in her keepsake shoebox and her gnarled, arthritic fingers struggled to close the lid. She slid the box onto its shelf and rang for the attendant to help her into bed.

Her mind hadn't faded and she recalled the events surrounding her "discovery" in every detail as she drifted off to sleep. *Me an' Bel decided we had to get even with Sgt. Fatty since he'd been yellin' at us every day for a week not to ride our bikes on the sidewalks in town. We thunk it through and splashed him good, but I was goin' too fast and hit the store.*

Scared! I run straight home an' hid in my room bawlin' my eyes out wonderin' how I was gonna pay for another bike. And ... why didn't I hurt after such a crash? Aw, hell, I knew something weren't right. I'm no dummy. I seen kids get hurt all the time, falling off bikes, trippin' an' stuff ... all that crying and bleeding! I felt fine. No bleedin', no scratches, not even a loose tooth!

Mama come found me and yelled at me, wonderin' why everyone was lyin' about me gettin' myself killed. I broke down an' told her what happened. So she hauled me to the Doc's, but he said I was fine. Even Sgt. Fatty said later that I should be dead after hittin' the wall like that. Mama figured I'd been saved for God's own reason and praised Jesus aloud 24/7 for the next couple of months.

I wasn't so sure. I thought back on it. Never once do I remember getting hurt, bruised, or even scraping my knees. And I wasn't no saint. Even fell out of a tree once—a good fifteen feet—came up without a scratch. I'd been like this my whole life, never needed a single Band-Aid ... some kind of freak.

*

At lunch the next day, they put a new resident at our table. They told us Angie had been moved to hospice. The man's name was Lars Gun ... Gund ... Gunder-something. We all said hi and Mickie, ye gods, she went to askin' him a ton of questions until I got tired of her voice and told her to shut up and leave the man to eat.

He'd been polite an' all, but mostly he kept eyein' me, his forehead all crinkled up. I finally got uncomfortable enough and excused myself.

At dinner, though, he started askin' the questions. I got five for everyone else's one. Mickie got pissed off and told him that she was there, too, and I wasn't the only lady at the table. I finally told 'em both to be quiet, but he kept looking at me like I was someone he knew. That's when Mickie turned on her charms, oozing all sweet and suggestive. We all knew she was man-crazy. Hell, she told us all too often that she'd been married five times and had always had "a man or two on the side."

He finally give her a big toothless grin, reached out and took her hand. He said, "I'm flattered you find me attractive Miss Mickie, but I have a heart only for my dear departed wife, an' my body's too wore out to please even me." He let go of her hand and went back to eating.

Mickie just nodded and didn't say another word to him. I wasn't sure, but that Lars, there was something different about his voice just then. But that seemed to break the mood and we all just finished our dinners. At least until Mrs. Crawford, the head nurse, swooped to our table. I wished I could be invisible 'cause that woman gives me the creeps. She's all plastic smiles, always talking down to us just 'cause we's old. She introduced herself to Lars and said she'd be seeing him and his family tomorrow at nine. Then she reminded me that I had my medical evaluation tomorrow morning at ten. She'd have someone come get me so I won't be late – again. After she left, I saw he's still lookin' at me all scrunchie faced. I just squinted back at him, shook my head and rolled myself back to my room.

About nine-thirty that night, I wheeled myself into the commons room 'cause I couldn't sleep. Lars sat there all alone watching a TV show with a huge grin on his face. Wouldn't you know it turned out to be one of them X-Men movies! The last thing I'd watch was a film about good guy mutant freaks. But he musta heard my chair 'cause he turned and saw me as I'd started leaving.

He called me over. "Evenin', Miss Norah. Hey! I said hi."

I would have kept ignoring him, but he called, "Hey, Repel." That was my superhero name.

I froze. Couldn't think straight enough except to deny it outright. "Wha ... Wha ... what you talkin' about? Who's Repel? I ain't no Repel."

He stood up and, with his walker, started waddling my way. I spun my wheelchair to beat a path to my room when I felt something on the back of my head. Then came a loud crash! I stopped and twisted around to see him standing in the middle of the room, teetering on his own. His walker was bent up and resting on one of the tables next to a broken lamp. As everyone came running in, he said to me, "The hell you ain't."

*

61

The clock glared back: 2:38 a.m. *What's happened? For so long I'd been able to hide, blend back in. I don't want to be Repel again!* My thoughts drifted back ...

Couple of days after I crashed into the store's wall, a TV lady from Raleigh come knockin' on our door saying she'd heard about the "Miracle Girl" and wanted to do a story. I said no, but Mama wanted the whole world to know I was blessed, chosen somehow. It turned out to be a whole-town kinda story. It included us, Sgt. Fatty, my friends and others who'd seen the accident. They showed pictures of what was left of my cousin's ~~bike~~—I had to promise to buy him a new one— and the broken brick wall of the building I'd hit. I thought back hard and vaguely remembered pushing my face into those poor old busted bricks. Only felt like I's snuggling my pillow.

About a week after it aired, a woman and man wearing business clothes showed up at the house. They said they were from Washington D.C., flashing IDs, and wanted to talk to us. So we sat down in the living room all solemn and quiet. Every time the woman asked a question, Mama would go off with another of her "Halleluiah" rants. They exchanged a quick glance. I saw it. Then the woman asked Mama to show her to the bathroom. When they left, the man grinned at me for a second, then picked up the soda bottle in front of him and threw it—hard— right at me. Before I could even blink, it hit my forehead and splintered into a thousand million pieces! I barely even felt it, didn't even have the sense to fake cry.

It got ugly right after that, but we ended up going with them 'cause I had my "special gift" and they convinced Mama that they would show me how to use it to help people, just what Jesus would want me to do. Never even got a chance to say goodbye to Bel and my other friends. It would be near twelve years before I got back home. The town stayed pretty much the same, but all my friends, like me, had grown up and changed. But none quite the way I'd changed.

*

"Can't we go around the long way?" I asked the nurse as she wheeled me down the hallway to my eval meeting.

"Why?" she asked in a dull voice, not seeming to really want to know. "We don't want you to be late."

I didn't think it'd help if I told her that I hated Mrs. Crawford, so I just said, "I love going down the ramp next to her office."

"That dangerous thing? They should take that out and put in a wider, safer ramp." She sounded condescending, like a teacher to a first grader. So we went the short way and in another minute I was left alone outside Mrs. Crawford's office to wait.

Ten minutes after ten, her door opened and Lars Gundersven—I listened this time—and his family come out and they was talking all happy and gushy with Crawford. He spared me only a sideways glance as he passed.

Then the head nurse's plastic voice greeted me loud enough to be heard by all as she wheeled me into her office.

"So, Norah, how are we today?"

She needs to just turn it off. "We? I'm fine and you're late." I sat stone-faced. Something about pushing this woman's buttons appealed to my darker side.

"Well, about that, our new resident's meeting took a little longer than I anticipated." She shuffled some papers as she spoke and continued, leaving me no opening. "You are here for your semi-annual medical review. We will go over your health, your medications, therapies, overall prognoses, nutrition, and how well you socialize with our other residents. Understand?"

I sat flexing my jaw as she droned on about how healthy I was and that I took fewer meds than any other resident, blah, blah, blah. I only really paid attention when she stated that Mickie had complained about me always being rude to her at our table.

"Why that dried-up old fish keeps hittin' on all the men, especially Lars, the new man who was just in here."

"So?"

"So? I ain't got the stomach to sit and listen to all her oozing on that poor man. Ask the others."

"I have. They think it's cute. You'll just have to be more tolerant."

"No, I don't."

"Really? Then you leave me no choice." She scrawled something on her notepad. "You will sit by yourself at the green table for a week."

I said nothing then, nor when they brought me back to my room. *The "sad table."* I hate that woman, and now Mickie's on my list, too. I'm not a vengeful person, but this is just wrong. I wonder what I could do? I know what Repel would do.

*

They put me in a special school. I got just one teacher all to myself first off, and then I worked on my "powers" in the afternoon, kinda like a long gym class. I got to liking it. It sure was fun to throw myself against stuff and just bounce off. We practiced gymnastics, tumbling, and trampoline. At first, all I had to do was land on my feet. Shoot, that weren't hard at all. After supper, I'd spend time with

Mama and Papa, but that became less often after about a month.

Finally, they sat us down and told me the truth about my powers. Seems I was born with an extra pair of genes. They said it was rare and I was one-of-a-kind! Mama stood up and started ranting about me being God's work and that we had to leave. Papa finally said, "Shut yer trap and just listen for once in yer life!"

The government people said Mama couldn't take me 'cause of some special legal stuff that they argued about for a long time. They finally asked me if I wanted to keep doin' my superhero training.

I got all excited and said I'd stay. That ended the meeting. Later, my teacher complimented me for choosing to stay, but that the hardest and most important part would be to keep it a secret. She said most people don't feel comfortable with differences, especially like mine. Yep, I'm a superhero in training. Cool! I even saw it on my teacher's clipboard, but I started laughing so hard I had to look away. They used those initials ... S.H.I.T. Swear to God!

Visits with my folks only happened now about once a month and lasted just an hour or so. One day Mama come alone and told me that Papa got sick. I had to stay strong 'cause the government would be moving them to Arizona for medical care. That was the last time I saw them. Shoot, I don't even know where they's buried.

My training became more focused. Instead of bouncing off things, they wanted me to focus to keep going. A few weeks later, I started breaking through walls, wood ones and brick ones! Wow! Clark's Pharmacy wouldn't have a wall if I did then what I can do now!

Then came the big change. I got my period. All of a sudden I was unstoppable! They told me my chemistry had changed and somehow made my powers even stronger. After just a few days of practice, I could bounce myself across the gymnasium and break through the floor where I landed. That's when they started shooting at me.

*

The second evening that I had dinner at the "sad table," Mr. Gundersven joined me. Karen, our meal helper, brought his tray for him. I guess the look on my face told of my astonishment 'cause he started chuckling.

"You can't be here," I told him shaking my head. "I'm in jail. This here's the 'sad table' for rule breakers and people Mrs. Crawford don't like. Did you piss her off?"

"Relax," he said and grinned. "We're safe. I have a knack of getting my way."

"Good," I said. "You gonna need that 'cause Crawford's heading this way." I put my head down. Mama always said that staring at people weren't polite.

"Mr. Gunderson! Why are you sitting here? I'm sorry but you have to stay at your assigned table." She'd blasted that all out in her loud plastic voice in about one and a half seconds. As she lifted his tray, Lars snagged her by the wrist. She froze and her eyes fixed on him in her "Oh-No-You-Didn't" stare.

Lars started speaking in that different voice again. "The name is GunderSVEN, Mrs. Crawford. I assure you, I am doing just fine with my friend, Ms. Broxton. She seemed so lonely here and I just couldn't be happy or even think of eating knowing she was all by herself. We have so little time, don't you think, to be happy?"

Crawford looked confused. "Well, I, uh ... I guess ... but, you see ..." she stammered. Her brow furled and her eyes shifted quickly as if looking for an answer to something. "You, uh, you need to sit at your own table," she finally managed.

I watched Lars's deep blue eyes narrow and his voice went softer, yet held more authority than hers even when she spoke to us all using the room's microphone system. "You told me this morning that I could join Norah at dinner, you remember, don't you?"

"I, I, uhm, yes ... I guess I do. Uh, it must have slipped my mind. Please, enjoy your dinners." She released her hold on his tray, straightened up, and shot out of the dining hall.

"Whew!" Lars sighed as his fork pierced the pork chop. "I haven't had to work that hard in a very long time." He looked up at me and smiled. "How are you?"

"How'd you do that?"

"Do what? What did I do ... he paused, "Repel?"

I ignored his reference. "You hypnotized her! You put that thought in her brain. How did you twist her thinking?"

"This kind of thing's pretty easy for any, uh, oh, let's say ... superhero. Don't you think?"

*

The first couple of times actually hurt, basically 'cause I'd never felt pain before. They started with a pellet gun, then a small .22 caliber, but then they worked their way up to .45 and even .50 caliber bullets. The bigger ones actually started leaving light bruises. It took some getting used to! The skill I had to practice was to focus my repelling powers to send them bullets right back where they come from. By Christmastime, I could return a .45 caliber bullet fifty yards and come

within two feet of the gun that fired it. They said I was ready.
    For what though, I ain't sure.

*

Lars and I met in the common room that evening to talk about what each of us had gone through.

He started. "I didn't even know I had powers until I got caught by the IRS and given the chance to join up or go to prison. I thought I was just a good con man. The feds ended up calling me 'Hypno.' How blasé. I used that ... what you saw me do to Crawford, but most of what I did was to listen in on interrogations and let them know whether a person was telling the truth or lying.

"I helped them with a lot of international crimes and spy stuff. Got myself captured once, shot once, too. Got to the point, though, where I just wanted to go home and be left alone, too much hate and deceit out there. Everything I did had to be hush-hush. I was some kinda secret weapon. I wasn't like you getting all the TV time."

"So how'd you know it was me? I had a mask."

He gave me another toothless grin. "Your eyes. Saw it right off. I could never get enough of your eyes."

I tsked a few times. *What a charmer!* I told him about Clark's Pharmacy and the TV lady. "After my training, they moved me to New York City. My first case was the Metro Bank robbery.

"They snuck me into the bank to get caught so I could size up how they held the hostages. I got the four baddies to forget all about them when I cut loose. Ten minutes after I'd been 'captured,' we all were talking to the press and the world found out about me. After that they gave me a costume with a mask to hide my 'secret' identity. Sheesh, I lived in a building surrounded by government goons.

"Most of the time I broke up crimes in progress. Then, after twenty-some years of being Repel, some new FBI deputy director thought I should do PR for the department, too. That's when I knew I was done. Nothing so demeaning than to take the freak and put on a show."

"What about that Hoover Dam thing?" He sounded hesitant, like he shouldn't bring it up.

I shook my head. "That just proved that when someone really wants to hurt themselves, we can't prevent it. They brought me in 'cause they suspected he was more than just a whacko in a hot air balloon. No one knew about the bomb until it went off. Thankfully, it wasn't powerful enough to do any damage, except to the idiot in the balloon."

"I'd heard that you threw some kinda of force shield to protect the dam."

I chuckled. "No harm in telling things honest now. Nope, never knew how to do that. That was something some desk jockey come up with to impress the newspeople. I had to practice that for six months after. They thought I could save more people that way, but I never figured out how to do it. Near as I could tell, this power of mine was inside me. It wasn't something I could shoot out, not like that. But then they never said that out loud. Nope, didn't want me falling out of favor ... couldn't bear the thought that their superhero wasn't so super."

"C'mon, Norah, every one of us, even our comic versions had their weaknesses, their kryptonite."

"Lars, you know better'n that. They could've killed us any time they wanted. Shoot you in the head, drown me and we're both dead. Too simple? Hell, I lost count of the times I considered it myself, managed to not jump off that bridge at least half a dozen times."

Lars took my hand. "Why? Even I never had thoughts that dark."

"You can let go my hand, Lars. I ain't about to lie to ya."

He smiled, and I paused. That old geezer'd be right handsome if he had a few teeth.

"No worries, my lady. My power has never worked on anyone with their own powers. They checked into it. Never figured it out."

"Who else you knew with powers?" I asked, not sure I wanted to get an idea how many of us they controlled.

"Just one. A fascinating woman with telekinesis. We worked several cases together. Ended up marrying her. She also never forgot anything." He quickly wiped an eye then sat there, blinking and grinning like a fool.

"How long you been alone?"

He sighed. "Too long. Just over a year in real time, forever for my heart. But we had two beautiful kids. You?"

"No. Never felt comfortable enough about myself to want to share with anyone. Couple of guys I met were tempting but, you know, life got in the way."

"Too bad. I remember watching you on TV. You were hot! Even when you got older."

*

"I don't care!" I screamed at the top of my lungs. And yes, I slammed my fist on his desk and that beautiful oak shattered.

"I've been your pet for more than twenty-five years. I've jumped through every hoop you threw my way. I've stopped criminals, prevented crimes, saved lives and monuments." I fought back the tears as my inner dam finally broke.

"You've tucked me into cars, trains, planes, and the back of a garbage truck—you remember that one? All at a moment's notice and I never said no, never hesitated to do my job. Then you put me on display like a trick dog to show off my 'magic,' which you all somehow took credit for. Every interview I gave was so well scripted.

"Then there's the movie. Very inspirational! So, tell me who was it about? It sure as hell weren't me! And I'm not even going to mention the book. What? An autobiography? I never knew it existed until some poor little kid held one out wanting me to autograph it! No, I'm done. You all sucked my life dry."

*

Norah blinked from the recollection, but still managed a smile. "Thanks, Lars. You're a dear, but I never felt 'hot.' I remember feeling used. After a while the thrill of being 'super' just became a burden. All them people out there expectin' me to show up an' save the day. They started criticizing why I was somewhere else doing something else. The demands of their expectations became overwhelming.

"Like after Hoover Dam, there were months of complaints and ... oh, hell, let's just call 'em suggestions about how I could be a better superhero.

"Those government people gave me all kinds of lip service, but were doing things behind my back. When I found out they 'authorized' that dumb-ass movie and my so-called autobiography, I quit. I changed my hair color and style and started living in homeless shelters. It wasn't comfortable, but at least I could be me."

Lars sat silently for about a minute. "That's crazy. I mean, I'm sure you saw the papers. We all wondered what happened to you. I was worried for you. You were kind of my idol, uh, among other things."

"Lars!"

"Don't worry. Fantasies were never my thing. But I did always read the stories about you and looked just a bit longer at the pictures. I don't think my wife ever noticed. I wouldn't let that happen."

The night shift head nurse walked by just then, but stopped

abruptly when she saw us. Checking her clipboard, she came over to us tsking. "Both of you need to return to your rooms. It's late. I'll help you, Mr. Gundersven." She came next to him and took his arm to help him from his chair.

Lars, once in contact with her, kicked his superpower into action. "Stop," he said simply and she did. His eyes narrowed and he tipped her chin to face him. "Why are you doing this?"

Her body stayed still, making her seem like a mannequin ready to fall over. In a very monotone voice, she replied, "Mrs. Crawford left a note on my chart to keep the two of you apart."

Lars and I exchanged a glance, eyebrows raised. "Why?" he asked.

"I don't know. She left no explanation, but when this has happened before it usually is because the residents don't get along."

Lars looked at me. "We'll talk more." Then he told the nurse, "You will forget our conversation. It never happened." He then clapped his hands twice. The nurse blinked.

"Oops! I'm sorry. I slipped!" Lars said, leaning back in his chair.

"Oh, are you all right? Here let me help you up and get you to your room."

They left and I sat a moment longer fuming. *Mrs. Crawford stirred my ire. She'd gone too far. Time for Repel!*

*

I only used my powers once in a get-you-back kind of way. I'd beaten out four big jocks to get a job as a bouncer at a college club in Queens near St. John's University. Surprised 'em all I did. You don't 'spect a girl keepin' the peace in a place like this. One night two groups of frat boys got into a spat and were about to take it outside. I wanted to diffuse the whole stupid thing, but they were really tanked. So I challenged them in wrist wrestling. The side that could defeat a girl would be declared winner. Obviously, drunk or not, they bought into it and of course neither side won. They left still trading insults about being beaten so badly by a girl, but their spat had been replaced by their embarrassment.

Karl, the manager, liked my style with a fifty-dollar bonus. After closing, I headed home and, surprise, met two of the boys from the Kappa Pi group. After ignoring their penny-ante threats, one of them took a swing at me. I let him connect with my jaw and he fell to the sidewalk cradling a broken hand. I laughed at him, telling him that's what he gets for hittin' a girl. His friend pulled out a knife and threw it at me. I focused my repelling and sent it right back hitting him in his crotch. The TV news reported that two fraternity men were attacked by a group of unknown assailants. Sure, male ego ... this girl could count on it every time.

69

*

Now I had a new foe to face. I had to be discreet about using my powers. Too obvious, and I'd most certainly be sent to County, the hellhole of nursing homes. Age had been the only foe I couldn't defeat, so I needed this damnable nursing home. Hell, most ninety-four year olds do. I confided in Lars and he said he wanted in on the action.

Two weeks went by. Lars said at lunch one day that we needed to watch the new X-Men movie tonight. Isn't he clever? He knew that no one else liked that kind of movie. So I went into the commons room about 9:15 that night and there he sat, right next to Mickie! Of course, she was doin' all the talkin' ... goin' on and on about her husbands and her affairs. How could she just be happy with one man? But, now she saw everything she could want in Lars. She was giving me snarky glances all the while she clung to his arm, even rubbing his leg. Lars, or rather Hypno, 'suggested' she had a nasty headache and wanted to go to her room.

With her neatly sent off, he never said a word, just held up a new package of balloons he'd pilfered from the staff lounge! I giggled so hard I damn near wet myself. Gave him a big hug, too! Now this had to be done just right, so the two of us superheroes plotted our revenge on the evil Mrs. Crawford.

*

About three years after I'd demolished the Deputy Director's desk, I saw a headline in the newspaper. It seemed I was dead. I never did like to watch TV news. Didn't believe a word they said. I'd been there and I knew what had happened in my interviews and how they told their pretty little lies and half-truths.

The paper said I'd died of unknown causes. Lots of conspiracy theories followed. Who did it? Why? How did they kill off a superhero?

Dignitaries from all across the country attended my "funeral." Amusing, the desperate lengths they went to. But the public's reaction ... truly heartbreaking. They did love me, or at least who they thought I was. The eulogy my old boss delivered clearly held a hidden message. The public heard them say the likes of me would never be seen again. I distinctly heard them say I'd best never show my face again. No problem. I could appreciate this "dead" thing. Oh, I don't doubt for a second that they'd known my whereabouts all along. All that matters is I was allowed to be free!

*

70

On the appointed day, Lars and I took the long way around the nursing home until we neared the top of the ramp. I cradled two overfilled water balloons on my lap under my blanket.

We'd practiced our attack for more than a week, exercising old skills and coaxing old habits back from dormancy. We'd rehearsed the thing several times in the wee hours of the night. Only got caught once, but thanks to old "Hypno," no one ever really remembered how that wall got damaged.

Lars stood behind me. We waited.

Mrs. Crawford loved routine and could be counted on to do everything on a very tight schedule, all to our advantage. Today was Wednesday. At 2:15 p.m., as scheduled, she opened her office door to begin her rounds of the East Wing.

Lars pushed my chair hard. I came a flyin' down that ramp faster than any wheelchair should travel. The commotion caught everyone by surprise and I let loose my balloons, guided by my Repel power and soaked old Mrs. Crawford head to foot. I repelled my wheelchair all the way to my room.

Thank you, superpowers! She got wetter than Sgt. Fatty!

An hour later, Mickie had been packed up and was awaiting transfer to the County Elderly Care Center on the other side of town. The staff couldn't believe she had attacked Mrs. Crawford with water balloons!

Everybody remembered seeing her do it.

***

More Powerful than a Locomotive
by Paul K. Metheney

He would be lying if he said that he didn't mind giving up being a celebrity. Just once in a very great while. And he tries not to lie. Flying around the world, flexing his power, getting his way, nothing could stop him. It often made him feel nearly invulnerable. It's true that *everything* he had done in his past wasn't totally in line with "Truth, Justice, and the American Way," but all those moments were long behind him. She had changed him completely. More than that. He wanted to be a better man FOR her.

He once thought he was the smartest, most powerful, person alive. Until he met her. He could explain how molecules interacted, how universes were formed, but she understood how people worked. She had a strength and humanity about her that he would never match. He loved her for years before actually telling her. Holding that truth in was the hardest thing he had ever done in a lifetime of unbelievable feats. There were obstacles to their life together. One particularly large obstacle. Eventually, it was her, not him, who overcame that problem and their relationship blossomed.

The feelings he had for her were more powerful than anything he had ever known. At one time, he was considered high above almost everyone, and now all he wants is to be by her side.

He remembers the day Lo told him they were going to have a

baby. Other than the day Jonathan was actually born and the day they got married, this would forever remain the happiest moment of his life. He immediately told her that he would give up his other life. Forever.

"You don't need to do that," she said.

"I do. My new mission in life is to protect our new family."

*

Retiring

He, in his more public persona, held a press conference later that week, but gave the exclusive interview to his sweetheart. In his press announcement, he simply said he was retiring from the world at large and that he had new priorities. As far as everyone else was concerned, he would merely disappear. Harder than it may sound for someone as publicly recognizable as he was, but not impossible, given his earlier feats. One day he was everywhere, the next he pulled a Howard Hughes.

*

"Chief ..." she began.

"Don't call me 'Chief,'" her editor snapped. "Whatever you want to expense or wherever you want to go, the answer is No!"

"It's not that—" she started again.

"What is *he* doing here?" He turned toward her husband. "Are you here for moral support or to be the muscle?"

"No, sir. I think you should listen to what she has to say," he said timidly.

"Well? Out with it. What kind of fantastic nonsense do you want to cover this time?" the editor asked.

She looked at her husband. She turned her gaze downward.

"I'm quitting."

"WHAT! Very funny. You couldn't live without the thrill of chasing of some story. What do you think you could do? What kind of joke is this?"

"We're going to have a baby," she said quietly.

For the first time in ten years, the editor was speechless.

"I'm going to leave in about two months, before I really start to show. We want to focus on raising a family and maybe write a few books. Besides, you don't need me around here. You're constantly saying how I eat up your salary budget and we know things in print journalism are getting tighter and tighter." She didn't go so far to say that print journalism was dead, but danced all around it. It helped that Perry had passed on a few years earlier. She didn't know if she could tell her former boss to his face. Perry would never have accepted that his best investigative reporter abandoning him.

She insisted that if her husband could give up his life and identity to raise a family, retiring from the life of a reporter was the least she could do.

Finally, the editor could speak.

"Great Caesar's Ghost!" he turned to her husband. "So, this was what that press conference was really about the other day! Is this about more money? I could—"

"No, Chief, it's not about money. You know very well that with his power and abilities, we will never have to worry about money ever again. We're having a baby and investigating stories the way I always have is just too dangerous for an expectant mother. It's time for a new chapter. This is about focusing on what's important now."

The editor looked at each of them.

"Well, I wish you the best of luck," and squared his shoulders, "But, don't think I'm going to take it easy on you traitors for the next few months. And I mean both of you! Get out there and find some news! And you," pointing his unlit cigar at her husband, "go do whatever it is you do. It's obviously not working for a living. Whataya waiting for?"

"Yes, Chief," they said in unison.

*

As soon she told him she was pregnant, he flew to Switzerland and the Cayman Islands and established new, untraceable bank accounts for them, trust funds for the baby, and had their wills re-worked. From now on, he wanted to live under the radar. Way under the radar.

*

That anonymity wasn't always appreciated, especially by a certain Kansas City bank manager.

"Ms. Siegel, what is this?"

"It looks like a cashier's check, Mr. Schuster. Made out to the bank," the lead teller at the Kansas National Bank said. "Based on the memo, I would say it's to pay off a mortgage."

"But there's no sender's name and it's drawn from a bank in Europe," the bank manager stammered. "This is all highly irregular. What am I supposed to do with this?"

"Looks like to me, all we *can* do is pay off the mortgage and send this lady the deed."

*

"New bank accounts, huh? What about your rule of always telling the truth?" his wife asked him when he returned.

"I didn't lie. I gave the Swiss banker my birth name, and I am fairly certain he recognized me. I may have done some business there in the past. None of that money was obtained illegally. And for the record, I didn't say 'always.' There are times when I need to protect our identities and I may have to genuflect a bit."

"So you just paid off Ma Kent's mortgage just like that?"

"And hired a neighbor to help with the chores. And created a savings account for her. I only did it because I know you feel about her. I guess I should have talked it over with you first."

"Damn skippy you should have! Why didn't you insist she come live with us? I love her to death and who has more experience taking care of a special child more than she does?"

"Honey, I *did* try to get her to move in with us, but she won't give up the farm and the community she's lived in for decades. When she wouldn't move, I did the next best thing I could think of. She did say she would come for extended visits to help out. Sorry again."

"Don't be obtuse, Boy Scout. Technically, that's your money, but even so, you did exactly the right thing. Like you always do. Is it hard being so perfect?"

"It *is* a curse. And you know I hate it when you all me that."

"Why do you think I do it?"

*

Thanks to her Pulitzer and her well-(and sometimes self-)publicized exploits with his former identity and his adversaries, every major publishing firm in the country was in a bidding war to contract her story. Her agent procured a sizable advance which further concealed their actual net worth. They honestly declared all her income, including the advance for her book, on their taxes. Their finances would not bear up under intense scrutiny, but who was going to look closely at the tax returns of Mr. and Mrs. Joe Average? She was careful to separate her written exploits from their current life. She refused to do book tours, but it was hardly necessary to make the book a best seller, with both of their past exploits.

*

Solitude

The couple bought a home in the Florida Keys to be as far away as possible from any temptation to investigate unusual stories and to avoid any tempting criminal activity. They purchased the home under their newly assumed identities. They paid cash for the house, which raised an eyebrow with the realtor, but avoided a pesky credit check. They needed to buy a home and not rent so they could make some extensive renovations to it. She moved in upon leaving the paper and he commuted in his own unique manner. She worked on her book, in a quiet, rented office in nearby Islamorada, while he renovated the house as quickly as he could. He also called in few of his past associates to help with the more laborious aspects. They were more than eager to assist the happy couple. Someone had escaped "The Life" and was going to be part of a normal family. Well, mostly normal.

He insisted that every room have red solar radiation emitters in the ceilings, just in case. He powered those through solar panels on the roof. A nice touch of irony, he thought. Solar-powered protection.

Thanks to his familiarity with high technology, the house was kitted as the smartest smart-home ever built. Besides voice commands, the home's AI often anticipated their needs and was programmed additionally for the baby's safety.

While she was busy writing offsite, he installed some discreet and passive defensive measures in the house such as Kevlar-tungsten-lead alloy reinforcement behind the sheet rock. Bullet and radiation resistant glass in the windows and titanium cores to the doors. Radar, sonar, and slightly more exotic sensor arrays monitored the skies, sea, and land around their new home, practically a fortress. Less passive were the futuristic weapons systems hidden in the landscaping. He didn't *hide* these alterations from her, but also didn't tell her about them. He didn't want her to worry about his past coming back to haunt them. She had enough on her plate with a baby on the way and a book to write. She would have thought all these precautions ridiculous, but there was someone in both their pasts who all these preparations may not be sufficient. Someone who may hold a grudge. Besides, who doesn't have robotic, Krypton-powered laser cannons retracted into the front lawn?

Along with the more discreet features of the house, they installed a panic room (which she insisted they call a "secure-room," because *she* doesn't panic). The room hosted a multitude of security monitors to scan both the interior and exterior of the home, an independent, uninterruptible power source, and was large enough, and stocked so well that they could stay there a very long time if need be.

*

Looks Ain't Everything

Given her status as an up-and-coming best-selling author and their pasts, they decided to alter their appearance to further any connection to their previous lives. Before any changes, she had plenty of publicity photos taken for her book jackets. She wouldn't look that way for a long time. She published the book under her original name, but lived in her new identity. Kind of a nom de plume in reverse.

He hired specialists to help with their transformations. Thanks to his past life, he was very familiar with people who specialized in both secret identities and discretion. She had her hair cut extremely short and colored sunny blonde. Coloring his hair was a bit more problematic, so he opted to go with a strawberry-blond wig that was so realistic, she had a hard time telling it wasn't his actual hair. He also grew a Van Dyke beard to further change his appearance. She thought it ironically made him look slightly villainous, but she couldn't deny it changed the shape of his jawline and hid the dimple in his chin. She jokingly suggested he wear glasses and a withering look from him ended that suggestion. A fake earring stud and colored contacts completed the transformation. She even let him smoke an occasional cigar, which he found surprisingly relaxing, as long as it wasn't in the house or near her. Add a colorful Hawaiian shirt and it all added up to a man not even his own mother would recognize. He would still have to slump to hide his physique, but he was used to creating that illusion, so people would constantly underestimate him. Eventually the wig would get phased out, but not for a while. The public's memory of him needed to fade a bit. Okay, it may take more than a bit.

*

Day Off

The couple took a rare day off. Funny how busy they were for two, supposedly, retired people. Her first book was off to the publishers for a final review, and she was well on her way to outlining the second. Her baby bump was showing, but they decided that they wanted to spend the day off at the beach.

"You know, honey, we could just buy up all the property around us so we could have it all to ourselves," he suggested, eyeing her for her reaction. "In fact, we could just buy the whole Key."

She reacted. The beach remained public to property owners and their guests.

He stretched on his beach chair. The sun's rays seemed to energize him and revitalize his strength. In his past life, he never really took the time to just *sit* in the sun. He still had to use tanning sprays to get some color, a fact of his genetics he believed he would have to live with for the rest of his life. He glanced over at his beautiful wife. She spent most of her time indoors, writing, but still managed a beautiful, golden tan. Not quite bronze, but a nice warm, healthy look. It went well with her now blonde hair color.

He daydreamed about the day he would play in the surf with Little Jonathan. Teaching him the mysteries of the galaxy, advanced science, throwing a frisbee, how to talk to girls. He was determined to give the boy as normal a life as he could, given Jonathan's lineage and heritage. Lo would help with that. Even if her own childhood was not exactly loving, she would show the boy how to be more ... human than he could. That adventure would begin in earnest in just a matter of months, but right now it's just a relaxing day next to his honey, stretched out in the Floridia sunshine.

A couple of tanned, young women in scanty bathing suits walked into to the surf several dozen yards to the south of their beachfront. He subtly lowered his sunglasses to see them better. No one needed telescopic vision to appreciate the sights on this beach.

"Eyes front, mister." She didn't even lift her head from her magazine.

He grinned. "Yes, ma'am." She never let him get away with anything. Another reason he loved her so much.

*

Sneaking Off

He might've tried to say that he couldn't remember the circumstances under which he snuck out of the house, but that would have been lie. He had an eidetic memory. He never forgot anything. Usually a boon to his lifestyle, except when he was trying to make honest excuses.

It started innocently enough, watching the evening news. Thanks to her help in him changing his life, he regularly ignored stories of enormous gem shipments, possible bank heists, and international coup d'etats. But even under her watchful eye, it was impossible to turn blind eye to natural disasters like earthquakes, avalanches, and even solar flares. Tonight, she was online, shopping for baby furniture, when the story broke on the national news. A hurricane had suddenly changed course and was heading right for the Florida Keys.

"Babe, I'm going to go out for a bit, get some air," he called out, heading for the door.

He made his way quickly to a nearby hangar-like building, at their private airstrip he bought without her knowledge, changed his clothes to something more appropriate, and from there, flew toward the heart of the hurricane.

Numerous well-placed super-heated explosions, air-shattering sonic booms, and artificially generated wind storms later and the hurricane diverted harmlessly out into the Atlantic.

Flying quickly back to his hidden warehouse, he changed from his flight suit and ran back to their home.

She was waiting at the front door.

Arms folded. Feet apart. Toe tapping. The one eyebrow up. The right eyebrow. This was not good.

Where was an apocalypse when you needed one?

"Get enough air?" she asked cooly.

"Baby, I just—" he started.

"Don't baby me! We have a *baby* on the way and the last thing he needs is his daddy flying out in front of a hurricane doing who knows what? His LYING father, I might add."

"I didn't lie. I did get some air."

"I know. It's all over the news. Evidently, a hurricane plane got video of you diverting the storm. What were you thinking?"

"I was thinking that storm was headed straight for us," he said.

"You and our baby. I needed to do something. Then once I started, I started thinking about all the other people in the way of that thing that didn't have someone that could stop it, and I just had to do what I could. And you know what, honey? It felt good. Yeah, I do miss being in the spotlight, but more importantly, I miss doing *big* things. Things that only I can do."

She softened at that. He looked up and she, in her raw emotion, forgot about their cover identities and used his real name.

"I know. I was just so worried. You're not invulnerable, you know. If something would happen to you, Lex, I don't know what I would do."

✳✳✳

Leave It Alone
By Steve Rouse

"I'm tellin' ya, Commander," warned D'Armin, "you're a damn fool if you even consider makin' off with that, that, whatever it is."

Commander Makale Natallo eyed the scientist with a tired gaze. Drawing in a long breath, she exercised all of her military self-control. "Mission Specialist Gerali D'Armin, we have had this conversation three times already. The first happened within an hour after the anomaly's discovery. The second happened during our staffing ten hours after its discovery. The third time was earlier today in the cafeteria when you chose to interrupt my breakfast.

"Each time I have referred to policies written in the *Code of Ethics for Space and Planetary Exploration*, third edition, 2186 AD. Since that has obviously not made an impression on you, I will paraphrase. It is our job.

"Specifically, we are to '... explore, mapping and measuring any stellar masses, any orbiting masses, and any other items or anomalies encountered.' Now here is where your confusion lies, 'This includes discerning as closely as practical, if such items or anomalies are of a natural or technological origin.'

"Since we have found one, this is how we are proceeding. You have the right to personally disagree, but I will not allow you to interfere with or jeopardize any phase of this mission. Is that clear? Any such action on your part and I will put you in Stasis."

"Really? How will we get home if I'm frozen?" she asked.

"I'll pull your settings from ship's systems."

D'Armin frowned. "You are intent on retrieving this thing?"

"I am ... our job." Natallo leaned back in her chair. "Just like I said."

"Then I insist going on record opposing your plan, regardless of how you choose to justify it, and I hope to Heaven and Hell that you are charged with our murders, posthumously, if necessary."

"So noted. You are hereby confined to quarters during retrieval. Ensign McKinney will escort you to your quarters." Natallo turned to her aide. "See to it that she stays there. Fuse the door, if need be." Commander Natallo turned to her communications panel. "Oh, and your systems access is hereby limited to 'Read Only.'"

*

Ignoring her confinement, Astro-physicist Gerali D'Armin completed a review of the propulsion readouts from their voyage out. The ship's propulsion system, a radically improved plasma drive with a modified ionic fusion interchanger—one that she had designed—had allowed the *Nebular* to reach further into space than ever before. It synced the ship's plasma coating resonance to the frequencies of the environmental radiation sources allowing the ship to interweave with those cosmic flows instead of plowing through it as traditional ships' propulsion systems did. Physical distances were inconsequential with this type of phase-drive. Thus equipped, theirs was the first ship to explore outside of the Orion-Cygnus Arm of the galaxy.

They were currently in a geosynchronous orbit above a planet about three times the size of earth, but only about sixty-four percent of its mass. It held oceans of an as-of-yet undetermined liquid. It had a thin methane-based atmosphere and a landscape of desert-like plains with ring-shaped mountain ranges from meteor impacts and a massive continent at its southern pole riddled with mountain ranges and volcanic activity, indicating continental drift.

Its uniqueness came from the fact that it followed a wobbly figure eight orbital pattern around both of the suns within the binary star system, according to *Nebular*'s sensors and computer projection. Its surface then would be alternately frozen and superheated. Hence, no surface plant life or even subsurface indications of life.

Upon its arrival, the *Nebular* had routinely launched multiple scanning orbiters. An anomaly was discovered on the first pass of a suborbital scan of the mid-range of its southern hemisphere, showing up as a patterned energy source. Subsurface scans showed no geologic explanation. A lander drone was dispatched, but ship's control lost contact when it entered the targeted zone. The same thing happened to a second drone. Plans were made to drop a manned lander to survey and retrieve the drones and the anomaly, if possible. The unique readings coming from the scans piqued her interests. She'd accessed those records and soon lost herself in the anomaly's bizarre readings.

*

Three hours into her confinement, Commander Natallo entered, waving her ever-present aide to remain in the hall. "We have a problem."

D'Armin looked up and feigned surprise. "Besides me? Whatever can we do?"

The Commander had no sense of humor according to most of the crew and D'Armin saw no sign of one now. "Our problem is the one you anticipated. The manned lander has also shut down, we're assuming, since we've lost contact with them. As our senior energy engineer, I want you to…"

"Excuse me?" D'Armin sat aghast, mouth open. "You have the audacity to come in here and demand that I help you with this, this madness!"

Natallo stood, fists clenched at her sides. "I am going to remind you just once that you are a non-commissioned officer aboard this vessel. As such, you are required to follow all military regulations and protocol that govern the operations of this ship," Natallo spoke at a controlled pace. "I need your expertise to retrieve my crew, our technology and, hopefully this alien technology as well. If you refuse this order, you will be arrested, put in stasis, and then tried for insubordination and mutiny when we return. When you are found guilty, you will be hanged. Do I make myself clear?"

"Perfectly. If I am to assist, putting my expertise on record, it has to be somewhere other than in your pocket."

Natallo raised an eyebrow. "Meaning?"

"Listen to me! Don't ignore facts and just do things the way you think you're supposed to. Your precious rule book was written based on what the human race anticipated we might find. It can't predict everything especially when so much of what we are experiencing hasn't been experienced before.

"I seriously think this anomaly of yours is some kind of power cell, but it seems to either absorb or somehow nullifies our power sources. Let me show you," she said and turned to her computer.

*

An hour later, after a bumpy ride through the peach-colored atmosphere, Gerali D'Armin, and her pilot, Carlos Esser, hovered high over the target site. The stark alien landscape stretched out before them.

The gentle terrain belied its history of ancient collisions. They targeted a crater bottom, shallowed from erosion and pot-marked with more recent hits. To the north a ring of peaks rippled the horizon like a row of cobalt teeth. Nearer, the rocky surface sparkled with pastel pinks and tans to clusters of darker purple and rust-colored outcroppings.

The manned and remote landers were clearly visible in the lander's display as they descended. But, she couldn't see the anomaly itself, despite the targeting computer's graphics. Esser glided their craft two kilometers passed the other ships and landed. D'Armin radioed the *Nebular.*

"Roger that and congratulations, D'Armin. Good call." Natallo's voice betrayed her relief. "Any updates on Krueger's lander?" The stress was back.

Esser responded. "The ship is a bit banged up, sitting at an angle. We saw their signal from the front viewport as we passed over, a double flash. So, both are alive. We're going EVA and will keep in constant communication."

D'Armin added. "If you lose us, you'll know we got too close."

"Confirmed. Continual enhanced visual and audio streaming. Natallo out."

Yeah, out of her mind, D'Armin thought. After checking each other's suit, they left the ship.

"Hard to tell, but only a bit more than the moon's gravity," Esser said as he stopped and scooped a bit of soil into a test tube. "Looks crystalline."

She agreed. "Amazing, considering its size. Very low density for a planet with an active core. Keep an eye on your suit ... readings, its feel, the sound of it, everything."

"Gotcha."

They walked in silence for the next fifteen minutes until they reached the lander.

"Yep, they hit hard. See, the port suspension is shot, Lucky they didn't puncture the hull." Esser poked at and rattled a displaced piece as he spoke, more to the ship than to her.

They rapped on the hull, waved at the faces of the crew and then heard the grating sound of the manual crank to open the outer door.

Both the pilot and engineer were in evac suits. Briefly, Krueger, the pilot, advised that their lander lost power at an altitude of seventy-eight meters above the anomaly.

Esser opened his tech-pad. Its blue screen tinged the lander's interior.

"You got power! How? How does yours work when everything we have is dead?" Krueger asked.

Esser smiled, but it was D'Armin answered. "We're not sure, but it's all about 'Bob,' I mean the anomaly." She shrugged at their curious gazes. "Hey, I just got tired of calling this thing 'the anomaly' all the time. Anyway, 'Bob' works with proximity. You got close enough. We haven't, at least not yet. And, speaking of the little devil, I haven't even seen it yet."

Madsen, the flight engineer, pointed to the starboard porthole. "About 150 meters out, sitting about four degrees below the horizon. Looks like a grapefruit."

D'Armin looked out from the port and noticed something roughly ovoid in shape. She couldn't be sure of its color due to the variances of the light of the twin suns and dust from the swirling winds. "Hi 'Bob,' she whispered."

She checked the power system of the lander with her own diagnostic computer and found no problems, except that all the power levels read zero. After some discussion, D'Armin and Esser left the stranded lander to test D'Armin's idea about conflicting power sources.

She and Esser walked side by side toward the anomaly. About twenty-five meters from the lander they stopped. D'Armin turned her suit's power off, something she hadn't cleared with Natallo.

"Are you sure about this?" Esser challenged yet again.

She faced him and put her finger to her lips. She touched her helmet to his. "Can you hear me?" she asked.

He nodded and then held up his index finger. He spoke into his suit mic, then nodded again to Gerali, gesturing that his suit's comlink was off.

Her rationale had swayed them. "Besides," she'd reasoned, "if it doesn't work, I'll still have the nineteen minutes of in-suit time before my air gets too thin and the temperature becomes a problem."

They continued walking with her suit powered down. Seventeen meters later, Esser tugged on her arm. His suit's power failed. The two stood there in silence. Two heartbeats later D'Armin's suit powered up. She'd touched nothing. She paused, checking the readouts twice. *Hadn't expected this.*

She signaled to Esser and made certain her comlink was deactivated. They returned to the lander, all the while Esser fidgeted with his controls trying to power up his suit. With Esser safely on board, D'Armin walked back quickly and soon stood next to the anomaly, about half the size of her head with a featureless surface. The scientist in her took over. D'Armin dropped to her knee and touched 'Bob' with her gloved finger. Call it a dedication to duty or a desire to learn, but the scientist in her knew this was too big an opportunity not take the risk of studying it.

"D'Armin to *Nebular,*" she radioed. "Hey, Natallo, you'll never guess what I did now."

The commander's voice sounded wary. "We lost both your signals. Surprised to hear you now. Tell me something that will make me happy."

D'Armin had correctly anticipated her commanding officer's reaction and wasn't even concerned when the commander threatened to throw "the book" at her for breaking "several dozen" safety regulations. Her tirade ended when D'Armin offered to dump the artifact and simply return to the ship.

*

The most difficult aspect of her plan, bringing the object on board the *Nebular,* was next. Because she was the "expert" on the ship's power supply and the lead investigator on the anomaly, D'Armin had to return to prep the system before 'Bob' could be brought aboard.

Without overwhelming Natallo with the math and formulas of quantum physics, D'Armin explained. "There exists a natural flow to the energies utilized in operating everything from a light switch to sensors to a propulsion system." The artifact worked on some levels of physics she admittedly did not understand, but she was able to extrapolate from the ways their systems had responded to it.

"'Bob' seems to be a power supply. But it reacts to the presence of other energy flows by either overriding them, or maybe just absorbing them. We don't know which 'cause we don't know how to monitor the damn thing to that extent. Anyway, then 'Bob' takes over as the power source. And, boy, what a job it does! But, and this is huge, any system drained by 'Bob' can't be restarted. We've exhausted all of our tech on attempting to restart the remote landers, the manned lander, and Esser's suit. We've followed protocol in recharging them, but nothing has worked.

"When my suit started up on its own on the planet's surface, all of my readouts went off the charts. Everything topped out. My suit's sensors picked up the ship, not the landers, but *Nebular*. I recognized the ionic signature of its main drive."

"That is impressive," Natallo admitted. "A suit's sensors aren't designed to extend beyond a range of about ten kilometers and the ship's in a three hundred kilometers orbit. But I'm a wreck. It defies everything I know to shut down my ship. I need to advise Mission Control."

The commander dismissed everyone to communicate with Earth. Their response was clear, "SECURE ARTIFACT."

D'Armin and her staff were given the full use of ship's data and processing to calculate a safe approach distance before initiating the ship's power down. Not knowing how long the *Bob*-initiated restart would take, the main concern was for the ship and crew's safety. Orbit degradation was the critical concern. With calculations done and rechecked a dozen times, D'Armin returned to the surface.

*

She nestled 'Bob' into the simple storage box she'd lined with some towels from her cabin. She estimated its weight at about three and a half kilograms. But even that seemed to be heavier by the time they'd walked the five kilometers back to the lander. Esser offered to help, but D'Armin, in her own terms, felt too maternal toward it.

The recovery had worked as anticipated with power downs of their excursion suits and the lander resulting in increased power on restart with 'Bob' providing all the energy. They lifted off, carefully following a flight path into an orbit designed to eliminate proximity to *Nebular* until docking. Their calculations estimated 'Bob's' influence to take effect at 210 kilometers. They set a 250-kilometer distance as their holding point while *Nebular* completed powering down.

Natallo handled the communications with their lander, reading out the distances. Just after the three-hundred mark had been announced, the comlink went dead.

D'Armin held her breath, actually looking around to be sure they had power. Esser repeatedly called *Nebular* and fiddled with adjustments to his panel. Nothing changed. He activated the video link but no signal was received. They homed their video to locate and focus on the *Nebular*.

The image sent chills up D'Armin's spine. The ship hung against the network of foreign constellations. No lights showed. No signals were evident. "It looks dead," she whispered, glancing at Esser.

"We have to get there, now!" Esser adjusted controls as he spoke.

"No!" screamed D'Armin. "We have to wait until we're sure it's powered down or 'Bob' will ..." Her voice quaked. "It'll never start up again."

"Look at it! No lights, no signals, no readings of any kind. They are ready. Look at the timing. So, they're three minutes ahead of schedule. Close enough." He keyed the computer-guided craft to accelerate. Neither of them took their eyes off the viewer, nor verbalized what they both obviously feared.

Thirty minutes later, they held position just off the still-closed flight deck hangar door. It was supposed to be open. Panic set in. Esser moved the lander into position twenty-five meters to their left to the emergency port. They suited up. The hiss of air pressurizing *Nebular's* airlock made them both smile. The docking procedure completed, D'Armin and Esser opened the hatch.

They were greeted by Natallo and three others, all ship's officers. D'Armin handed 'Bob' to the First Officer and removed her helmet.

Natallo stepped forward and punched D'Armin in the face, knocking her down. She screamed "You bink! You screwed up and now you've killed us all! *Nebular* is dead! You were wrong! We've got no power, no reactor, no batteries, nothing! And it's all your fault, you damn bink! You planned it all along, didn't you? You've been against retrieving this artifact from the beginning. And you were willing to destroy us all in the process!

"Now you pay, bink. Back up." Natallo crowded her energy officer's still-prone form and began kicking her. Esser moved to intercede when the ship's commander pointed an old-style pistol at him. To D'Armin she hissed, "Get back on that lander!

"Mission Specialist Gerali D'Armin, as commander of the *Nebular*, I hereby charge you and find you guilty of sabotage and hold you responsible for the destruction of the *Nebular* and its crew. I hereby sentence you to death, just like you've sentenced us." She reached across, took 'Bob' and tossed it back into the lander. She then shot the hatch control panel.

Its deafening report startled everyone. Sparks erupted from the lander's damaged circuits and the hatch whirred shut. "What are you doing?" screamed Esser. "She'll die out there."

"Just like us, Lieutenant. Except we get to die in here. Unless you want to join her." When he didn't respond, she continued. "I thought not. Murphy, close our hatch."

The inner hatch sealed and Natallo stepped up and turned the manual release. The thud of explosive bolts reverberated along the hull and the lander drifted away. She turned and walked away followed by her staff. Esser stood in disbelief.

*

Eighteen hours later, *Nebular*'s orbit had decayed. After maneuvering her lander under *Nebular*'s hull and firing its engine for the last five hours, she sighed to find that her efforts to save the ship from the inevitable resulted in only an additional two hours. She'd no idea how long the air would hold out for the ship's crew with no power.

Just don't want them to burn alive. She assumed the atmosphere would do the same as Earth's, but she didn't know enough of the physics. Regardless, she resolved to follow them down to her own demise.

The lander's sensors indicated the ship's interior mean temperature had already dropped to 12.6 degrees centigrade. She sat at a relatively toasty 20.3 degrees centigrade because her lander had 'Bob'. *I've got all the power this lander could ever use, but it's not designed to be able to take me back to Earth.* It sat in its box, a sandy yellow.

The miscalculation—*what else could it be!*—plagued her relentlessly. The numbers checked each time, so she must have erred in setting up the equation about what distance 'Bob' would affect the *Nebular*. The computers failed to identify it, though.

Subconsciously at first, something tugged at her. Looking at 'Bob', she realized it was no longer a passive dusty color. It pulsed in a triplet pattern, one-two-three. She listened intently, but could hear nothing.

Next, 'Bob' repeatedly ran through and, she presumed, beyond the visible light spectrum, still pulsing sequentially.

Her peripheral vision saw it first. She turned and, from outside her viewport, saw a matching array of lights. 'Bob's owners had returned.

A craft drifted just below *Nebular*'s bow, pulsing and shifting to match 'Bob.' But, it also shifted aspects of its physical shape. Thickening and waning, extending arms and flattening with the same variations. But its main configuration remained, looking ever so familiar. She focused on it exclusively. A *Mobius strip!* While the ship appeared a solid shimmering metallic, it acted as a fluid but maintained the basic closed, one-sided form.

It moved under *Nebular* and approached Gerali's lander, stopping a mere ten meters or so away. She estimated it to be about a third the size of *Nebular*. If it would just hold still! she thought. A thin thread, about as thick as her thigh, extended out from the ship toward her. It reached the lander and expanded to envelop her front view screen. 'Bob' stopped pulsing.

Gerali stopped sensing things. She heard, felt, saw, even smelled nothing. She did know she wasn't alone. A presence filled her mind like a second person in the same chair. That realization was immediately followed by the question, *"How have you the morika?"*

"Morika?" she questioned.

She became instantly aware of 'Bob.'

"We found it, and, uhm, we ... we took it, hoping to study it." She experienced guilt and sorrow, not sure if she'd received or sent that.

"Not yours," came the response. But it also came as if needing an explanation.

Gerali wondered if their actions were being judged. How could she let this being know that she was against the idea and fought to prevent it.

"You did initially," it offered.

Damn! You are in my head! The idea repulsed her as an invasion of the worst kind. Every thought, memory, and impulse was exposed to whatever this thing was. But then she calmed. *How better to explain what happened than through my own memories?* She thought back, letting her mind run the course of events from the time they first located the artifact.

There was no immediate response when she'd finished. After a few moments, a different presence addressed her, questioning the science of her ship and of her kind.

This exchange continued for a considerable time. Then the connection ceased.

She stood next to the pilot's seat in her pressure suit, holding 'Bob'. The thread still covered the viewport. But then it changed. The covering had some sense of dimension, as if inside the lander. A thin swishing filled her ears.

She watched intently as a spherical protrusion extended toward her. 'Bob' vibrated slightly and rose from her hands. The extension stretched out and touched 'Bob', the morika. It flashed like thousands of diamonds and was drawn into the thread. A wave of warm satisfaction washed over her.

Another protrusion appeared and extended toward her, lightly touching her forehead. She sensed dozens of questions and felt suddenly elated. She smiled as the protrusion spread over her, enveloping her.

Gerali next realized she was watching *Nebular* from within the Mobius-like ship. Her old ship had power. Its lights were on, preparing to leave. A second lander had docked with the one she had been in, and were entering *Nebular*'s docking bay. She watched as its hatch closed very slowly. She felt nothing toward them. It was good that they should leave here. They did not belong here, not ready to be out here.

Nebular receded, getting rapidly smaller as it powered away. A part of her that still could smiled, knowing she'd won. The morika was safe. She had new friends and a future of learning new levels of science that humans could never understand.

***

The Other 1963
By Paul K. Metheney

"Ah'm tired of lying for you, brother! No more!" stress exaggerating his New England inflection, his vowels stretching as tight as his nerves. "Ah've paid too dear a price."

His older brother bowed his well-groomed head in a way the cameras loved, then stared into his shorter sibling's blue eyes and said, "I need you here. More than ever. If Father ... "

"Father? Our dear father never intended it to be you! It was always supposed to be our brother. But when he disappointed Father by going off and getting killed, our loving father had to settle for his second choice ... you," the younger's voice colder than the November gusts outside. Invoking their late brother would rip open the old scabs, inflict the most pain. "I was never even a contender. I guess I wasn't handsome enough, tall enough ... war hero enough. Damn shame Germany and Japan had to go and surrender before I got my shot at it."

"Did Ethel put you up to ...," the older brother started.

"You leave her out of this," the younger brother's voice a low growl. "She sacrificed more than you will ever know. She raised an entire family while I was out handling your dirty laundry. All these years, while I was busy with your campaigns and back-room deals and cleaning up your messes, she was raising a family a man could be proud of."

"I'm sorry. I never meant to imply that ..."

"Don't even say her name. Not with the same mouth that does who knows what to those women while your own wife is just down the hall. My wife's name doesn't come out of the same face that looks gangsters in the eye and tells them what they want to hear. The same pretty mug that lies to the American people. You will never say her name again. You hear me? Never."

"What can I do to make this right?" the elder brother asked, his tone soothing and apologetic.

"Step down," the younger sibling's voice cold and hard. "Step down and take care of your wife and children. Lord knows you've done enough. Enough for this country. Enough for the whole world. And everyone in this family has paid with their very souls to give you that chance."

"You know I can't do that," his intonation changing, strengthening, hardening with an edge he usually reserved for the military.

The argument had been brewing for ages. Tension had been building like a nor'easter, but instead of gale winds and barometric pressure, the rough seas here were triggered by unions, mob money, and repeated infidelities.

The younger of the two inseparables glared at his elder's courageous profile for a long while in the dimly lit, circular room. With a sigh of exhaustion and resignation, he lowered his slim frame into a Queen Ann arm chair, chosen specifically to keep dignitaries and underlings from getting too comfortable. In this office, everyone was an underling. In this office, it was easy to feel uncomfortable.

Looking up from the chair into his older brother's greenish gray eyes, "In three days, I'm going to announce my candidacy."

"Excellent! You'll make a great senator," the elder brother smiled, relief flooding through him. "Maybe New York. I'll come out and ..."

"I'm not going to run for Senate," the younger statesman announced quietly. "If you don't step away from this office, I'm announcing my candidacy for President of the United States."

It was the older brother's turn to go weak-kneed. A twinge of pain ran up his spine, as he lurched against the antique Resolute desk.

"You can't be serious. You don't stand a chan—" he couldn't stop himself in time.

"Don't stand a chance?" the younger man smirked. "You arrogant bastard. The sad thing is, you're probably right. I don't think anyone can run against you. They love you too much. They love her too much. You're right. I don't stand a chance. I'm not doing this to be president, you big galoot. I'm doing this to save you ... from yourself. You've done so much good, but I love you too much to sit back and watch you lose any more of your soul. This is too much power for you. It has to stop—one way or the other. I'm begging you to step away from all this."

Like dust motes in the light from the circular office's windows, a silence hung between them.

"I told you, I can't do that."

His baby brother sighed, "I know that you won't."

"It will tear this nation apart. You can't be serious. Do you even know how insane this sounds? It will tear our family apart!" In reality, his mind reeled with the potential impact to his administration.

"You mean the family that put a philandering pimp into this office? The same family that had an entire movie made to sensationalize you wrecking a damned boat in the war just in time to get you re-elected? That family? Well, that's the price our family will have to pay for buying our way to the top. God always demands His due, dear brother. As for tearing the nation apart, what I think you really mean is, this will tear you apart. This nation is a hell of a lot stronger than you give it credit for. I will always love you as my brother, but I hate what you are becoming."

"Pimp?"

"You're right. 'Pimp' isn't exactly accurate, unless you count your interns. Maybe 'John' would be a much more appropriate term," the younger brother's voice a meld of irony and accusation.

The elder brother's face froze, eyes hardening. It was the face his younger brother had seen an October ago. Back then, it was only about global destruction. Now, it was serious. It was about power. Now, it was about disappointing the family.

"You can't win," the older brother's New England accent threatening to erupt. "You're as dirty as I am. You were by my side the entire time."

"You're right. I am dirty. As dirty as you? Not even Hoover is that dirty. But I am willing to face this country, and our family, and clear my conscience. Will this great nation forgive me? Maybe not. Will the family? Never. Do I have your charisma, following, or power base? Hell no. Can I win? Definitely not. But I can split the party. I can tell the truth. Coming from me, somebody will listen. Hoover will listen. And you won't win. Not with this."

Bobby held up a worn, brown leather satchel, thrusting it into his brother's hands. "Step down now. Don't make me use this. I love you and have done everything you or this family has ever asked of me, but don't make me a blackmailer just to save you."

The older brother opens the case and pulls out some of the papers to study them.

"Where ... where did you get all this?"

"Some crazy, white-haired old man in a weird metal car showed up at the house and gave it to me. Said that if I used this, I could 'stop you.' I knew about all this before, but this is proof."

"There are photographs, dates, even films," the elder moaned. "Hoover has to be behind this. Who else could gather all this?"

"It's not Hoover. The old man gave me a file on him, too, some stuff you won't believe. Stuff that makes your antics look like child's play. Trust me, Hoover will fall in line now."

The Attorney General continued purposefully as he walked to the door, "I want you to take this case and study what's in it. Study it well, Jack. Because in it, is every dirty lie I've ever told to protect you. All the agencies and unions we've ever screwed over. All the women. All the money. Every deal you ever made to be king. You read every page and look at every photo, Jack, because everything is going to be different. Nothing will ever be the same when you get back. Nothing."

"Okay, Bobby. You win. Let's talk this over. We'll take the whole weekend, if necessary. Jackie will be disappointed, and the Secret Service will flip, but I'll cancel the Dallas trip."

***

Eddie Kruks
By Steve Rouse

A dusty bus creaked and groaned as it rocked over the last of the ruts, finally rolling onto the gravel parking lot. The sun shone through the trees and into the streaked windows of the Twin Cities Youth bus as it finally came to rest. The metal monster of the road seemed strangely out of place in the tranquil greenery of northern Minnesota, having traveled five hours from St. Paul to the Wilderness Base Camp in the Boundary Waters National Forest.

Two people came out from under the shade of a nearby tree as a worn looking woman stepped down from the bus with clipboard in hand.

"Can it get any hotter, Cal?" They hugged and she wiped the sweat from her forehead. "It's got to be a hundred degrees in there," she gasped, using the clipboard as a fan.

"Could be, Sylvia," the camp director replied. "It was about ninety-six degrees at the lodge an hour ago. Let's get them off before they bake. This is Marilyn, our new coordinator."

The women shook hands. Sylvia looked back at Cal. "You know Eddie's in there," she said, tilting her head toward the bus.

Cal's shoulders dropped with a sigh. "Seriously? Just our luck. Well, we survived him last year. I suspect we can do the same this year."

Sylvia McClelland, counselor for the Twin Cities Youth Co-Op, managed to whisper "It'll work out." She turned toward the bus, blew her whistle and called for the children to "hustle on out." With a mixture of curiosity and sleepiness, twenty-one sweaty twelve-year-olds unloaded themselves. The sole source of any commotion was the fourth, thirteenth, and last student off.

A somewhat taller Eddie Kruks was the fourth child off the bus. His feet no sooner touched the parking lot, when he groaned, turned, and salmoned his way back in. A similar thing happened the next time Eddie came out. This time he made it about ten feet when he dropped his backpack, slapped himself on the forehead, and with a rather long and large "Arghh" ran back into the bus. He reemerged after everyone else carrying his eight-pack of diet soda, one of which he drained as he stepped onto the gravel for the third time.

"Ah, sweet and wet!" he smacked. "Beats salty sweat any day."

"Sorry, Eddie, you know you can't bring in any pop," Cal told him. "It'll attract bears and other animals that we don't want coming into camp."

Eddie waved him off and kept walking. "Ah, what do you know? I snuck a bunch o' stuff in last year and never saw any bears." As Eddie walked past him, Cal snagged the soda. "Whatever," said Eddie, still waving his arm and never breaking stride. "There's more where that came from."

"Okay, Mister Kruks, Freeze! Drop that pack. I need to see what you've got in there. We do have rules for everyone's safety."

Eddie stopped and turned to face him. "Seriously?" When Cal didn't budge, Eddie opened his backpack and dumped it on the gravel lot. Sixteen candy bars, four bags of chips, and a package of chocolate chip cookies later, Eddie was allowed to catch up to his group.

Cal looked at Sylvia and Marilyn and sighed. "It's going to be a long week," he said. They turned and followed the trail toward the lodge. Cal noticed two ravens fly from a nearby tree, cawing loudly.

*

After orientation, the group counselors took the campers to their cabins to assign bunks and get them to their swimming test before dinner. Meanwhile, Cal returned to his office with Sylvia to go over the itinerary for their stay.

"You know," she started. "Eddie's not a bad kid. He's a child who needs to, uh, to test things."

"Yeah, like my patience," interjected Cal.

Sylvia continued. "I've watched him in our after-school program. He's smart, really smart. He's interested in how things work. I think he could be an engineer someday."

"Look, it took us nearly three weeks last year to put everything back together after he left. Eddie's only interested in how things come apart. Let's see ... there was a lifesaving vest, our wildlife center's mammal display and ventilation ducts, the main kitchen's freezer ... Should I go on?"

"Cal," Sylvia said softly, "you know deep down that Eddie is exactly the kind of kid who needs this camp."

Cal sounded tired. "Yeah, I guess. But there are a score of other camps between—" Just then a voice hissed at them through the static of the camp radio.

"Jim to Cal. Over."

"What's up Jim?"

"Cal, there's a problem at South Bunkhouse. Over." Jim's voice trailed off. The pause became painful.

After waiting, Cal prompted. "What kind of problem?"

"One of the campers dislodged the wood stove's vent. We've got soot all over the cabin. Over."

"That bunkhouse should be empty. Who's in there?"

Another pause. "Sylvia's boys. Over."

"They're supposed to be in Hilltop. Why are you putting them in South?"

"One of them took a swat at a spider on the screen door with his sleeping bag and busted it out. I figured they could bunk here until I fixed the door. Over."

"Tell me it wasn't Eddie."

There was yet another uncomfortable pause. "No can do, Cal. Over."

Cal sighed. "I'm on my way. I'll get a couple of people to help fix the door. Just get the kids down to the beach for their swimming test." He paused, then added, "Over."

"Roger that. Out."

Cal started out for South Bunkhouse after calling and assigning three of the summer help to cleaning detail there. He took the long way along the lagoon path, his favorite. The heat was less intense beneath the pine, sycamore, cedar, and birch forest. The trees scented the air and relaxed him, even amidst the perpetual buzz of insects. A raccoon called to her kits and four scurried out of the brush near him after her. Cal watched them waddle passed the lagoon and head into the open water of Red Rock Lake, crossing to the nearest of its many islands.

As he watched, he noticed an unusual number and variety of birds flying around it and a wolf on its shoreline. Not usually so close. Something must have died there, he thought. He turned and walked toward South Cabin to assess the damage.

Half an hour later, Cal arrived at the beach, summoned by another radio call. Sitting off on his own, Eddie watched glumly as everyone else strained pulling the twenty-passenger birch canoe out of the water. A broken paddle and a cracked thwart, the gunwale brace dangled as the canoe was emptied.

Standing over Eddie, Cal worked hard to control his voice. "Tell me how this happened."

"I, uh, I ..., I just jumped off the end of the pier, Mr. Cal!" Eddie blurted. "I'm sorry! I didn't know the big canoe was there. Honest!"

"All 'Geronimo' here had to do was look," Sarah, the camp's lifeguard, added as she joined them.

"Geronimo?"

"It's what Eddie screamed as he ran down the pier to jump in." Both adults looked at Eddie.

He gulped. "I, uhm, I'm sorry." He looked up as a tear silently rolled down his cheek. "I don't mean to keep breaking things."

Cal's look eased. He reached down and took Eddie by his shoulders. "All right, Eddie, mistakes happen, more for some people." He softened his voice. "Just promise me you'll be extra careful from now on."

"I promise. Thanks, Mr. Cal!" Eddie turned to go, but Cal still held his shoulders.

"You weren't hurt, were you?"

A huge smile flashed across Eddie's face. "Not this time." He turned and ran off to rejoin his group. Sarah followed him toward the beach shaking her head.

"That was impressive," the voice came from behind him.

Cal turned and saw Marilyn and Sylvia grinning at him. His face reddened. "Wha, what do you mean?"

"When we heard the radio call, we thought you might kill him. We figured we could get here and help, but you got here first, all soft and understanding." Marilyn grinned.

Cal's features hardened. "You know, the two of you could be assigned as Eddie's personal escorts," and he brushed past the women.

Sylvia looked at Marilyn. "Is he serious? Can he do that?"

"I'm not about to find out," Marilyn chuckled and the two headed down the path behind him.

*

After dinner Cal heard Marilyn yelling at someone. He followed her voice and found her and Eddie packing dirt around a tree trunk.

"What's going on here?" he asked.

Marilyn nudged Eddie. "Go ahead. Tell him."

"Not fair! Why am I always getting in trouble?" He folded his arms hard against his chest and sighed. "Okay, I did it, but it wasn't wrong."

"Did what, Eddie?" Cal asked.

"There were all these little bald, pink things running in and out of this tiny hole right ..." He pointed at the base of the tree. "... well, it was there. I watched 'em for a few minutes and I just had to know how many of them were in there. So, I found a stick and started digging."

"You and I need to talk." Cal showed Eddie where to sit. He sat next to him and Marilyn sat opposite.

"What stick did you use?" Cal asked. Eddie pointed and Cal told him to get it. "I want you to balance that stick on your fingertip, like this." Cal demonstrated.

Eddie managed after several tries to get the stick to stay level.

"That stick is Nature, and one of the most important things about Nature is that it has to stay balanced. Is your stick balanced, Eddie?"

'Uh, yup," he answered after glancing at it.

Cal picked up a smaller stick and put it on the end of Eddie's stick, which promptly fell. "Now, tell me why it fell."

"It fell 'cause you put something on it, duh."

"Just like you, Eddie. Every time you mess around with something, you put things out of balance. You may not mean to, but that's what happens. Whenever you do something to an animal or plants, or even bugs, it changes things for them. Nature must stay in balance or something bad's gonna happen to it. Do you understand?"

Eddie nodded. "Yeah, I gotta think it through, though."

Cal felt his tension release. "Good, you do that. Now, go back to your group."

With Eddie out of earshot, Marilyn said, "That was marvelous. Nice job."

"Well, it was either that or, I don't know, punch a tree."

"Seriously?"

"I don't know what to do with this kid, Marilyn. He pisses me off. He doesn't think. He just acts ... does stuff without any thought about what might happen. He's digging into a vole hole to see ... see what? He doesn't realize that what he's doing is destroying the stuff he wants to know about. Sweet Jesus! Honestly, last year ... by the end of his week, I just wanted to throw him out into the forest and ... whatever happened, blame it on the animals. And now he's back ... back doin' the same crap." Cal tossed the stick.

"Well, from what I saw just now, I think you know exactly what he needs. Your one-on-one with him works! You'll see, it makes a difference. Just keep workin' on him before he burns the place down."

Cal managed a smile. "Now there's a plan. What the ...? Look over there just passed the twin birch."

"Is that two raccoons? It's a little early in the day for them, isn't it?"

"Early, yes, but it's a 'coon and a skunk. Together, I mean. I, uh, whoa ... they don't do that." Cal's face stayed crunched as he stared. The two critters backed from view behind the tree and scampered away. "Not only do we get Eddie, but even the animals are acting weird this week."

*

Two days later, six canoes quietly made their way northwest through Lake Saganaga. The previous day in camp had been surprisingly calm. Eddie had "not been feeling well" after deciding to eat some wild berries he'd found the morning after his arrival. He'd spent a very uncomfortable, but busy day running to and from the outhouse. The berries, it turned out, were not quite ripe.

Off on a two-night outing, the group was about an hour out of Twin Cedar Point where they'd had lunch.

"Why is it so quiet?" asked Sue, one of the campers. "I haven't seen any loons, or eagles, or even a stupid crow since we left this morning. They were all over the place last year," she added.

A few canoes to her left, Cal and Marilyn exchanged a glance, then at Eddie, who was sitting between them. He still looked a little pale but was growing restless. And for Eddie, that could only result in one thing.

Later that afternoon the canoes pulled out of the water at their American Point campsite. Cal, Marilyn, and Eddie were the last ones to arrive and the only ones who were wet. Marilyn grabbed Eddie by the arm along with her pack and pulled them up where some of the kids were already pitching tents. Cal beached the canoe and tipped it over. Gallons of water spilled out, forming little rivulets that ran down into the lake. Sylvia watched as he lifted drenched packs from the canoe.

"He saw a fish," was all that Cal would say.

"What can I do?" she whispered.

His lips parted to answer but then pressed closed as he shook his head. "Just pray."

Once the tents were up and wet clothes had been replaced with dry, Marilyn took a dozen of the kids on a nature survey. The rest were collecting firewood. In a low, shallow swamp area about fifty yards inland, they spotted a moose. Chomping marsh grass and ignoring his audience, it stood about eight feet tall.

"Dude! That thing's as tall as the basketball hoop on my garage!" said Damon, one of the campers. Before Marilyn could add anything, a loud scream came from behind them. Everyone wheeled around as Eddie came crashing through the group, bellowing at the top of his lungs. Something very large behind him came swooping down from the trees along the edge of the clearing.

Its high-pitched "kreeeeee" added to Eddie's scream, and everyone who was still standing, dropped to the ground. Swooping mere inches above their heads, the bird landed in the tree just above the moose. The obviously angry bald eagle still kreed, as if scolding the human boy.

"What did you do?" yelled Marilyn at Eddie as they all stood.

"Nuthin'." A panting Eddie muttered with a shrug of his shoulders.

"Nothing?" echoed Marilyn, gesturing wildly. "Nothing? Okay, if you did nothing, then I'm sure that bird will leave you alone. At least you'd better hope so 'cause we're going back to camp and you're staying here."

Eddie's eyes widened. "No! I mean, uh, you can't, you can't leave me here."

"Why?"

"'Cuz, cuz you're supposed to take care of me out here."

"But you said you didn't do anything to that eagle," Marilyn continued. She glanced over to where the eagle had landed. It was gone. Turning back to Eddie, she asked, "...or are you lying to me?"

Just as Eddie opened his mouth, the eagle swooped in again. Even with its outstretched talons, though, it passed about a foot over Eddie's head.

"Okay, okay." Eddie whined and wrung his hands. "I saw it in a tree and threw a few rocks at it. But, honest, I just wanted to see it fly."

"Oh, Eddie." Marilyn turned toward the group and in a suddenly tired voice said, "Everyone, let's head back." No one had to be told twice, and fourteen sets of eyes nervously scanned the treetops the entire way.

Later that night, Cal stirred the embers of the campfire with a stick. Sparks softly drifted out over the lake, swirling up into the starry darkness. "Well, no one was hurt," he said at last. "I can only hope that even Eddie got the message that the bald eagle isn't going to put up with his antics. Hopefully, we won't have to either. Well, we made it through the day. Are all the kids in their tents, Marilyn?"

"Yep, and the bear pack is up in the pines next to the canoes. Are you sure you want Eddie in with you?" she asked.

"No one else wanted him," Cal noted, "and even I don't think Eddie can cause much trouble in his sleep. And, since I like to have my tent away from the others, it will remove the temptations that close proximity brings to a campsite."

They all nodded and chuckled. With that, Cal said "It's been one of those days. We'd better sack out. Tomorrow's on its way." He reached for the water bag next to him and doused the campfire. The others yawned their soft good nights and retreated to their tents. Cal sat for a while, again stirring the hissing embers and gazing at the stars and the shimmering of the Aroura Borealis. He finally stood up, stretched, and headed for his tent. He noticed things looked different and lit his flashlight. He found lots of animals' tracks, but his tent and Eddie were gone.

*

Eddie had gone to Cal's tent shortly after Cal had told all the kids about the Northern Lights. He laid in his sleeping bag for only a short time when he heard shuffling and snuffing noises outside. He knew it was just the other campers. After what had happened today with that eagle, the other kids would almost have to try to scare him. Just when he thought they would charge the tent, Eddie threw open the tent flap all set to yell "Boo."

What greeted him were the yellow eyes and massive teeth of a very large wolf just a foot away. Its deep, throaty growl was the last thing Eddie heard before he fainted.

*

Cal and everyone else were on the move to find Eddie. No one knew anything. Everyone brought flashlights. Marilyn set them up in search parties.

Sylvia called Cal over to her. "All of your tent pegs were yanked out. See? You can see where it dragged across the dirt.

"And look at all these animal tracks! I followed them from the tent site to the water's edge. Look at all these different kinds!" She pointed with her flashlight as she spoke. "Wolf, fox, that one looks like a bobcat," she said waving her *Wildlife Tracking for Dummies* book. "But here, this big one ... it's a moose, Cal! And look down here at the sand and all these displaced stones. It's like the whole tent got pulled into the lake!"

*

When Eddie came to, he couldn't move. He found himself weighed down by the dripping folds of the tent. He struggled and slithered against the canvas and ropes, and then slumped back against a stump to catch his breath. He looked up and saw stars and the soft light of the moon behind scattered clouds. Around him was a clearing of sorts, about as big as the gym at his school. He couldn't really see much else, but he could hear lots of animal sounds.

"Where am I?" he called out.

No answer.

"C'mon, you guys, that's enough! Get me outta this!"

He heard a grunt very close to him and he froze. Then more long, breathy grunts directly behind and above him. He stretched his neck back and could make out the outline of a moose's head and antlers just above him. A muffled scream escaped.

"Silence." The moose looked right at Eddie.

"Wha ...?"

"Silence!" repeated the moose, moving down to just inches of Eddie's face. Its face dripped water onto him.

Eddie wiped his face, but shrunk down, not quite believing what his ears had just heard. *Can moose talk? Stupid question! Of course not!* "Did you just talk to me?" Eddie asked.

The moose lifted its head up and said in a louder voice, "Any creature that will not trust its own senses will not survive, even this K'sibe cub."

Just then the clouds covering the moon drifted off. The full moon shone brightly into the clearing, revealing more animals than Eddie had ever seen. He recognized the moose, a pack of wolves, lots of deer, a skunk, fox, some kind of a wild cat—*about twice as big as Aunt Martha's fat tabby*—raccoon, and a whole bunch of things he didn't recognize. There were eyes up in the trees, too!

Eddie's brain whirled. *All these animals ... way too close ... and none of them in cages!* He gulped but didn't have time for any more observations as the moose spoke again, loudly to the crowd of other animals.

"This cub, for two seasons, has shown itself to be a danger to us." A din of animal noise ensued. "What are we to do?"

A wolf came out of the darkness and stepped up to Eddie, who leaned back so that the stump dug into his spine. It sniffed him and with a low, ominous growl softly said, "Eat it."

At that moment a great flurry of feathers brushed against Eddie's face as a bald eagle landed atop the moose's antler. The great bird's kreeing became a voice.

"This one attacked me today, but the K'sibe, the humans do not eat my kind. It wandered away from its herd. Look at it. It is but a cub and does not know our ways. We have watched and seen that it struggles even with its own kind.

"Those of the water, the land, and the air all know that young must be guided. My own must learn to trust the wind. Mi' Taal, who would eat this one," glancing toward the wolf, "must teach her cubs to hunt. Keeya' Rasa," bowing toward the moose, "keeps her calf through the cold times to learn how to forage. All of this place and of all other places need to teach their young so they may live, grow, and be strong." Another chorus of animal voices resounded.

"Why, then, should his own kind, the K'sibe, be beyond this need? He is not a rogue! He simply has not yet learned. We remember he came here during the last warm suns and was a danger. Then he left."

"Now he returns and is a danger to us again." A new voice, deep and angry, interrupted the eagle. A large bear rambled up to the stump. Eddie shrunk back further, now between the moose's front legs. "He should be taken into the deep forest and left to die," it growled.

"What say you?" roared the bear, glancing repeatedly around the clearing. Many animals' voices rose in response to the bear. The moon went behind a cloud.

"No!" kreed the eagle. "Killing is not our way!" She flapped her wings rapidly, as if calling for attention and order. "If this one is killed, more harm will come to us. The rest of the K'sibe will come out and destroy our place, destroy us. If they cannot teach him, we must! Not for his life, but for ours!" The animals responded through clicks and chitters, growls and roars, barks and howls, and more.

*

Cal, Marilyn, and Sylvia each led their own groups of campers in canoes to explore the neighboring islands in the hopes of finding Eddie. Cal's group were nearing Birchbark Island, the closest to their campsite. As he dug and pulled with his paddle, Cal prayed that Eddie would be all right and reprimanded himself for his own intolerance. Never again, he thought. I'm here to help them learn. I've failed Eddie just because his way of learning didn't fit my way of teaching. Never again!

As they reached the shore, Cal heard animal sounds. "What in the world is going on here?" he said aloud and remembered the odd behavior of the animals he'd seen the past few days. Fearing the worst, he sent the kids to follow the shoreline in the other direction with the warning, "Make lots of noise but stay together!" Cal watched their lights bounce off trees and shrubs as they shouted along. He headed in the direction of the animal sounds he'd heard.

*

Through the distance, more familiar sounds reached Eddie's ears. People sounds! Their lights bounced along in the distance. He heard voices and their thrashing through the bush. Many of the animals wimpered, growing nervous at the approaching K'sibe. Eddie heard some of the smaller mammals scrambling off into the underbrush.

109

The bear moved closer and placed his massive paw against Eddie's chest, covering it. "Tsi'Golya speaks wisely. Your death will only bring death to our place and us. You must learn how to live here if you are to be here! Many of your kind have and they are welcome. If you cannot learn, do not come," it growled loudly, jaws wide and head askew.

At that moment, a light on the far side of the clearing cut through the darkness. Eddie heard Cal's voice yell, "Eddie! Oh, God, no!" Immediately the light jerked wildly up and down. The man holding the light was screaming as he ran.

They all saw the light and heard the man. Eddie watched as the animals fled. The wolf and moose bolted into the blackness and the eagle launched herself into the night sky. The bear roared and swiped his paw at the stump, splintering it. It then lowered its head inches from Eddie and growled, "Remember, learn how to live here if you are to be here! We all will know." It then charged off into the forest with a speed that left Eddie in total awe. Seconds later, Cal reached the Eddie.

"Eddie, God, Eddie, are you okay?" Cal kept asking, even though he was out of breath. He grabbed the boy, patting him to look for any injuries. "Oh, thank God!"

"Yeah, yeah, I'm fine. Did you see how fast that bear ran? God, he was fast! He's so big! Can they all run that fast?"

"Eddie, stop. You're okay. How did you get here? What happened?" Cal stood and fired his flare gun into the night sky…the signal to return to camp.

Eddie kept staring after the bear. "What? Oh, yeah, here's the tent," he said pointing to the folds of canvas in front of them. "They, uh…can they, uhm, can they talk to each other? How do they see in the dark?" Hundreds of questions continued about bears, moose, eagles, and about a dozen other creatures even after they'd returned to camp. Eddie had finally slumped over asleep next to the fire in a makeshift sleeping bag, shielded by a tipped canoe.

Cal and Marilyn weren't as lucky. Cal shook his head. "All I really saw was that bear right on Eddie! He was that close to being killed," he said indicating with his thumb and forefinger.

Marilyn huffed. "What I don't get is how he got across to the other island. You said the tent was pretty wet, but Eddie was dry? I don't understand." Then she chuckled. "It only makes sense if you figure the animals kidnapped him."

They both laughed and Cal added, "I guess maybe they had enough of him, too. It's weird. If I didn't know better ..."

*

The bus was finally loaded and the goodbyes had all been said. Cal and Marilyn were standing with Sylvia next to its open door when a gust of noise surged from within, just ahead of Eddie.

"Mr. Cal," Eddie said, somewhat shyly, "I, uh, I just wanted to thank you for everything you did for us, um, I mean, for me."

"Not a problem, Eddie," Cal replied. And he actually meant it. Those last few days after the "kidnapping," as it was now called, showed everyone a strange, new Eddie. He showed an almost insatiable interest in the forest and hadn't wrecked anything.

"And," added Eddie, "I want to apologize to you for all the trouble I caused."

Cal put his hand on Eddie's shoulder. "And I have to apologize to you. I didn't know how to reach you, how to get you to understand about Nature. Thank you for teaching me, Eddie. I'm a better man for it, too."

Eddie's eyes widened as his excitement returned. "But you have! I've learned my lesson. You'll see! I'm a changed man! I'll be back and you don't even have to worry 'cause I'm gonna find out about all the animals and how they live. I'm gonna help you guys next year teach all the other campers about all the animals, too."

"That sounds like one big job, Eddie. I hope you do. But for right now, get your butt on that bus. It's time to go. And, yeah, I'll see you next year."

*

Eleven years later, a dusty bus creaked and groaned as it rocked over the last of the ruts and rolled onto the gravel parking lot. The sun shone through the trees and into the streaked windows of the Twin Cities Youth bus as it creaked to a stop. The metal monster of the road seemed strangely out of place in the tranquil greenery of the Boundary Waters National Forest.

As its door opened, a young man came out from under the shade of a nearby tree and walked toward the bus. When the children had piled out of the bus and collected their gear, he blew his whistle.

111

"Welcome to the Boundary Waters, kids. My name is Eddie and I'll be your guide while you're here. You guys aren't gonna believe some of the awesome stuff I'm going to teach you about the wilderness!"

***

Cancer-Free
by Paul K. Metheney

"When something seems too good to be true—"

"A pessimist comes along and ruins it for everyone," Jeremy's lab assistant, Dell, snarked.

"When something seems too good to be true," Jeremy repeated, "it probably is."

"Doc, what could possibly be bad about aliens that have come to Earth to remove all our cancer?" Dell asked.

"I don't know, Dell, but that doesn't mean there isn't ... something."

"I admire the hell out of you, Doc, but at times," Dell told his mentor, "you can be a real buzz kill."

"Yeah, like I haven't heard that ... today," Dr. Jeremy Hamilton said. It may be true. Hamilton's friends, colleagues, students, and ex-wife had all made a point of his cynical nature at one time or another. His ex-wife had said that he was living proof God had a sense of humor to put such a pessimistic personality in a ruggedly good-looking, intelligent, specimen. That was shortly before she left him to live with a physics professor tenured at the same university. *It's not the size of the ship, but the motion of the subatomic particles in quantum flux.* She claimed it was Hamilton's sardonic nature to cause her to nickname him "Eeyore." He called her "Polly." Her name was Allison. She never really connected, or appreciated, the Pollyanna reference.

The aliens had appeared several weeks ago, announcing their good intentions in all languages. In the U.S., a drone ship landed on the White House lawn. In other countries, they landed at the residences of their respective leaders. They claimed they came in peace. To demonstrate their benevolence, they proposed that they would effectively remove all the cancer cells from human bodies. They suggested Earth send a delegation to interview and investigate their claims.

An enormous starship hovered in geosynchronous orbit around the globe. Ironically, their ship wasn't shaped so much like a saucer as a large crystal pyramid. While the ship seemed to be crystalline, it was both clear and opaque at the same time. Another mystery needing solved. The extraterrestrials offered very little data on their systems. If they were friendly, why not share their technology?

"If not to help us," Dell asked, "why DO you think they came here?"

"Just because we don't know the answer right now," Jeremy answered, "doesn't mean there isn't one. Or the one they so readily provided."

"Well, what I know, is that if they do what they say they are going to do, you are going to be out of business," Dell said, "and I picked a horrible field."

Again, Jeremy had to admit that his assistant was not wrong. As one of the leading oncology researchers at the university, the eradication of cancer would leave him adrift and make Dell's selected career path ill-chosen. Jeremy hoped that the alien's claims were true. He had lost his mother at an early age to cervical cancer and his father to prostate cancer. Two more reasons he had chosen the path he had. He hoped to help eliminate cancer in his lifetime. Now that all seemed irrelevant.

"Dell, I don't know what their real motives are, but nobody, not even little green men, travel across the universe out of the goodness of their hearts, no matter how many they may have," Jeremy stated, looking out the window of his lab. "Let's find out why they did."

*

"We have an application from one Dr. Jeremy Hamilton," the committee chairman said, as he passed around copies of Hamilton's dossier. "The good doctor has impeccable credentials, St. Jude's, Mayo, and currently at Princeton. While not yet tenured, he has done well for himself, making several minor breakthroughs in carcinoma metastases and then in neoplasia growth inhibitors, whatever those may be. He teaches and researches at Princeton while regularly making rounds at the Princeton Cancer Center."

A dozen men and women the president hand-picked and United Nations approved, gathered to choose a select team to interact with the aliens and investigate their proposed methods for eradicating cancer. Since the aliens' arrival and suggestion for an investigative envoy, applications and resumes of those wanting to meet the newcomers inundated governments around the world. The committee ranged from esteemed medical research professionals to accomplished political operators to intelligence officers. They were evaluating possible applicants from the thousands of candidates who volunteered to interact with the extraterrestrials. The powers that be tasked the committee with selecting a small team consisting of a medical researcher, a security analyst, and a diplomat.

"Especially for such a young man," said one of the elder committee members, best known for his political aspirations and manipulations. "Why hasn't he tenured or moved higher in his field?"

The chairman flipped through Jeremy's folder, finally stopping toward the end. "It seems while academically astute and one heckuva researcher, our good Dr. Hamilton has himself a bit of an attitude problem."

"What kind of attitude?"

A committee member from a leading intelligence agency picked up a different folder.

"It seems the good doctor is a bit of skeptic. He spends as much time disproving others' findings as he does generating new ones for himself. He values the truth above all else, no matter who it hurts. He's not very popular amongst his peers because of it and even his superiors are put off a bit by his cynical attitude and personality."

The chairman eyed the intelligence folder from the end of the table. "Is he any kind of security risk?"

The intelligence officer looked at the folder a bit more and glanced up. "Just the opposite, actually. The ex-wife has her own income, resources, and romantic interest with a physics professor at the same school. Despite that, the divorce seems mutual and amicable. No debts to speak of, no affairs, no gambling issues or vulnerabilities that we can find. Seems like the doc is clean. And more importantly, incorruptible."

The elder committee member spoke again, "What about this penchant for cynicism? Do we really want to send a 'Debbie Downer' on a mission to establish diplomatic relations with our first contact with an extraterrestrial race? Don't we want things to go as smoothly as possible?"

"He does seem the sort to muddy the water wherever he goes," the chairman added.

The intelligence officer looked at each man, one at a time, with each sentence.

"Gentlemen, Dr. Hamilton doesn't care about politics. He doesn't care about popularity. He doesn't care about any single person. He only cares about ending cancer and the truth. He can't be bought, blackmailed, or dissuaded. I couldn't pick a better candidate. Worst-case scenario, we *take* the anti-cancer technology from E.T. And if Hamilton muddies the water a bit, well, it's still wet. You never know. He may drown himself in it."

*

Dr. Jeremy Hamilton, now approved to be a part of the Extraterrestrial Integration Operation (E.I.O. - governments love their acronyms!) possessed two first-class airline tickets and a car sent to deliver him and his assistant to the rendezvous point. For security's sake, the intelligence agencies involved selected mid-state Kansas as the initial meeting point between the extraterrestrials and the E.I.O. The car drove Jeremy and Dell to a private airfield in Kansas City, where a military helicopter picked them up to deliver the scientists to a barren spot about seventy miles northwest of Topeka.

Jeremy stepped out of the darkened SUV into the middle of the hastily established Forward Operating Base (F.O.B.). Squinting in the harsh summer sunlight, Jeremy took in the immense temporary Quonset huts and military presence.

Not exactly diplomatic and welcoming, Hamilton thought, as he scanned the heavy artillery and personnel carriers. Automatic rifles and camouflaged BDUs were everywhere. *Perhaps not unwarranted. Evidently, I am not the only one with reservations about our new friends. But then again ...*

"You think this all here to defend us against them if it goes pear-shaped?" Dell asked.

Looking around at all the military presence, now noting a lack of anti-aircraft weapons and missiles. "No. I think this is to keep *us* in line."

"Dr. Hamilton?" an officer greeted them and extended his hand. "I am Major Vincenzo. I will be your liaison officer. If you need anything, please let me know, and I will see what we can do. I'll give you a quick rundown. You will be part of the first three-person team to interact with the extraterrestrials. They picked the number. We wanted more, but they insisted. Your assistant will have to remain here and help organize your data and reports in your absence. The extraterrestrials will transport you and your fellow delegates to their main ship above the U.S. where you will talk with them about their science and diplomatic relations with Earth."

"Is E.T. going to shuttle or beam them up?" Dell asked with a smile.

"Yes," the major said. "When we asked, we were told 'both.' Before they are shuttled to the main ship, they'll be 'beamed up' part of the way. Another technology we would love to know about."

"Roddenberry would be so proud," Dell joked.

A craft floated directly over the base. Just like the White House craft, it appeared to be a crystalline pyramid with each side of the base about sixty feet wide.

"Looks like your ride is here, Doc," Dell said.

"I haven't had time to gather equipment, recording gear—" Hamilton stammered at the sight of the glass-like ship.

"We didn't have an ETA on when they would come," Major Vincenzo explained, looking up at the floating vessel. "Seems like it's right now. I wouldn't worry, Doc. I seriously doubt they plan to kill us three geeks at a time."

But Dr. Hamilton was already gone.

*

The three delegates stood in a large room in the center of the pyramid. The walls were transparent and they watched as the world sped away. There was no sense of movement inside the craft.

"What's going—"

"We apologize for the suddenness of your transportation," a deep baritone voice echoed in the room. "We will be arriving at the prime craft in moments. Please be patient."

Hamilton moved to the edge of the room, watching the pyramidal shuttle rise farther and farther from the Earth below. *We're not in Kansas anymore, Toto.*

117

*

The crystalline pyramid that carried the delegation rose to meet a much larger version of the pyramidal ship. Much larger. About a thousand times larger. The shuttle craft slid easily into a relatively small square hole in the bottom of the larger ship.

Hamilton's eyes never left the wall which was now whitely opaque. Two other delegates seemed to stand next to him without his noticing. Jeremy glanced to either side to see himself flanked by a serious looking, dark-skinned woman, about his age, of African descent, and an older, well-dressed man with a slight paunch and receding hairline.

Just as they had at the F.O.B., the delegates simultaneously and suddenly blinked out of existence, only to appear somewhere else on the ship.

Hamilton and his two teammates found themselves standing in a slightly smaller room identical to the one they had just occupied. They might not have noticed the difference, but the opaque walls were suddenly closer.

Three humanoid shapes slowly faded into view. *It's like they're coming into focus.* The new trio varied widely in appearance, but all wore a high-collared, knee-length, frock-like uniform, similar to an Earth priest's, but all white. White slacks and shoes completed the uniforms. Standing in the white light of the alien craft, they seemed almost ephemeral. All of the aliens were extremely human in appearance, but with a skin tone and characteristics that defied identifying a race or nationality. That is where the similarities ended.

The first member of the alien team was the tallest, at Jeremy's height. Clearly male, with a V-shaped torso, flat stomach, broad shoulders, and short dark hair that topped an inhumanly attractive face. The second was female, not just feminine, but the most beautiful woman Jeremy had ever seen. She seemed young without any signs of aging. With blondish brown hair and dark, somewhat Asiatic features, she appeared both exotic, mysterious, and approachable at the same time. The third humanoid was androgynous. Neither overtly male or female, but completely bald with petite features and a slender build. The frock on the androgynous entity made it impossible to discern a male or female body type. Jeremy's eyes immediately jumped back to the female alien. *No problem discerning a body gender there. That frock is a tad snug in all the right areas.* She and the first alien were so attractive, they could easily be models. The third was so neutral as to be almost immediately forgettable.

"Greetings people of Earth," the male alien's voice was the same rich baritone they had heard earlier and without a hint of sarcasm. "We welcome you in the spirit of sharing and peace."

"Hello. I am—" Jeremy began.

"Dr. Jeremy Jefferson Hamilton," the female alien interrupted, her voice as soft as a flower petal, while looking him straight in the eye. "Your governments provided brief dossiers on each of you, so we familiarized ourselves with your credentials, but not your interests, and as you learn about us, we would also like to learn about you, personally."

Personally? I wonder how she meant that?

"Dr. Nadaya T'doyo and Dr. Duncan Nelson," the androgynous alien said looking at Jeremy's teammates.

They're BOTH doctors? I guess that makes sense. If you've got to send people to meet space aliens, may as well make them Ph.D.s.

"And what are your names, if we may ask?" Nelson asked, his British accent apparent, directing his question to the male alien.

"Unfortunately, our true designations are not pronounceable to you. For the sake of simplicity and diplomatic expediency, you may refer to me as Alpha," the male alien stated authoritatively. "Refer to my colleagues as Beta," the female nodded, "and Delta." The androgynous alien lifted its chin. "I assure you this has no bearing on rank, gender, or preference. We have simply chosen designations easy for you to remember and universal to your life experiences."

"We are very familiar with your world, cultures, languages, and technology," Delta said coolly. "We have made no secret of the fact that we have been studying your planet for some time, prior to our recent contact."

"Our goal here is to make you comfortable with us, so that we can be friends," Beta said, again looking directly at Jeremy.

"All well and good, but I have a question before we even get started," Nelson said. "If you can transport matter, why did we come up in a ... shuttle craft, I guess you would call it?"

Hmmm. Seems like the kind of question an intelligence officer would ask. Sussing out their technological limits right off the bat.

"Our matter transference systems have a very limited range," Alpha replied frankly. "The closer they operate, the more precise their accuracy. From above your base of operations, it was a safe and simple procedure to exchange an equal mass of oxygen/nitrogen mixture for your mass. Transfer from our sub-craft to our prime-craft is much more accurate. To minimize our personal contact with your general populace, we thought it best if you transferred first to our shuttle."

"Interesting," Dr. T'doyo spoke for the first time, her voice carried an almost musical lilt. "You must have to exchange like masses or the instantaneous absence would cause a popping vacuum, while the simultaneous insertion of too much matter would cause intense pressurization. Is this done on the atomic level?" directing her question to Delta, *sounding more like a physicist than a diplomat.*

"On the quantum level," the androgynous alien said, "but the negative effects would be felt on the atomic and macro levels."

"Perhaps we could relocate our discussions to someplace more comfortable for you?" Beta asked, turning with a gesture to indicate a doorway that wasn't there previously.

What could possibly be more comfortable than discussing quantum mechanics with a beautiful alien in a crystal pyramid starship thousands of miles above the Earth? Well, I could think of maybe one or two things.

*

"I find it interesting that they separated us even more," Dr. T'doyo stated when the three delegates were later alone.

"It was likely more efficient to allow us to focus on our individual interests independently," Dr. Nelson said.

"Yes, there was no possible way it could be 'divide and conquer,'" Hamilton murmured to himself. T'doyo shot him a sideways glance.

After the initial meeting and the delegates sat more comfortably, the group spent considerable time reviewing the ground rules and parameters for the meeting. The delegates made a point not to refer to it as an investigation. From there, the aliens each accompanied a delegate to specific areas of interest. Alpha directed Dr. Nelson, T'doyo left the room with the androgynous Delta, and the beautiful Beta lead Hamilton to the medical bays. Jeremy expected Nelson to object to the pairings, but the Brit cheerfully followed Alpha down the hall. The feminine alien mesmerized Hamilton. He couldn't help it. *Ironically, that nearly shapeless frock makes her even sexier than a form-fitting uniform. I have GOT to focus on the investigation.*

After the tour, the three delegates returned to a small (again crystalline, but opaque) conference room to confer. The conference room seemed somehow recently tailored and configured just for the delegates. As with every space they had been in previously, intense white light seemed to emanate from slots in the ceiling.

"Did either of you gentlemen learn anything new about our hosts?" Dr. T'doyo asked as they sat at the table.

"I say, do you think they are monitoring this room?" Dr. Nelson asked his companions as he looked around.

That is exactly what an intelligence officer would think.

"Very likely. Be mindful," Dr. T'doyo glanced around at the featureless room. Besides the crystal table and chairs, there was nothing else in the small space except a bowl of various types of fruit and a carafe of water and three glasses. Crystal, of course. A quick investigation revealed that a second door led to very human restroom facilities.

"Not much new to tell. The technology they will use to remove the cancer is similar to their matter transport system," Hamilton reported. "They perform full body scans on individuals to detect the cancer cells with a hand-held device. Then in a different device, somewhat similar to an open MRI bed, they swap the cancer cells out for an appropriate substitute using their matter transference tech at close range."

"Appropriate substitute?" asked Dr. T'doyo, her soft, lilting voice tinged with concern.

"Yes," Jeremy explained. "Evidently for them, that is the difficult and most time-consuming part. And by time consuming, I mean a couple of seconds. The machine's computer figures what could be safely inserted into the affected areas of the specific patient. Sometimes, it may be a saline solution, sometimes plasma, or it can be a gelatinous protein substance we have no equivalent for, that the body will eventually assimilate. As we discussed, they just can't 'beam' the cancer cells out or the sudden vacuum created in the body would be disastrous."

"Did you learn anything about this matter transfer technology they use for the process?" Dr. T'doyo asked.

"That's the thing," Hamilton said. "They are very open about *what* they are doing, but very evasive about *how*.

"I fear I fared no better than Dr. Hamilton. The *why* to their purpose is also no more clear than when we began," Nelson interjected. "For all intents and purposes, they are using their cancer-eliminating procedure as a gesture of goodwill and to demonstrate their friendly intentions."

"Or so they claim," Jeremy stated.

"Claim?" Dr. T'doyo asked.

"I just find it hard to believe that an advanced extraterrestrial species would travel all this way to eliminate one of the banes of our existence just to meet new buddies," Hamilton frowned as he echoed a sentiment he had proposed to Dell earlier.

"Perhaps their intentions are exactly as they claim," T'doyo offered. "Maybe they are just trying to be good neighbors."

"Or ... cure a world's cancer once, that world owes you, and is at your mercy," Hamilton hypothesized. "Teach them the cure and they are set for life."

Nelson smiled. "Reminds me of an old saying: Build a man a fire and he is warm for a night. Set a man on fire and he is warm for the rest of his life." Neither of his companions seemed amused.

"Can I ask you two a personal question?" Hamilton looked at his companions. "Did you think that two of our hosts seemed naturally ... beautiful? Especially Beta."

"I would not have brought it up, but, yes." Nelson's eyes seem to defocus as he smiled and pictured the aliens. "I found Alpha, in particular, disturbingly flawless."

"Actually, Dr. Hamilton," T'doyo's said, "all three aliens were nearly perfect. As if designed to appeal to a specific gender preference. Delta would appeal to a person identifying as bisexual ... or at best, undecided."

"Perhaps their race genetically altered itself to remove all the 'ugly' genes," Nelson said.

"Maybe it was just me, but I found it particularly difficult to focus on their science while distracted by Beta," Hamilton said. Dr. T'doyo stared at him and Nelson for a long minute.

"Dr. Nelson, please feel free not answer this question if it makes you uncomfortable, but there is a reason I ask," T'doyo started. "Are you attracted to Alpha?"

"Wha—" Hamilton exclaimed. "Actually, Dr. T'doyo, I am. Very much so. Why do you ask and how did you come to that conclusion?" Nelson said. "Was there something in my manner that gave it away? In my line of work, I try very hard to be unreadable."

"No, you are fine, Dr. Nelson," T'doyo explained. "I just made a logical guess. I, myself, am attracted to Delta." The two men could barely contain their shock. "Dr. Hamilton is correct. They are very distracting. Almost intentionally so. It's something I myself would have done."

The two men looked shocked at the dark-skinned woman.

Jeremy, still reeling over the revelations of the sexual preferences of his companions, looked to T'doyo. "Why would a diplomat want to distract investigators with members of the opposite sex?"

"I can't speculate what a diplomat would want to do, Dr. Hamilton," T'doyo said frankly. "I am an intelligence operative."

*

The committee reconvened to discuss the report from the delegates. After the chairman called the room to order, the senior intelligence officer stood to address the committee. After reading from a rather sterile report of the facts, he looked at the group of politicians, doctors, and intelligence officers and provided his own insights.

"It seems our visitors are very smart. They separated our delegates and gave them tours of their ship, going into great detail about *what* they would do to show their friendly intentions, but being very evasive about *how*. They gave us practically no information about their teleportation or cancer-eliminating technology except to describe it in its most general terms. Nothing at all about their propulsion or weapons systems. They have shed no light on why they are being so magnanimous. In short, this was a very elaborate dog-and-pony show."

"What about Dr. Hamilton?" asked the chairman. "How is he performing? He was the wildcard in our selection."

"Actually, T'doyo reports that Hamilton is exceeding our expectations. He can sense something is amiss. He is the one who first vocalized that the aliens are not very forthcoming about the specifics of their technology. He also noticed something about their thought processes concerning their own personnel. It seems our galactic neighbors have specifically chosen representatives that are sexually appealing to our delegates in an attempt to distract them or even turn them. It is exactly what we would do in their shoes.

"Dr. Hamilton was also the one to point out about how little actual technology the aliens are divulging," the senior intelligence officer continued.

"The aliens ain't suspicious or on guard or anything, are they?" the chairman asked.

"It seems quite the contrary," the intelligence man replied. "According to our operative, the aliens act as if their seduction technique is working on Dr. Hamilton even more so than the others. Despite the great possibility that the delegates discussed all this in an insecure room, the visitors are continuing to move forward with that strategy."

"Is young Dr. Hamilton falling for it? Your earlier dossier on him said it's been some time since he was ... er ... in a relationship and may be primed for feminine attention."

"I don't believe that to be the case. If there is one thing the good doctor possesses more than a healthy, if somewhat neglected libido, is an obsessive dedication to the truth. The man not only cannot lie, but the very thought of it goes against his entire personality. Given that he knows nothing of strategic value and his naturally skeptical nature, I maintain we couldn't have picked a better delegate. He is utterly believable because he is utterly honest."

*

An hour later, the door to the conference room opened with the trio of aliens focusing into view just outside. Mindful of the delegates' earlier discussion, it was much easier for Jeremy to stay focused on the investigation and not his hostess's physical charms. But upon closer observation, Jeremy could now detect tiny laugh lines around her eyes and the faintest of smile creases in her face. When able to study her discreetly, he noticed a very small beauty mark near her jawline.

I know that wasn't there before.

These new 'defects' in her appearance were subliminally subtle and made him more at ease with Beta's appearance, not less. Her beauty could still be distracting, but those little imperfections made her seem more *real*, even sexier.

Wait! What am I thinking? Those things weren't there before. They must have listened to our conversations and made adjustments to make our hosts more human to us, to put us more at ease. That's not special effects makeup. How could they have made those changes so fast?

The other two delegates were led away to continue their tour and Beta brought Jeremy back to the medical bay.

"We have decided that the best way to allay your fears about our procedures is to demonstrate its effectiveness," the beautiful alien said. She indicated the scanner laying on a crystalline work table.

"You may take this device and use it to detect carcinogenic cells on your own, so that we may remove them as a demonstration."

The device on the table had a white handle, much like a pistol grip, topped with a small, smooth-edged white box. Mounted on that, a see-through screen approximately six inches wide by four inches tall, completed the device.

"We have modified it for human usage," Beta explained. "The screen provides both easy to understand instructions as well as interactive diagnostics."

"You know that we can't provide humans for trials without first doing tests on animals, right?" Hamilton asked his host.

"We assumed as much. It is your nature," Beta acknowledged. "We calibrated the device for humans, any biological actually, and will detect a wide variety of physical imperfections and maladies."

Unbelievable! This device is a godsend! A hand-held scanner that can detect any disease? And she's just giving it to me? This will change medicine forever.

As Jeremy picked up the device, it activated. Holding it out in front of him, he pointed it all around the room, adjusting various settings on the screen.

"There are restrictions however," Beta warned. "We have created this specifically for you, personally, to use. Any attempt to x-ray or dismantle the device will cause it to self-destruct. This is for your own protection. Until mankind is ready, it would not be beneficial for it to reverse engineer advanced technology."

Jeremy looked down at the floor briefly. That was the first thought that had crossed his mind. How could humanity duplicate this technology to advance human medicine? His shame quickly replaced by curiosity. *Would you look at that?*

"The device will cease to function and self-destruct after three of your days," Beta advised. "We hope that will be sufficient time to gain your trust."

"We appreciate your concerns and will bring up lab animals by tomorrow so that you can show us how your procedure works." Hamilton looked down at the scanner.

And I know just where to test this next.

*

The aliens returned the delegates to the F.O.B. the same way they left. A brief shuttle ride followed by an instantaneous popping out of, and into, existence. Teams of experts in their respective fields debriefed the delegates. Hudson deferred much of his debriefing brusquely.

"I'll get you full report as soon as I can, but right now, I only have three days to use this machine, do a thousand tests, find test subjects, and return to the ship for a demonstration of the procedure, so excuse me if I don't have time to sit around and talk about what happened."

"But Dr. Hudson—" Major Vincenzo began.

"Not now Major," Hudson said, standing and moving toward the door of the Quonset hut. "My fellow delegates can answer many of your questions. Now if you will just point us in the direction of a lab in all this, I would greatly appreciate it."

Major Vincenzo looked helplessly at Dell.

"What can I say Vinny?" Dell said with a smile. "I may be out of work soon, but till then, I'm gonna stick with the smartest guy in the room."

*

"Dell, I need you to round up as many test subjects as possible. Animal and human. Both healthy and with late stages. Get the major to fly them out here yesterday. I want all their medical records. Get us some lab assistance. Once the subjects are here, I want them to undergo every test possible to verify their conditions so we can compare it to what this thing says."

"What are you gonna be doin', Doc?" Dell asked.

Hamilton held up the scanning device. "I'm going to do some further testing and make sure I'm reading this right."

*

The man on the alien bed looked like a desiccated mummy. The white light from the alien ceiling emphasized his gaunt features even more. Jeremy looked down at him and squeezed his hand.

"Don't worry, this won't hurt a bit, Mr. Moore," Jeremy soothed the man. "They're will be some slight tingling for a minute or two and that's it."

"Then I'll be good as new, Dr. Hamilton?" Keith Moore asked weakly.

"No. I'm not going to lie to you. If everything goes as planned, this procedure removes the cancer cells, but your body will have to rebuild itself. It's suffered through quite an ordeal. It may take a long time to regain your strength and health, but the good news is: you'll have a long time to do it."

"Well, at least I'll still have my hair," Mr. Moore joked as he rubbed an emaciated hand over his bald pate. His once-thick mane destroyed by chemotherapy.

"Sit tight while I go check on some last-minute details," Jeremy said as he squeezed the man's hand. Mr. Moore looked as if he hadn't eaten in months. He barely cast a shadow on the alien bed. Skin stretched tight over emaciated muscles, the man on the bed looked more like a reject from a zombie movie than a man Jeremy's age. The chemo and radiation had done as much damage as the cancerous cells eating away at his lymphatic system. If this didn't work, Mr. Moore's ... Keith's ... remaining time could be measured in days, not years. Certainly not decades. His quality of life would be measured by the amount of agony he could endure. Jeremy prayed that the procedure worked.

At Jeremy's insistence, Dell accompanied him to the alien ship to assist with the work. Reluctant to let more humans access to their prime vessel, the aliens installed the necessary equipment aboard their shuttle and all of the work would be conducted there. After Hudson the approved the process, shuttles, carrying the equipment, would transfer the cancerous cells out of humans across the world. Once aboard, the gawking Dell was speechless for several minutes after first seeing Beta.

The animal testing of the alien cancer removal procedure worked flawlessly. Jeremy would like to have more time, years really, to observe the mice and other mammals for side effects of the alien tech that replaced their cancer cells. But they didn't have that much time. As assured by Beta, the animals seemed to experience no pain during the procedure and immediately began to show improvement. In a few days, Jeremy and Dell, under the watchful eye of the beautiful Beta, had "cured" hundreds of mice and even chimpanzees of life-threatening cancer. The aliens seemed patient and even understanding of the human need to test the procedure on as many animals as possible before human trials. He and Dell dissected random animals to make sure that the treatment eradicated all traces of cancer. The alien scanner confirmed their results. Jeremy presented his research, albeit rushed, to the E.I.O., the FDA, AMA, and the White House. Ultimately, it was the White House that overrode the others to allow Dr. Hamilton to begin human trials. Keith Moore had been selected the first among the thousands of volunteers and signed enough hold harmless waivers to fill a file cabinet. He declined having a lawyer look at them first.

"What are my choices? Sign these here papers or die? No, no. Please. Let's haggle over details for a few more months. Gimme that damned pen."

A few hours later, his white blood cell count and MRIs confirmed what the alien scanner reported. Keith Moore was the first human completely cured of cancer.

*

In a conference room identical to the one on the main ship, Jeremy slouched in a chair while Dell laid on the floor with his hands shading his eyes from the light pouring from the ceiling. Beta stood several yards away.

"Do you know what we just did?" Dell moaned.

"Yes," Jeremy answered. "I believe we just saved a man's life."

"No. No. No. If you jerk a guy from in front of a bus, THAT saves a man's life," Dell's hand still covered his eyes. "Do you know what we just did? We cured fragging cancer. Not just put it in remission, but fragging CURED it."

"No. You did not," Beta said impassively.

"Whoa there, Carmen Elektra!" Dell was sitting straight up now. "There's a guy on a bed not five yards from here who could live another fifty years. A few hours ago his ticket was scheduled to be punched before we flip the calendar at the end of the month. My guess is: he's calling it cured."

"No, she's right," Jeremy said flatly. He looked like he had just seen ghost. "We didn't *cure* cancer. We just transferred it. Where did we transfer it to, Beta?"

Beta was already fading from view.

*

Jeremy and Dell continued to operate the machine on numerous volunteers. Each seemed to undergo a miraculous change in health. Each patient now seemingly cancer-free. The alien matter transference tech beamed the processed cancer patients to a hospital in Kansas for further observation and testing. All tests reported them clean of the killing cells. Beta had not reappeared since Dr. Hamilton's questioning after Mr. Moore's recovery.

After several days of ridding stage four patients of cancer, the delegates, and Dell, met in the conference room to discuss their findings.

"Gentlemen, it is time for us to report our findings to our superiors," Dr. T'doyo said in her soothing sing-song voice. "What do we know? Please keep in mind, as Dr. Nelson pointed out, that this room may not be secure."

"Well, we have no more insights as to *why* and *how* our friends are helping us than we did when started," Dr. Nelson said.

"I know I am not an official delegate," said Dell, "but I can tell you that whatever this mystery process is, it works. We somehow cured over a dozen people of cancer. People who wouldn't have seen their grandkids, or run in the sun, or hugged their loved ones a year from now, could be alive long after we're gone. As far as I'm concerned, that makes it worth whatever they're after."

"Dr. Hamilton, do you believe they are being truthful with us?" Dr. T'doyo asked.

Everyone turned to Jeremy.

"I need to speak with Beta before I can give my final decision."

As soon as he said it, Jeremy Hamilton blinked out of existence.

*

"How can I help you, Dr. Hamilton?" Beta asked.

"I think after a few days of us eradicating cancer together, you can call me Jeremy." Hamilton looked around the crystal room he had just appeared in. Beta had faded into view just after he materialized.

"Very well ... Jeremy," Beta said hesitantly, "how can I help you?"

"You can start by telling me the truth."

"Why do you believe we are not being truthful with you?" the alien woman asked.

"You've been lying to us since you sent that drone to the White House lawn," Jeremy growled. "For starters, what do you really look like? You expect us to trust you and believe the story that you are just here to help us, but you aren't showing us your true form."

"Why would you say that?"

"Oh please. The bodies we first see are perfect in every way and almost *designed* to be specifically attractive to each of us and distracting from our mission. You bug our conference room, then 'overhear' us talk about your physical perfection and the next time we see you, just an hour later, you have subtle imperfections to make us feel more at ease with you." Jeremy points to his own feet. "You don't cast

129

shadows and you never touch anything, including us. The problem with a seduction technique is that eventually you have to touch someone. You appeared so sexual, I was acutely aware of not ever touching you, even casually. When I '*accidentally*' pointed the hand scanner at you, nothing appeared on the screen. Not even a ghost of an image. And finally, you don't blink in and out the way your matter transfer device does to us. You 'come into focus' when you appear. If I had to guess, I would say you are holographic projections of some sort. Tell me I'm wrong."

Beta faded from sight.

"Beta? Hello? Anybody?" Jeremy bellowed at the white walls of the room.

All three aliens came into focus as he turned around the room. All three had their hands clasped behind their backs in their usual white frocks.

"Dr. Hamilton, Beta has relayed your concerns and we wish to—" Alpha began.

"Put a sock in it, E.T.," Jeremy punched his fist into the alien's chest.

Alpha looked down at the arm protruding from his sternum with no shock, pain, or surprise. Jeremy's face, on the other hand, was ashen white.

"Well, that could have gone horribly wrong," withdrawing his hand from the alien's torso.

"Now that you have surmised the nature of our interface, how can we help you Dr. Hamilton? We *are* here to help," Alpha said.

"You can start by answering some questions," Jeremy said, looking at his own hand which seconds before he had buried in the chest of the alien in front of him.

"Are you sure you really want the truth, Dr. Hamilton?" Delta asked flatly.

"That's all I've ever wanted my whole life," looking at each of the aliens one at a time. "The truth has hampered my career, ruined my marriage, and now, is very likely going to stop humanity from beating its worst enemy. Despite all that, damn straight I want the truth."

"Which truth would you like to start with?" Alpha asked. Jeremy noticed that Beta was strangely silent. "There are many truths. Some more personal than others."

"For starters, where do the cancer cells go?" Jeremy asked. "We transfer in saline, or that protein gel, and we 'beam' out the cancer. Where does it go? What do you do with it?"

Beta spoke for the first time since reappearing, "It's simple ... Jeremy. We eat it."

"YOU WHAT?" Jeremy exclaimed.

"We, our species that is, digest the cancer cells to live," Alpha explained. "We transfer them to storage units inside our main ship, and when we harvest all the carcinogenic material on your planet, we return to our home world to supply our populace with sustenance."

"You *eat* cancer?"

"Much the same way your planet's population survives on vegetables you grow on your farms," Delta explained. "There is no plot to subjugate your world. We have no interest in being responsible for feeding or controlling another planet."

Jeremy collapsed to a sitting position on the floor. This was almost more than he could handle. He thought he was prepared for the holographic deception, but the reality of what these creatures did with the cancer cells was too ... *alien* ... to ... *digest*. Several minutes passed while Jeremy processed what the alien images had told him.

"Wait. You said 'harvested' and 'grow on a farm.' Did you plant the seeds of cancer in us?"

"Galactic mandate forbids the manipulation of the genetic structure of other races to their detriment," Alpha stated.

"But ...?"

"Given the severity of our home world's dire situation, we did find a way to adhere to that mandate and still enable our civilization to survive," Delta said.

"So, you didn't break this galactic law, you just bent the hell out of it," Jeremy accused the aliens.

"No. We did not violate the rules set down," Alpha explained. "We did however, visit your world and adjust certain non-biological elements to better fertilize your environment. Unfortunately, one of our shuttles crashed in your North American desert only to be discovered. We have since made our presence less obtrusive."

"Desert? This wasn't about seventy-eighty years ago or so, was it?" Jeremy inquired.

"By your method of calculation, yes."

"Hold the phone. You 'adjusted certain non-biological elements to better fertilize our environment'?" Jeremy quoted.

"You speak a truth," stated Delta.

"So you didn't tamper with our DNA, but you monkeyed with our world ... so we would more easily get cancer?" Jeremy asked incredulously, looking directly at Beta.

"I am not certain of your vernacular, but I believe that to also be a truth," Delta explained.

"You didn't put cancer in us, not because it was wrong or anything, but it was against some cosmic law that you didn't want to get busted for. Then you made nearly everything else in our world cancerous? Because you were hungry," Jeremy exclaimed.

"We were *very* hungry."

"Dr. Hamilton, you must understand. We have waited for millennia as you quantify time to harvest these cells. It has taken this long for your populace's biologics to reach critical mass. We do this for the survival of our species," Alpha explained, as if to a petulant child.

"Do you know how many people have died from cancer while you waited for our world to be 'ripe'?" Jeremy was nearly in tears. "My parents died because of what you did, waiting for your next meal, all the while you had the means to save them."

"We regret the inconvenience this may have caused you and anyone on your world," Alpha said, "but rest assured that once your governments accept our offer, that no one on Earth will suffer from cancer for several generations."

"Several generations?" Jeremy asked.

"Yes. The environmental and elemental conditions still exist on your world," Delta explained. "We will remove all cancer cells currently in any humans, but eventually, the environment will create carcinomas in new generations to come."

"But why?" Jeremy asked. "Why not just eliminate all those cancer-causing agents in our world?"

"Why does one of your farmers not burn his fields after a single harvest? He wants to harvest again next season."

"Next—" Jeremy was aghast. "You mean you're going to let cancer start growing in us again?"

"Yes," Delta said. "It will take several of your generations before it reaches a critical mass that justifies sending a craft back to harvest again. Surely you must realize this is not the only world we are 'farming.'"

"But you said our governments have a choice."

"We are not conquerors. We do not dictate the actions of others," Alpha said. "Your world has the choice to allow us to harvest these cells and be on our way, or forever allow cancer to decimate your population."

"That's no choice!" bellowed Jeremy. "What world would let so many suffer and die when there is a free solution?"

"Actually, Jeremy," Beta said quietly. "Your world's governing bodies await your verdict on whether we have their best interests at heart. They do not choose. You do."

"You expect me to decide if a large chunk of population lives or dies horribly? That's unfair!"

"More so than you think, Dr. Hamilton," Alpha stated.

"What could be more awful than that?" Jeremy asked of the alien.

"The scanner we loaned you for testing, transmitted data back to us as you used it. When you used it on yourself. We know."

*

Jeremy Hamilton appeared back at the F.O.B. soon after. Dell quickly hustled him into an empty Quonset hut.

"Doc, where have you been? What's going on?"

"Dell, there's some things I want you to do for me," Jeremy began. "I want you to write up all our notes into a paper—hell! several papers—and submit them to every medical and scientific journal in the world."

"But Doc," Dell said "they'll end up giving whoever writes those papers all the credit. He'll get the Nobel prize in medicine. He'll be on the cover of every magazine in the world as the man who brought the cure to cancer to Earth. It should be you who writes them. I'm glad to help, but you were the point man on this thing."

"No, I need you to promise me you will do this. Also, I want another promise from you. A serious one."

"More serious than taking all the credit for curing cancer? Sure, Doc, no problem."

"I want you to swear to me that you will continue to search for a real cure, or reverse engineer the alien transfer technology, so that we are not dependent on them to save us. Can you do that?" Hamilton gripped his assistant by both shoulders. "At the very least, inspire others to continue the work. There are things in the environment that are causing these cancers. Find them."

"Yeah, but why?" Dell asked. "In a few weeks, won't Carmen Elektra and her pals eliminate the need for oncologists, period?"

"Promise me."

"Sure, Doc. After all, you're forcing me to be the hero of the medical and scientific world, the least I can do is swear my life's work to a field that won't exist soon."

*

"And that, ladies and gentlemen, is my report," Jeremy Hamilton concluded to the E.I.O. committee.

"And that's it?" the senior intelligence officer asked. "You are telling us to trust the aliens and that this 'cure' they're offering seems legitimate and that they have no ulterior motives?"

Jeremy looked at the other two delegates seated to his side.

"Unless you have evidence to the contrary, yes, that is what I am saying."

"Well, Ah guess that's it then," the chairman announced. "Our experts are of the opinion that it is jest about impossible for you to lie about something so important Dr. Hamilton. We will let the alien shuttle crafts start removing cancer from patients in every major city. Free of charge. This will decimate the pharmaceutical industry." *Companies that have major interests and investments in my constituency.*

"There is just one other thing gentlemen," Jeremy interjected. "My assistant, Dell, will be publishing extensively on the data we collected and I expect your full support for him on this."

"Why aren't *you* publishing, Doctor?" the chairman asked.

"Because I am going with our new friends. First to their main ship and then back with them to their home planet once they have eradicated cancer from Earth."

The room silenced.

"Is it the woman, Beta?" the intelligence officer asked.

"No. She is not someone I can envision myself holding," Jeremy said. "I am going because there are more truths out in the galaxy and I wish to live long enough to discover them. I hope someday to be able to provide Earth with some of them. I also believe there are some galactic law makers that would love to talk to me."

*

Two days later, Dr. Jeremy Hamilton found himself lying on a bed in the alien craft.

Beta, or at least her image, stood beside him.

"You are sure this something you wish to do, Jeremy?" Beta asked.

"Yes. If you keep your promise to me."

"I will," Beta replied.

Moments later, the alien machines finished their work and Dr. Jeffrey Hamilton's body showed no signs of pancreatic cancer. Beta had promised him that she, in her real body, would be the one to digest his cancer cells. As of right now, he was cancer-free.

**

Part of the Family
By Steve Rouse

Kevin McKinley's marriage was finally just a week away. At thirty-eight, his family had pretty much given up hope. All that changed a little more than a year ago, literally by accident. Kevin ran late one morning and was accessing the morning's e-mails on his cell phone as his car approached the intersection of North 35th and East Ramsey. He failed to notice Janet Mitchell's car in front of him stopping for the red light. After the usual cussing and accusations, the two exchanged insurance information and phone numbers. Three months later, their exchanges included dinner and bodily fluids.

*

A week before their nuptials, Janet barreled out the door, heading to her bridesmaid's house for a marathon session of finalizing details. It was a girls' day, so Kevin had gratefully kissed her goodbye to dwell over his freshly renewed mug of coffee and ESPN's take on the upcoming collegiate football weekend. He hadn't told her, but he had over two hundred dollars in the office pool riding on Ohio State losing to Wisconsin.

Janet stopped on the porch at the top of the steps. At the bottom of the steps, a woman stood, looking somewhat uncertain. "Hello, can I help you?"

"Uh, hello. I'm looking for ... for Kevin McKinley," she said.

"Okay, and you are ...?"

"I'm a distant cousin, actually. My name is Beth, Elizabeth Jorgenson. My mother was a McKinley."

"Oh! Are you here for the wedding?"

"Ahh, a wedding? I'm sorry, is this a bad time?"

"No, no, not at all. It's next week. I'm Janet, Kevin's fiancée." She came down the steps and extended her hand. "Look, I really don't want to seem rude, but I have an awfully full schedule today. Would you mind letting yourself in? Kevin's in the kitchen, glued to the TV. You know, sports. He's probably got some money bet this weekend and needs to figure out how I'm not going to find out about it." She grinned. "Just let yourself in. I'll be back about six-ish. We'll talk then, I hope." She continued to her car.

Beth stood and watched as she backed out the short driveway, waving as she drove off. Beth sighed before climbing the steps to the house. Directed by the sound of the TV, she walked toward the back of the older, two-story home. She admired the stylish, almost rustic décor. "Too bad," she murmured.

*

"Oh, Good God! Who the hell are you?" Kevin startled, jumping back and spilling coffee over the newspaper, his green flannel shirt, and new khaki pants. "How'd you get in here?"

"I'm sorry. Are you Kevin Michael McKinley?"

"Yeah. Who are you and what the hell are doing just walking into my house like this?" His voice had raised an octave and about twenty decibels.

"Are you the son of Philip John McKinley and Stacey Jo Pierce?" Almost at a yell this time, "Who are you?"

"My name is Beth Jorgenson and you and I just might be related."

"Related? How?" he asked. At least she'd answered his question. Jesus!

She said more deliberately, "That depends on your answers." Beth still stood in the doorway between the kitchen and the dining room. As Kevin grabbed some paper towels, she came and stood next to the table, the old wooden floor creaking slightly as she passed the refrigerator.

"Look, I am sorry. I had no intention of scaring you like that. Your fiancée, Janet, told me to come in when we bumped into each other as she was leaving."

As Kevin dabbed at the coffee stains on his pants, he eyed this woman carefully. She was not quite pretty. She seemed about his age with brown hair, just short of shoulder length, and green eyes. His fight or flight reaction had worn off by this point, so Kevin felt he deserved an answer. "Who are you?"

"Can I ask you just one more question before I answer yours?" The sincerity of her voice and the fact that she'd sat down on a damp kitchen chair reduced her threat factor.

"Okay," he conceded.

"What is your birth date?"

"Are you with the IRS?"

She smiled, despite what Kevin felt was a pretty lame attempt to hide it. "No, I am not with the IRS, but I need to know."

"October 12, 1983. Your turn."

Her smile disappeared. "I'm your sister."

The chuckle began softly in his belly and then spread upward, quickly involving his entire frame. Within seconds, the kitchen table he rested on was shaking, threatening to spill the rest of the coffee left in his mug. An uncontrollable smirk streaked across his face as the laughter gushed forth.

"Oh, God, I can't believe this. You're really very good! Did Carlos put you up to this? Who hired you? Sweet Jesus! Seriously, how much are they paying you? Oh, Lord! I didn't expect any pranks until the bachelor party. But this, this is really a good one."

"Kevin, stop." Beth waited, patiently, for the guffawing to dissipate. As his laughter subsided, she sat, controlling her breathing as best she could. "Are you quite through?"

"Oh, come on. This is awesome!" Kevin leaned back in his chair, rubbing his face with both palms. "Tell Carlos or Frank or whoever came up with this gem that they got their money's worth."

"No one has hired me for any stupid collegiate prank!" She indignantly retorted, standing up quickly, sending her chair backward. It was Beth's turn to be loud. "I am being painfully honest with you and you'd better listen up real quick because there is a dire price that has to be paid!"

"What? What are you talking about?"

"Kevin, I am your sister, or would have been."

"Really? Well, my memory must really suck, 'cause you ain't in it! Where's your ..." That last word died away as her words registered. "What do you mean 'would have been'?"

She had his full attention. Beth leaned forward intently, both hands flat on the tabletop. One slid over and touched the mute button on the remote control, plunging the kitchen into an uncomfortable stillness. Distant outdoor noises, filtering in through the windows, were the only sounds. Kevin watched intently as she moistened her lips. Her voice followed, barely audible.

"What I am about to tell you is pure truth. I swear it on the soul of my—sorry, our mother. It's going to sound like pure fiction to you. To get started, I'd like you to see this." She held out a folded piece of paper. Kevin eyed her suspiciously. Without gazing at the paper directly, he took and unfolded it. He leaned forward. It looked old and official ... a birth certificate.

He looked at it, not really interested in reading the thing. He could only think that he wanted this woman out of his house. Prank or not, this had gone on too long. His inaction was not the reaction Beth apparently expected. She snatched it from him.

"Well, since you're obviously unable to comprehend what this is, I'll have to help." There was a distinct strain in her voice that wasn't there a moment ago.

"This is about a baby girl. Her name is Elizabeth Stacey McKinley. Oh, that's your last name Kevin. Now, what about her birth date? Oh, look! It says right here that she was born March 26, 1984." She glared over the paper at Kevin. "Make certain you listen to this part especially. Her parents are—look at this, Kevin—her parents are Philip John McKinley and Stacey Jo Pierce. Kevin, aren't those the names of your parents? Imagine that! What an amazing coincidence!" Her sarcasm came through clearly. He'd never heard anyone over-emphasize every single sound in every single word before. She sat back in her chair, with eyes intensely focused, like a wolf's on a wounded fawn.

Kevin sat mute, his mouth skewed up on the right side, with a bit of a squint to the right eye. He stared at this woman who glared back at him. This strange woman appeared in his kitchen doorway, uninvited, ten minutes ago. And now, sitting smugly at his own table, with some cock-and-bull story that was so outlandishly stupid, but which she obviously expected him to swallow. *What a psycho!*

For some God-forsaken reason, this woman—no, this bizarre, psychotic leech—felt she needed to attach herself to him. *Why? Who the hell is she and why does she have to be here?*

Janet! Thank God she'd gotten away when 'psycho-bitch' had shown up! Would she have been a threat to her somehow? Would his new 'sister' feel a need to hurt her? His mind raced over possible scenarios, all of which ended badly.

If he could only get her outside. Way more chances of running or getting help. He then felt his heartbeat, which had been going like a fullback's for the last minute or two, slow. *Okay, listen to your body. Calm yourself. Breathe evenly. Keep her calm and talking. Move to the front of the house. The living room, near the door, or maybe sit on the porch. Yeah, that's it. Get her to the porch and there's a huge improvement in the odds of seeing this one tossed into the back of a squad car.*

"That sure is one helluva story."

"Sorry, Kevin. That's not the story. That's just the introduction."

"Okay. So do I get to hear it or are you planning to keep me in suspense?"

She seemed to relax a bit. Good. *Now, to get out of the kitchen.* Kevin stood up and Beth bolted upright in her chair.

"Where are you going?" She said it like it was a single word.

"Relax. I'd still rather drink my coffee than wear it," gesturing to his clothes. "Do you want some?" Kevin walked to the cupboard to get her a cup.

"No, thanks. It always makes me jittery. Could I have some ice water, though? I'm a little nervous, and that always makes me thirsty."

Hell, you're nervous? He retrieved a tall glass and then walked passed her to the fridge. *I've got a clear shot at the front door. No! No way am I going to leave this wack-a-doodle alone in my home.* Half a minute later, ice water and coffee in hand, he announced, "Let's take this out on the porch, I love early autumn." Without waiting for her to reply, he walked toward the front door. He'd no idea how she might react.

He arrived there without her. He turned back and saw her standing next to the refrigerator, just staring at him. "Really? You're taking this much calmer than I thought you would."

"Well, like you said, that was only the intro. I want to hear, like Paul Harvey put it, the rest of the story." He watched her shrug and then join him on the porch.

They moved to the porch chairs and, as he put the ice water and coffee onto the glass-top table, a voice called from the next yard.

"Morning, Kev."

"Hey, Pam." Kevin smiled. *The one person I just didn't need.*

His neighbor, Pam Strakowski, stood next to the short hedgerow that had been her obsession for the past four summers. "It's getting close, eh? How are you and Janet?"

"All's good. Wedding's still on from what I know. Janet's spending the day with Georgia working on God-knows-whatever she hasn't spent the last five months making sure is set by now."

"You leave her be, Mr. McKinley. That woman's good as gold. I might even have to tell her that you're cheating on her already." She smiled as she said it, nodding toward Beth. But Kevin knew her enough to know that she probably suspected that was exactly what was going on.

Before he could muster up a response, Beth stood up, with a wave and a smile. "Hi Pam. I hate to spoil your news flash, but I'm Beth Jorgenson, Kevin's cousin from Minneapolis."

"Nice to meet you, Beth. You here for the wedding?"

"No, actually, a funeral."

Pam stood, mute as a statue. Her smile left her. She then shifted her gaze back to Kevin and the friendly look returned. "Kevin, you remember to mind yourself tonight. I know everyone who works over at Callahan's. Donny tells me he's offered to be your designated driver. But remember, he can't get there 'til after eight."

"Thanks, Pam, Donny told me. I'll be just fine."

"Well, you just be smart. Too much booze cost me my brother, you know."

"I know that story, thanks anyway. Beth and I and are going to catch up a bit now. See ya'." Kevin sat back down facing away from Pam and picked up his coffee. To Beth he added quietly, "Every neighborhood's got one."

Beth watched Pam huff, then head toward her backyard. She looked at Kevin and sighed. "How do I tell you?"

Kevin eyed Beth, who'd sat at the front corner of the porch. He sat in his usual spot, a well-worn burgundy director's chair positioned against the outer wall of the house, facing the street. "This one kinda sounds like it could start with 'Once upon a time.'"

Beth stared, mouth slightly, but politely, agape. "Exactly." She reached out and took a drink of her ice water, closing her eyes as she swirled it in her mouth before swallowing. Again, she sighed and looked at Kevin.

"When I was a little girl, I learned very early that Mom needed my help."

"Is this your mom, my mom, or both?"

"Look, this is hard enough. I don't appreciate being interrupted," she said tersely.

"Sorry. I promise, not a word until you're done."

She gave him a quick nod. "As I said, Mom needed my help a lot. I was her only child, her only helper. They'd only been married a short while when they were in a traffic accident. An older woman, who pulled out of the Shell station at Ramsey and 35th, hit them on the passenger side."

"Where?"

"Ramsey and 35th. Why?"

Kevin just shook his head. "Janet and I met there, that's all. Oh, sorry."

Beth looked perturbed, but continued. "Mom got the worst of it. Her right collarbone broke and her right elbow needed three surgeries. It healed, but in just a few years, she had increasing problems with arthritis. She learned how to do things left-handed because of the constant pain and limited range of motion.

"I spent most of my childhood helping her do the simple basics around the house. I also spent a lot of time in my room crying 'cause she hurt so much and I couldn't do a damn thing about it.

"By high school, I'd decided to go into medical school, you know, so I could help her. I started out at Boston College where I met Jeff Jorgenson, a physics major. He was a dreamy hunk of self-assurance and he had a full scholarship to MIT. I never wavered in wanting to do something that would help Mom, but my priorities very quickly shifted to Jeff.

"We married during our junior year and he was selected for some big secret project on campus. Rumor had it that the government had their hands in on it. I worked through med school and my internship at Massachusetts General.

"Then he got really sick one night, high fever, throwing up, and talking nonsense. The stuff he rambled about dealt with temporal inversions. He was delirious. I'm a doctor, but he needed help I couldn't give. I called his lab that morning and said he was ill and I was going to take him to the hospital. Seriously Kevin, within five minutes, a bunch of suits showed up at the door and hustled us out.

"To make a really long story shorter, he recovered and I joined his research team as a medical consultant. They'd been doing serious work on time travel and he'd volunteered for a 'trial run' and got radiation sickness. The longer I worked there, the more I got involved in the project. Finally, the day came to select a test time trip. I was inspired by an idea to go back and prevent my parents' accident. I had to fight for it, but with Jeff's insistence, it was selected! I was told it was because of its minimal temporal consequences. I was really going to be able to help my mom in a way that I'd never imagined possible.

"I got to go. It was really simple, too. After the time transport, I went into the gas station and talked to the older woman for a few extra minutes until I saw Mom and Dad drive by. That was it. My lifelong dream was realized! I felt great.

"When I came back through the portal, I was immediately arrested! They had no record of me! Since it was a time experiment facility and I had one of their coded tracking units embedded under my skin, they had no choice but to listen.

"The hardest part came when Jeff didn't even recognize me. But he still was a sweetheart. He helped me track down the reason no one knew me anymore in my own time line.

"Mom and Dad conceived you three months after the date they would have had the accident. That means, in my time line, Mom would have been in her fifth month of pregnancy with you when they should have conceived me. Bottom line is that, in this timeline, I was never conceived, never born.

"Now my problem is to undo what I've done. The University's Ethics Committee requires me to supply the project with your DNA as proof. That's why I'm here. I need a simple blood sample. Then, I'll leave and I promise you'll never see me again."

Kevin sat, cup cradled in both his hands just below his lips. "That is an amazing story. Same parents ... different timelines. Wow.

"What you're asking actually sounds reasonable." He stood and walked across the porch. Beth stood, but Kevin said, "I'm just going to the bathroom and get more coffee. Please, sit back down, relax. We have a lot to discuss."

She did. But, that changed the second she heard the front door lock.

"Kevin!" she screamed. "Don't be difficult." She moved quickly to the door and tested the handle. Locked. She then pounded on it with a closed fist. "Kevin!" Moving left, she looked in through the main window and saw Kevin talking on the phone, waving his arm toward her. He glared at her and flipped her off. She turned and ran down the street.

*

By ten p.m., *Callahan's* was in full swing. The tavern had a full front bar, but most of the din came from the private party in its basement lounge. She'd seen him come in at about eight o'clock with a few of his friends, but her back booth was safely dark enough.

She still sat there when, several hours later, he reappeared, obviously inebriated, sputtering loudly about beating all his friends at darts.

It wasn't difficult at all, given her medical background, to depress the syringe and collect the required sample when she 'accidently' bumped into him near the restrooms. He never looked at her and she doubted very much he'd even felt it.

*

She'd spent the night of her return time trip with her husband, Jeff. All was just as it had always been. She hadn't felt this alive, this energetic since her honeymoon.

She arrived at her parents' home the next morning, using her own key to go in, unwilling to wait at the door. "Mom? Dad? Where are you? It's me, Beth"

A distant voice answered. "We're all upstairs. Just a sec, sis, Dad and I are finally moving that big armoire."

She didn't recognize the voice. Things didn't feel right. *Sis? I'm an only child.* She ran to the steps.

Mom stood at the top of the stairway, all smiles. "Hi, Bethy. Thanks for coming over. The guys have things well in hand."

Dad came up behind her Mom. "Hi, Beth. Good to see ya. Kevin and I finally got around to moving your old cabinet. C'mon up and see."

"Who's Kevin?" She felt her stomach twist.

His now familiar face joined her parents. "Losing your memory already, Beth? Well, you are my **older** sister, even if it is by just three minutes."

***

A New York Yankee
By Paul K. Metheney

I remember everything. Right up until the gigantic cracker cold-cocked me. Oh, I remember a bunch of stuff after I wake up, but that has to be a dream, right?

My boys and I are doing what all professional ballplayers do just before the World Series: Partying.

The limo, an enormous, vintage, petrol-burner, dropped us off outside whatever "in" club in Manhattan reigns these days at one a.m. Artie told the driver to wait for us, "we'd be an hour or so." Artie adores the idea of giving orders to white guys. It may be 2056, but racial lines are drawn sharply enough you could cut yourself. White people are so afraid of offending us; they treat us like royalty. It's good to be the king.

Artie and L compete to talk trash to the same waiter, confident in the fact one of them will take him home. Whatever. Takes all kinds. While race issues became more volatile in recent years, sexual orientation has become a non-issue. Artie and L leapt out of the closet when they were kids, and as the two best outfielders in the league, no one cares. Care? Some feel it makes our team that much cooler.

I surpass my physical limits of alcohol consumption and am rounding third on a hookup with a red-headed, young hottie sitting at the bar, wearing about half a dress. She was wearing the dress. Not me. My motto is: "*What Mrs. Patricia Morgan, and the MLB, don't know, won't hurt me.*" (One will slap my hand with a fine, and one will make me dance on the end of a butcher knife. I'll let you guess who will do what.) I slide my iPal out of my inner jacket pocket to pay the bill. Evidently, *we* bought the house a couple of rounds. Makes me think of money. I pause to send an encrypted vmail to Rudy. As I swipe to send, a shadow eclipses the lights from the dance floor.

The eclipse turns out to be the most massive white man I've ever seen. By far. And I play professional sports. Godzilla screams at me, red veins popping out on his non-existent neck. All I can hear is part of the word "girlfriend" over the music as he hauls a ham-sized fist back to bludgeon me. The world moves in slow motion. Artie and L will never make it in time. I slide the iPal back into my jacket to cover reaching for my nine out of my back waistband. A million thoughts race through my head at once. I hesitate. If I pop this giant, my multi-gazillion dollar contract disappears, and ... oh yeah ... my baseball career. On the other hand, if he removes my head from my shoulders, which looks to be a solid bet, that would likely end it too. We could fight, and even as mountainous as I am for a ballplayer, Godzilla is much BIGGER. I have as much chance against this guy as Artie and L have of going straight. The press won't see it that way. The commissioner won't see it that way. I'll end up sued. Again. Turns out, I have no choice in the matter.

The last thing I see before all the lights fade: a tarnished high school ring. Real, real close.

*

Crash Landing

Damn! Someone used my head for batting practice. I push my way into what might be loosely described as an upright sitting position against a tree, just as some yahoo rides up on a horse. An honest-to-God horse! You see them in zoos but even mounted cops are motorized these days.

I stand up to see who can afford to own a horse, much less ride one. And there it is. A guy in a suit of medieval armor. Museum quality. Makes perfect sense. Brain damage. Godzilla scrambled my eggs pretty thoroughly.

"Who be your master, boy?" he demands. English accent. Snotty as all hell.

"Watch that 'boy' shit, cracker." I try to be as race neutral as I can be, but Armor-All has crossed all kinds of lines.

"Impudence! If you be a free-roaming Moor, then I claim you for House Gwalchmei." He pulls out an extremely long sword and points it at me, still sitting in the saddle. I search around for the camera; sure my boys are screwing with me.

Or maybe not. He presses the point into my jacket lapel.

I can still sense the nine in the waistband of my jeans (Thank God!), but I don't consider Mr. Hallucination here as *that* much of a threat. Plus, if this *is* a practical joke, it might suck all the fun out of it if I cap this racist tin can here and now.

I step back a pace or two, pick up a hefty fallen tree branch, tap it on the bottom of my shoe, and line drive his ass right off the back of the horse. His dismount looks painful and sounds worse.

I stand over Armor-All, teeing-up on his bucket head.

"I ... yield," he stammers. "State your terms, Moor."

"The name's Morgan. Not Moor. Henry Morgan." I pick up his sword. It's much heavier than I imagined. I take a long dagger from his belt. I don't see a gun on him. "Stand up. You look stupid laying there."

"I require ... assistance."

*

What's in a Name?

It takes both of us to haul him off the ground. His suit of armor weighs a ton. I help him take his helmet off. Whoa. Long, brown, greasy hair; dirty, unkempt beard; and smells as if he hasn't bathed in weeks. Except for being short and white, he could be a professional basketball player.

"Did you state that your name be ... Morgan? By chance, be you related to Morguause, of the House Lot?" the knight asks.

"Not that I know of. Born and bred in the city so nice, they had to name it twice. 'Hammerin' Hank Morgan, starting catcher for the New York Yankees. You probably saw me on TV. Sorry, man, I can't do autographs. I licensed my signature to Hallmark last season."

Armor-All doesn't know what to do with that. Clearly not a sports fan. Bitch.

"Do you know who my mother is?" Armor-All asks.

"No. Do you?" I'm still a little heated over the whole "master" and "boy" thing.

"I ask of your relationship to Morguause, as I am her son, Gwalchmei, loyal nephew and knight to our liege, the King. My aunt's name be Morgen. If related to her, it begs to ask in regards to your ... lineage." Old Gwalchmei knows how to sugar coat the fact auntie dearest may have been doing little "slumming." Well, she wouldn't be the first white sister looking for the LD, won't be the last.

Gwalchmei shakes his greasy head. "'Tis no matter. You bested me, albeit in a somewhat unorthodox manner. How say you, Henry of the House Morgan? What be your terms?"

"G-man, I just want to catch a ride back home and make the Series."

"Even bested as I am, I cannot offer a Moor to ride while I walk alongside as a knave, but I can walk beside thee."

Give him credit. He's offering me the back of the bus, but at least he's back there with me.

"I know not where your home is. Truthfully, I understand little of your strange speech. But I can offer you hearth, home, suitable attire, and sustenance. Perhaps an audience with Our Majesties."

"Lead on, McDuff."

"No. It's Gwalchmei."

*

Yay for Chinese Manufacturing!

As we walk, I slide my iPal out of my jacket. It's undamaged, thankfully. One improvement over the years involved toughening these things up. You could hit one with a hammer and not ding it. Unfortunately, Godzilla hit a whole lot harder than a hammer. They measure battery life in months now, not days.

No chips, cracks, or dents. Or signal. How is that even possible? Decades ago, the entire country went WI-FI3. Years before, wireless networking blanketed the globe. It should be impossible not to detect something. I check the latest download date. Last night. Just before we hit the town (no pun intended). At least this thing has most of the Internet downloaded to it.

"Pal, why am I not getting a signal?" I ask the screen.

"I don't understand, my dark friend," Gwalchmei says believing I am talking to him.

"*I can theorize we are not in the United States as the Internet Accessibility Act of 2032 provided for free, unlimited access to the Internet and mobile communications to all within its borders, with certain restrictions applying.*" Okay, maybe calling my iPal's female-voiced assistant software "Pal" strikes even me as a little weird.

"WITCHCRAFT!" Gwalchmei screams. Stepping back as fast as his steel plate will allow, he looks around for a woman.

"Relax, G. It's just my iPal. Surely, they're all over ... Hey! Where are we?"

Gwalchmei never takes his gaze off my iPal, eyeing it with suspicion and fear. "We be but a few leagues from my home inside the castle of Lord of all the Britains."

"Great Britain? Maybe they don't maintain universal access here." Not beyond Artie and L to ship my unconscious ass to England as a practical joke. I can't see them doing it just before the Series, but as I mentioned, there was more than a little alcohol involved.

"Pal, call Coach." He will fly me back to the States and the playoffs on the fastest thing moving. If he doesn't fire me.

"*I am unable to detect or connect to any mobile communication or WI-FI networks at this time. Please try your call later.*"

"I do not understand, Friend Henry, but the wizened Myrddin will fathom this sorcerous peril."

"Smartest guy at the Renaissance Festival, huh? Fine." Rolling with it. "Pal, is this England?"

"*I am unable to connect to any GPS signals at this time. Please try again later.*"

Damn. GPS is *global* positioning. Maybe I did break the friggin' thing.

*

Okay, NOT the Renaissance Festival

These guys must be some sort of re-enactment freaks, dressing up in Days of Yore. Still doesn't answer how they got here. No parking lot. In my few days here, not one person breaks character or uses an iPal, or any modern convenience I can see. No running water. No refrigerator. No microwave. Not even chewing gum. These guys are good. Too good.

And then there's the smell. Shit. I mean real shit. I see people throwing sewage out into the street. The smell of animals and manure hangs far and wide, and that's just marginally worse than the people. Gwalchmei's home boasts an outdoor "privy," essentially, a semi-enclosed hole in the ground. Go ahead. Ask me about toilet paper. "Personal hygiene," two words these people can't even spell. One thing worse than their body odor is their breath. When you get close (and don't!), check out some of these people's teeth, you'll see why. I used to fancy Gwalchmei as ripe. After meeting some castle dwellers, my boy G's all but surgically sterile.

If it's a re-enactment group, they're dedicated to the point of bag-of-hammers crazy. The food's so disgusting, you won't see it on a reality show and the drinking water is not quite brown, but it's well on its way. I settle for some undercooked meat and wine.

*

Middle Ages

I learn something a few nights later I wish I hadn't.

"Friend Henry, how old be you? I hold no experience with Moors, so I bear no way to gauge your age," Gwalchmei asks during some confusing, but polite, conversation.

"I am not a—never mind. Well, G, you've hit a bit of a sore point with ball players. I'm coming up on thirty-six, which is up there in Major League years."

"Ah. Beyond middle-aged. 'Tis disheartening facing our twilight years, but t'is God's will."

"Whoa! Hold on there, Armor All. Thirty-six ain't old. My whole life's ahead of me. I could squeak out a few more years of ball if I take care of myself." I am more than a little pissed. Racial slurs I can swallow, but trash talking a ball player's age and it's game on. I size Gwalchmei up and down, figuring him in his late-fifties. "Uh, how old are you, G?"

"I meant no offense, Friend Henry. I am in no position to cast aspersions on your vigor. My mother bore me mid-month of May, in 492 Anno Domini. So I am unquestionably old as well. I am approaching my thirty-second winter."

"Thirty-second! G, no apologies necessary for me, but I thought you are a LOT older than—WAIT! Did you say '492 Anno Domini'? As in 'AD?'" I do some quick math, never strong suit for me. I sit for a moment, taking it in. "Is this 523 AD?"

"Aye, my dark friend. I know, more than ever, Their Majesties will wish to meet an enchanted Moor of advanced years, who appears so youthful, *and* can cipher. In truth, it be beyond imagining."

No. Shit.

*

"Friend Henry, I secured an audience with Their Majesties a fortnight from now. I did not presume it possible to procure an audience so soon, but it seems Her Highness has never seen an ensorcelled Moor before," Gwalchmei announces.

"A fortnight? What's that? A couple of days from now?"

"No, my tall friend. A fortnight be fourteen days."

"G! I need to shag my butt back to the States *right now*. The World Series starts soon, and if I am not at practice, I can kiss my sweet, sweet contract goodbye."

"I'm sorry, Friend Henry, but Their Majesties cannot see you until then, and the sole chance you to return you home involves a mounted escort and letters of conduct from them."

"They'll want me to mount an escort?" I ask incredulously. Clearly, the bar hottie did not work out as planned. I avoided "Trish Da Bitch" for longer than our usual few weeks and mounting an escort sounds pretty tasty right about now.

"If your audience goes well, His Majesty may grant you a boon to ride all the way," Gwalchmei says.

"Okay. I'm up for it if she is." Somehow, I don't think we're talking the same thing.

*

I Am So Screwed

I've decided to not fixate on what I can't figure and focus on the few facts in my possession.

I seem to be in Great Britain. At any rate, the lot of them speak with a barely understandable British accent.

My iPal can't find a GPS, mobile, or WI-FI network. But it works. Just no connectivity. Just no way to communicate with anyone. Great.

I am in a castle. Out in the sticks with nothing around for miles and miles.

I am not going to make it back for the Series. Thank God I got a vmail off to Rudy.

I still carry my Ruger, though I gave Gwalchmei back his sword and knife. I wouldn't know how to use them anyway, and he didn't stab me as soon as he got them, so I have that going for me. Pretty sure I'm safe since he put me up in his home and feeds me, be that as it may.

Until I see proof to the contrary, I am going to accept (and it pains me to even consider this) I am stuck ... in the sixth century.

Oh yeah, I'm the sole brother in the castle.

*

My Kingdom for Cheeseburger!

I thought I could take it, but I can't.

"G, I need to eat some real food, a bath, and some clean clothes."

"Dost thou imagine the food be fictional, Friend Henry?" Gwalchmei thinks I'm simple *and* possessed.

"No, I appreciate what you've done for me. At least, let me help out around here. I have some ideas to make this place much cooler," I try a different tack.

"Art thou *hot*?" Gwalchmei a lot of things, but speedy on the uptake is not one of them.

"No, G, I mean with a little work, we can hook you up with the most bitchin' house in the whole castle."

"Why would I wish to tether my house to dogs, Friend Henry?"

"Never mind. Just tell your servants to do what I instruct them to do. Trust me."

"It shall be as you will, my dark friend. And I do trust you. You defeated me soundly and gave me back my blade. You speak true, though strangely. No man could ask for more."

I can.

*

Clean water. It all depends on clean water. G has servants take care of his household, and while they do all that I ask, they do it when not doing their usual chores for Gwalchmei. Can't blame them for knowing the relationship of their bread and buttered, I guess. I coerce G's maids into boiling well water on a regular basis to purify it. Boiled water supplements what we fetch from a nearby stream ... from upstream. You do not want to know how the water smells downstream. While collecting water, I take time to bathe and wash my clothes. I notice Gwalchmei's maids peeking and giggling. They've never seen a brother before. Well, once you go twenty-first century, you never go back.

*

Now we can drink safely, wash our clothes, cook and clean. I convince G's staff to bathe at least a couple of times a week, but many suspect this is how the Devil enters. After many arguments, I convince the women through their sense of smell. First, I had to convince them *why* they should smell better. I can't find it in myself to launch into a lecture on microscopic germs, viruses, and bacteria, so I do what Mamma used to, and say, "Because I said so." And now I know why she said it: it works.

The men are easier. The household women would withhold their "favors" until the men did not smell pig-like. Same rules apply to using a homemade brush and powder to clean their teeth. It takes a while, but eventually, we enjoy the cleanest, most satisfied staff in the castle.

The maids are duty-bound to submit to Gwalchmei's advances whenever he chooses, but even he starts to notice the difference and begins bathing on a regular basis.

*

Now with hygiene improved, I turn my attention to nutrition. Not a lot of citrus fruits or bananas (i.e., none), but I find apples, pears, grapes, nuts, berries, and plenty of greens. In the event I ever return to civilization (or my time), I will be lucky to still hold a career, so I need to be in the best shape of my life to *earn* my spot back on the team. Something I haven't had to do in years.

With some borrowed woolen pants, I start running and working out. I was wearing some pretty decent kicks when I got clobbered, so I use those as running shoes, and just peel off my shirt. At first, the castle inhabitants assume I'm crazy, or worse, running from—or after—invisible spirits. A half-naked black man jogging laps around the castle in 523 A.D., not something they see every day.

One of my first runs takes me back to where G found me. I am hoping to find a portal, spaceship, or *something* I could use to return my time. I see an old tree and some fallen branches. Not exactly a DeLorean.

My days consist of rising at dawn (say what you will, these people do *not* sleep in) to "breaking fast" with whatever fruits I can scrounge, time-managing the chores of the household staff, overseeing water and cleaning projects, lunch on leafy greens, and then a few hours of exercise. Gwalchmei's house is a picture of clockwork efficiency. If there was such a thing as clocks. Did I just invent the black butler? I am setting race relations back a hundred years, or forward fourteen hundred? Either way, I can pretty much stop expecting a Christmas card from the NAACP.

*

We Will Never Be Royals

The day of my Royal Audience arrives. I dress up in my original clothes. My jeans aren't tight when I tuck my nine in the back waistband, up under my jacket. My recent workouts and diet trimmed me down. Who am I kidding? I am in unbelievable shape. In just a few weeks, I dropped all the flab around my middle, and my muscle tone is denser than it was fifteen years ago.

I wear my twenty-first-century clothes for a reason. If my "in" with the King and Queen centers on the fact I'm something unique, then I am going to give them a show unlike any other. Gwalchmei coaches me on what to expect and how to act during the audience, and in turn, I tutor him on hygiene, nutrition, and some modern first-aid techniques. I spend my afternoons preparing. I will either become the next court jester, end up running this place, or beheaded, but one way or the other, I am going to show them some shit they have never seen before.

*

When called in, Gwalchmei leads. The Royal Hall appears a noticeable step up from the rest of the castle. Polished marble and tapestries cover walls and floors alike. The guards at the door tell us it's standing room only. Few in the kingdom ever beheld a Moor before, let alone an enchanted one. The style of dress, materials, and thicker waistlines indicate this crowd fares much better than the common folk outside. More than clothing and jewelry, these people reek of entitlement. And they just plain reek. I would take the lowest servant of Gwalchmei's house staff over any one of these smelly snobs. G treats his crew fairly, but for the first time, the class segregation strikes me right between the eyes.

*

On Gwalchmei's cue, we both take a knee until addressed.

"Step forward, noble knight. Regale us with the tale of your capture of this creature," commands the blonde woman on the throne.

A bearded guy, with dirty blond hair, a little older than Gwalchmei, sits next to her on the larger throne. I'm no Sherlock Holmes, but I'm going to guess: "The King."

"In truth, Your Highness, it was *he* who captured *me*. After a pitched battle lasting three days and three nights, this Moor defeated me through the use of great and powerful magicks."

Great and powerful magicks? I whupped him with stick in less than three seconds. Whatever.

An ancient turd of an old man steps up next to the King. "If this is sooth, how do you both stand here?" He speaks at Gwalchmei, but his eyes never leave me.

"Ah, wise and wizened Myrddin, this Moor, named Henry of the House Morgan, granted my freedom and life and asked for naught, but my hand in friendship," Gwalchmei says.

"Methinks he be the loser of that exchange," Myrddin croaks.

With a sharp glance at the old man, the Queen continues, "Pray good knight, what magicks does this dark man demonstrate? We hear of many strange tales from your household. Surely, they be false."

"No, my Queen, in the fortnight since Friend Henry has taken residence in my meager home, my servants be happier, healthier, and with nary an instance of illness."

At this, the Queen sat up straighter. "You let a Moor sleep under your roof? How will you ever expel the fleas?"

Yeah. She said that. It was all I could do to keep my mouth shut, but G explained to me how critical it is I not speak until spoken to. All this time, I didn't recognize what a looker she is. Overwhelmed by the whole spectacle, I never noticed the age difference between her and the King. A girl, actually. Blonde, buxom, and so pale, she borders on translucent. Men in any century would consider her extraordinarily hot. Between her looks and the twinkle of intelligence in her eyes, it doesn't take the aforementioned Mr. Holmes to see the King is batting way out of his league.

Still, fleas? Really?

"To the contrary, my Queen. While his humanity may be in question, Henry here has purged my home magically of all pests and pestilence. His spells, which he names 'science,' cured my household of all its ills and he has beguiled even the lowest of my servants to bathe."

"Bathing? A clear sign of being in league with the Devil. Slay him before he can enthrall the Royal Court." Myrddin points both the index and pinky fingers of one hand at me.

"Tell us, Henry of the House Morgan, use you *dark* magicks?" the King asks. This is the first time he spoke. And the first time anyone here spoke to me.

"Your Majesty," I say with a deep bow, just as rehearsed, "I do not use dark magicks, but common knowledge where I am from. I hail from a far-off land and wish nothing more than to return. But until then, I hope to use my knowledge for the benefit of your kingdom."

"Do you deny bewitching common folk into bathing, which all know as the Devil's welcome?" bellows Myrddin.

"I just convinced them they would not be as prone to illness if they bathed more. It doesn't hurt they also smell better. A lack of pain I heavily recommend. Even from here."

"Do not claim your dark arts more powerful than mine own gifts, monkey-man! An incubus sired me. I have been the Sorcerer Royale since before you were a swaddling," spit comes from Myrddin's lips as he screams. He is *pissed*.

"Actually, you weren't," Gwalchmei states flatly.

Myrddin wheels on the knight. "What! Of course I was! This ape-ling can be but a few decades in age, while I have presided as the King's wizard since His Majesty was but ten and three."

"But Henry of Morgan be thirty and six in years. And more. He conjures and speaks with spirits. He can count, read, and do mathematics. In his head," Gwalchmei says.

"NO! No man, and never a monkey-man, can do as you say! I, alone, age backward! Begone!" Myrddin is losing it. Waving his arms, a bloom of smoke puffs at my feet. All the bystanders step back in awe. "Hie ye away, DEVILSPAWN!"

There it is.

*

I glance at G. He gives me a slight signal, but looks really worried. I turn to the King. With a flourish, I bow low at the waist, never taking my eyes off the blond guy on the throne. "With permission, Your Majesties." He nods.

Batter up, bitch.

*

Going to The Show

"Old man, I stood here politely while you called me a monkey-man, ape-ling, and devil spawn. Quite frankly, I have had about all of *that* shit I am going to take." Many gasp. It seems no one has ever talked back to him before. (And in an instant, I invent "uppity.") "Puffs of smoke ain't gonna cut it from here on in, Gandalf. Pal, give me something I can dance to, full volume."

Waves of bass thump from my chest. Background singers chime in. Electric guitar strains pierce the room. In case I hadn't mentioned it, the audio systems in the latest iPals are a thing of beauty. I would love to lecture you on all the cool micro-technology, but in reality, I don't know, nor care. All I know is: the sonic waves coming off that thing are so intense, my clothes actually vibrate.

To the room, it must appear as if I am summoning the music of Hell.

The entire room, Myrddin included, steps back. The King sits back in his throne, mouth open.

"Pal, play 'Amazing Grace,' full choir rendition, full volume."

Hearing the hymn's bagpipes, the King leans forward again. When the sisters in the choir kick in the vocals, the room belongs to me. I wait a moment after the song has finished before I speak again. I'm not a math wizard, but I know how to put on a show.

"Pal, what is 3,722 times 4,201?"

"*15,636,122,*" a female voice says, out of nowhere.

"Pal, who am I?"

"*You requested I refer to you as 'The Greatest Wizard on Earth.'*"

*

"ENOUGH! Sir Lancelot, strike down this speaker of demons! Slay him! NOW!" Myrddin screams.

A suit of armor, more massive than most, lurches toward me, sword in hand. G reaches for his weapon, but I put a hand on his shoulder to stop him. The King does not move to either stop or encourage the apparent slaying of the Greatest Wizard on Earth.

I speak to the knight in armor but am looking at Myrddin. "This will not end well for you."

I pull my nine millimeter and shoot Lancelot in the center of his chest.

A number of things happen simultaneously.

The impact knocks the knight in armor a foot off the floor, laying him out with a gigantic CLANG.

The crowd runs terrified for the exits, hearing the thunderclap of the gunfire and seeing the effects of the shot.

The King leaps to his feet, both hands on the arms of the throne.

The Queen puts her hand over her mouth and cries out.

Myrddin screams like a little girl.

That's my favorite part.

"G, with me." I move to the knight on the floor. Between us, we remove his chest piece. The hollow point round flattened on impact, on the outside of the steel plate. It leaves a fist-sized dent in his armor, a mighty bruise, and a few cracked ribs in its wake. I had a fifty-fifty chance it wouldn't penetrate. Luckily for both of us. Him, more than me, actually.

I turn to the throne.

"Your Majesty, I ... wait. '*Lancelot*?'" It's a statement, but it comes out as a question. I stare at Myrddin. "Then, he is ...?"

"The old wizard, who seems to have ... soiled himself?" Arthur says, somewhat amused.

"Gwalchmei called him Myrddin." I am having a hard time shifting gears here.

"Gwalchmei still clings to the old Welsh. Here, he answers to Sir Gawain. In Wales, Myrddin means Merlin."

"So, you must be ..."

"I am King Arthur, Lord of the Britains. To my left sits Milady Guinevere, and you've met Sir Lancelot."

Oh. And. Shit.

*

Excuse Me While I Whip This Out

Merlin and most of the royal suck-ups disappear. Arthur, Guinevere, many of the knights, including Gawain, and I, talk till the wee hours.

"With what magical instrument did you best fair Lancelot?" asks the Queen.

I hold the Ruger up briefly. "This has many names, but many refer to it as a 'Nine.' Where I come from, people carry these for self-protection."

The Queen watches me tuck it into the back of my jeans.

"Any kingdom would be foolish of heart to attack a people with such magic," she says, looking at me.

"Yeah, and this one of the smallest."

Did no one else see her lick her lips?

*

At the end of the meeting, Arthur names me the new Sorcerer Royale.

"Merlin seems to hold that We don't comprehend that all his 'miracles' happen solely when no one can witness them. Through disguise and whispers, he manipulates and schemes. While you, black wizard, bested our finest with but a wave of your hand in Our Very Presence. You manifest voices and music from the ether. You are a true magician," Arthur states. "I bid you: use your magicks to raise Our kingdom to even loftier heights."

*

Making Magic

So I do. I expand my hygiene, nutrition, and exercise programs. It doesn't take long to transform Camelot into the healthiest, cleanest kingdom in the world.

With some technical advice from my iPal, I instigate irrigation, crop rotation, and selective breeding systems to enhance their farming.

I (and my iPal) "invent" manufacturing. From artillery weapons to clothing, to upgraded farm implements, to even paper production, we use assembly lines, blast furnaces, and spinning wheels to create better goods than the rest of the world will produce for centuries.

The Cameloteans ... the Arthurians ... whoever ... these folks aren't yet able to mine the mineral resources to manufacture gunpowder and build cannons, but I do teach them how to build trebuchets. This advances the castle's defenses nearly six hundred years ahead the rest of the world.

More importantly, I motivate Arthur's craftsmen to make some rudimentary gear, and I teach anyone who will listen the game of baseball. I need to keep my skills up. Arthur, in particular, loves the sport. In no time, baseball surpasses jousting in popularity since anyone can play it, from royalty to commoner. Soon, every village in the kingdom has a makeshift diamond. Now, *that's* what I call civilization.

I do experience a failure here and there. For the life of me, I cannot convince the knights to utilize guerrilla warfare. "'Tis dishonorable." Because lining up, charging into a fray, and getting slaughtered by the dozens is so much more honorable. What can you do against centuries of programming?

I keep a few agendas I don't exactly run past Arthur and the Church. First among these must be education. At this point in history, only priests and a few nobles can read. After swearing students to secrecy, I create underground schools and educate the peasants how to read, write, and do math. The writing exercises consist of copying primers to teach others. The Church has all the books—uh, Bibles. A few exceptional adult students, I push them to start their own schools. I encourage students mastering the basics to move on to more advanced studies, such as simple chemistry, alternate trade skills, and even rudimentary biology and medicine.

My education scheme is more than a little complicated as peasants must also perform their daily duties (in essence, slavery for the high-born) and not allowed to travel too far from their hovels. They must stop whatever they are doing to pray several times a day. For generations, the royals conditioned the peasants to see slaving for the nobility as an honor and God's Will.

Since I am re-inventing education, I decide to make this world a better place. I integrate accounting, business, technology (with my iPal's aid), social studies, and even race relations into the lessons. I invite the more curious of the students to touch my arm to show my skin, while darker, feels no different than theirs. I can't tell you how many times I prick my fingers to show them I bleed red too. Few of these people ever laid eyes on a black man and all they know springs from superstition, fear, and ignorance. I am determined to enlighten them.

Along with teaching racial equality, I try to imbue to the male students the essence of how a real man should act. But it's the sixth century, and my gender-related lessons seem to fall on deaf ears. Hopefully, some of them get it.

While secretly teaching the masses, I too, learn more than I suspected. Many a late night I spend with Arthur discussing honor, leadership, humility, and statesmanship. From Gawain and Knights of the Round Table, I learn duty, loyalty, camaraderie, and fidelity. I don't imagine how soon I will find those lessons useful.

All goes pretty much as planned. Arthur delegates a humble staff of servants to me, who, after some private education, I promote to 'middle management,' supervising my various improvement projects. Manufacturing, defensive measures, hygiene, health, and quality of life soar to an all-time high. The underground schools churn out more enlightened graduates each day, reducing the gap between nobles and peasants.

Right about then, the summons arrives to attend the Queen's chambers.

*

The Queen's Weapon of Choice

"Henry of the House Morgan," she begins, "I would have you tell me of your world. Have you a bride? Does your kind even marry?"

"Yes, Your Majesty, my 'kind' does marry, and I am. Mrs. Morgan and I don't see each other much, probably why we're still together. We have an understanding. I understand if she catches me, I'm a dead man." An old joke, but for some reason, I'm nervous and trying to break the tension.

"That I DO understand. So. Moorish men and women have relations, just as we do here?"

"I don't know any Moors. I'm from New York, and I don't know relations from relativity here. Been a tad busy," I reply.

"Have you not taken a woman since your arrival? Gawain's maids and mine own eyes tell me you are larger than the men of our kingdom. Perhaps there lies the reason."

She's right there. I am at least six to eight inches taller than all the men of this era, except for Lancelot, and he has just a few inches on me. Wait. Did she say Gawain's maids? Why would ... Oh. And. Shit.

"Show me your 'Nine,'" she commands.

"What?"

"Your weapon. Pull out your weapon."

"Your Majesty, I don't think I should ..."

"Henry of Morgan, I desire to see the weapon that bested Sir Lancelot."

"Oh." I reach behind me and pull out the Ruger.

"Come closer so I may touch it."

I eject the round in the chamber, re-engage the safety, pop the clip, and step forward to hold the empty gun to her.

163

She grabs my crotch.

"This DOES best Sir Lancelot."

I jump back several paces. I'm shocked. Not just at her actions, but at my own.

"Your Majesty! I can't believe I'm saying this, but as gorgeous as you are, and frankly, as much as I would enjoy it, I *am* married. Maybe this place is rubbing off on me, but I guess an oath should mean something. I hope you understand."

"Ah, Black Wizard, I fear you do not. Whoever holds such a weapon, can rule the world. I intend to possess it. One way or the other. I will hold your Moorish weapon in my hand."

To say I couldn't escape her rooms fast enough qualifies as a monstrous understatement. I'm still backing up well into the hall. Slamming right into a waiting Merlin.

"Enjoy your audience with Her Majesty, Friend Morgan?" the old wizard asks, straightening my jacket and vest. "You appear ... bothered. Most find a visit to Her Majesty's chambers ... invigorating."

"Well, the Queen does give good conversation. Sorry, Gandalf old boy, but I need to go. So many illusions, so little time. You know how busy it is being the King's sorcerer and all. I mean, you used to."

"Yes, Friend Morgan," he whispers. "I do."

*

The Purloined Pal

That sonuvabitch! He lifted my iPal. I was so flummoxed from my audience with the Queen, I all but handed it to him. I need to speak with Arthur. Now.

*

"What proof do you offer the old man stole your magic slate?" His Majesty asks. "A trickster and charlatan, yes, but he has never sunk to thievery."

I explain what's going to happen. "Your Majesty, I propose we ride to Merlin's tower, we shall see, or rather, hear, for ourselves."

*

Our entourage approaches, and even a few dozen meters from Merlin's tower we hear the klaxon echoing from the stone walls.

Arthur looks at me aghast and with a touch of sadness. He turns in the saddle to his guards. "Arrest Merlin. Do not harm him. Touch not what you find there."

*

As they hold Merlin bound and gagged, I pick up the blaring device. "Pal, unlock." The voice and facial recognition and fingerprint scanner disengage the alarm. Arthur strides away from the tower without a glance back.

*

Arthur does not order Merlin's imprisonment or execution, as much out of nostalgia as anything. He strips the old man of any titles, lands, position, and exile him to the life of a commoner. For someone of Merlin's nature, it may have been more merciful to kill him.

*

Joust in Time

"I challenge thee, Moor." Lancelot bellows.

"For the last time, I am not a—oh, forget it."

"I will not allow you to besmirch Her Majesty's honor. I hear gossip that you, a sub-human ape-ling, has had relations with Her Majesty. It is beyond tolerance."

Ape-ling? This starts to ring a little familiar. Plus, who knows I had a private audience with the Queen? I'm going out on a limb.

"What's Merlin feeding you, Lance?"

"'Tis true, the wizened one spoke to me, but with mine own eyes, I see how she looks at you. Most likely, you ensorcelled her affections. You will answer for your perfidy. Choose your weapon, monkey-man."

"Okay. I choose nine millimeters."

"Alas, I do not possess 'nine millimeters.'"

"Yeah. Sorry about that." In reality, I'm not.

"Choose again."

I mull it over. I need to eliminate any of his advantages. "Well, I don't own a sword, so if we must do this, let's fight hand-to-hand."

"Nay, 'tis unseemly. Hastilude in the lists. The next tournament sets but a fortnight away. My varlets will supply you with a charger and suitable accoutrements," Lancelot announces, turning to leave.

"Hastilude?" I ask Gawain.

165

"Jousting."

Phenomenal. In two weeks I need to learn how to beat a guy in an event in which he is undefeated. No problem. Now, all I need to do is invent the DeLorean.

*

Gawain offers to teach me jousting, and while I manage the lance, I can't get the hang of riding on horseback.

No. If I am to survive this insanity, I need to think outside the box. Given these people don't even own boxes; how hard can it be? With iPal in hand, I move into Merlin's vacated tower.

*

The night before the joust, a few peasants collect Lancelot's armor, saddle, and his horse's armaments for polishing. Lancelot doesn't give them a second look, and his personal squires rejoice with the reduced labor.

The next morning, I watch as they lower Lancelot on to his horse.

"Squire, why does my armor glisten so? Who cleaned it? Why does my mount's armor not shine as well?"

"Peasants, milord, from the castle. Ones never seen before. As to the horse's armor, they thought you would prefer the Royal Eyes solely on you."

"Find out the secret to the polish. I would'st all my armor sparkle so at every occasion. You say you don't know them?" Lancelot looks in my direction, eyes narrowed. "Make secure the bindings, as well ensure all is in working order. I trust not this black fiend."

"Yes, milord. We were suspicious as well and checked the armor thoroughly. It will work as never before."

He got that right.

*

Lancelot rides slowly to one end of the lists. I walk to the other. His armor glistens in the sun. My twenty-first-century apparel shocks all in attendance.

"Friend Henry, I implore thee. Don armor at least," Gawain begs. "Lancelot will slay thee in a single ride. His lance be not blunted. Without armor, he will pierce thine heart in his first pass."

166

"G, with any luck at all, Lance won't even come close," I reply, not sure who I'm trying to convince. Gawain sure as hell isn't buying. Time for me to give one last try.

I yell down the lists, "Lancelot, any chance if I ask you not to do this, you would pass? For your own sake?"

"Prepare to die, black dog of Hell." Well, as long as he's conflicted about it.

We both salute the King.

Lancelot kicks his steed to a bouncing gallop toward me. I step forward, hands spread wide and empty in the air. I see what I am waiting for and yell, "SHAZAM!"

Hey, it's the sixth century. I don't need to be original.

Lancelot's suit of armor explodes into flame.

Merlin runs toward his champion as fast as his ancient legs will carry him, grabbing a bucket on the way.

I see his intent in an instant and yell, "Not water!"

When the bucket of water hits Lancelot, the flames spread farther.

I grab the bucket from the old wizard and fill it with sand and dirt from the lists. Bucket after bucket I toss on Lancelot. I finally smother the fire.

Taking off my jacket, I wrap my hands in it to extract Lancelot out of his armor. Layers of chain mail helped protect him, but he will be looking at living with some nasty burns. Squires take him off the field, and Gawain follows them, utilizing some of my first aid training. Guinevere follows them in tears. A few too many tears.

Merlin stands in awe and confusion. Arthur looks at me.

"Wizard Henry, how did you set brave Lancelot aflame with a wave of your hand? A blaze Merlin could not quench?" Even Merlin looks at me for the answer.

"Science, Your Majesty." I'm not feeling exceptionally heroic. I just set one of history's bravest knights on fire. Now granted, it beats the hell out of him puncturing me with that oversized stick, but I am still not too proud of myself. What I'm *not* telling Arthur is the night before, I had some of my students polish Lancelot's armor with a waxy gel, similar to Napalm mixed with gelignite, created with the help of my iPal. Camelot doesn't own sufficient quantities of the right minerals to use this technology in defense of Camelot, but Merlin's tower has the proper ingredients, plus whatever Pal instructed my students to find in nature, to coat a suit of armor. When cleaning

Lancelot's gear, they swapped several ornamental pieces on the saddle with similar ones, made of roughened quartz. When Lancelot's armor bounced up and down in the saddle, it scratched the flint creating the spark igniting the Napalm-like coating of his armament. His chain mail would have protected him, if not for Merlin's water seeping into the crevices.

*

Who Da Ho?

Life never fails to surprise you. I'm back in time fifteen hundred years. I outwitted Merlin the Magician (twice), defeated the greatest knight ever born (twice), dodged the clutches of a power-hungry, nymphomaniac, adulteress queen, and became the second most powerful person in Europe. Oh yeah—and singlehandedly changed civilization. One would assume I would be blessed with the smarts to stop there. Go figure.

I ask to speak to Arthur alone. I'm struggling with whether or not to break it to him His Queen is an unfaithful ho. Not something you tell the King of all the Britains every day. Or, you know ... ever.

I try to speak with Gawain on the subject, but he slams his fist into the table and stomps from the room. Evidently, royal infidelity, not a subject he warms to.

The day of my appointment with Arthur arrives, and we sit at a modest, but not round, table.

I ask about the Queen. I ask how Lancelot's doing. I try as diplomatically as possible to communicate the point. As a diplomat, I make a phenomenal catcher.

The last thing I see before the lights fade: a tarnished signet ring. Real, real close.

*

Back to the Future McFly

My head hurts. Stop with the shaking already. Did I mention my head hurts?

"Hank, you okay buddy?" Artie asks, genuine concern in his voice. I manage to force my eyes open into some retina-burning stadium lighting. Artie looms over me, close enough to kiss me. His face a mask of concern.

"What happened?" I manage to mutter.

"Wow. You really got nailed. It's top of the eighth, and France's pitcher figures you less of threat on first than busting the fence. So he beaned you." By now, Coach and the umpire stand over me.

"I guess that's one way to keep a brother down," I murmur.

"Whoa, son," the umpire says. "I don't know where that kind of talk came from, but I'm writing it off to a hit to the head. There's no need for racist trash talk in His Majesty's Baseball League. Go sit down."

"I'm good. Help me up," I say. Coach sends a designated runner to first and the crowd cheers as I am half-carried to the dugout. I study the lineup. "Where's L?"

"Hank, maybe we do need to have you checked out." Artie looks into my eyes for signs of concussion. "L passed years ago. You know that."

"What?"

"Yeah, man. Swallowed his nine. Guess he just couldn't stand folks finding out." Artie hangs his head down, his voice a mere whisper. He lowers me to the bench. "Being gay—well, he couldn't take it and just took the off-ramp."

"But, Artie, aren't you ...?"

"WHAT!? What're you gonna say, Hank? I got two kids and a wife. I'm a world-class athlete, play the most popular sport in the world, and am winning the World Friggin' Series. What're you gonna ask, Hank?"

The World Series? Oh. And. Shit!

*

I spy the scoreboard. I grab Artie's jersey. "Is that the score? I need an iPal. Right. Now!"

A batboy hustles mine from the locker room. "Pal, call Rudy." I walk to the far end of the dugout.

"Rudy, it's Hank. Tell-me-you-didn't-place-the-bet." I snap at the image on the screen.

"Hank, calm down. You okay? I saw that beaner on TV. He genuinely nailed you, and then some." Rudy seems more ... together than ever before. Is he wearing a tie?

"I'm fine. Rudy, I just saw the scoreboard. We carry a five-run lead. Tell me you didn't place that bet." I am now pleading.

"Henry, first of all, you know damned well I'm a stockbroker and not a bookie. Secondly, you know baseball is all but cheat-proof. You couldn't bet on it if you wanted to. And thirdly, what the hell are you talking about?"

"Thank God." I am not sure if I feel more relief he didn't place the bet or that I didn't. I can't conceive I ever wished to.

*

We win the World Series. Reporters. Champagne. I go through the motions of dressing in a fog. Was it all a dream?

I contemplate the locker room. The average physiques of ballplayers I'm used to seeing now display chiseled abs and zero body fat. So. Not a dream.

After the other players have left to celebrate, Artie and I sit in the locker room.

"Hank, I'm sorry about going all medieval on you out there. I don't know what gets into me."

"Artie, don't give it a thought. I guess I'm a little fuzzy. You know I'm gonna love you like a brother no matter what, right?"

"I know," Artie's eyes well up a bit. "I thought that was cool you telling that reporter it was a team effort. Not your usual style at all."

"Maybe I've learned a few things lately. You know, grown as a human being. Learned some humility, or honor. Become a real man. Or ... maybe that shot to the head was harder than I thought." I finally score a smile.

Artie looks at the clock. "Grab your gear. Isn't your gorgeous girlfriend coming by in a few to pick you up?"

"Girlfriend? You mean *Trish*?" Artie knows I'm *married* to the Bitch from Hell. For years now.

"Trish? That goose egg on your swollen melon will acquire a twin if you call Gwen some other chick's name."

*

I pack my personal stuff in a duffle. I start to slip my iPal into my bag. It's thinner and lighter than I remember. Thinking back on it, the picture resolution's much higher as well. I flip it over. On the back, etched into the aluminum case, a logo of a sword coming out of a stone.

*

170

Excerpts from questioning iPal:

"Racial differences stopped factoring into societal interactions in the seventh century."

"Masculinity, fidelity, and honor remain highly revered characteristics in male behavior."

"Homosexuality is a criminal, moral, and ethical offense. The authorities prosecute alternate sexual orientations to the fullest extent of the law. See HM Penal Code 514.297"

"Great Britain conquered the majority of the civilized world in the ninth century and has since led the globe in technology, education, social reform, and baseball."

"No records found for 'the Revolutionary War,' 'Civil War,' or 'Declaration of Independence.'"

"Fitness and nutrition are at all-time highs with less than one-tenth of one percent of the population struggling with obesity or malnutrition."

"Baseball is the most popular sport in the world. Every nation on Earth competes in The World Series (see His Majesty's Baseball League *for more information). More money is spent on advertising in baseball than all other sports combined. Fan attendance dwarfs any other sporting event."*

"Football, hockey, soccer, and Olympic sports rank behind professional bowling and polo in popularity."

"No records found for the terms 'basketball' or 'NBA.'"

***

The Wall
By Steve Rouse

Amy had closed up Duffy's tavern at the usual one a.m., and now headed south on County Road 17 toward her mom's. They would be going to her niece's big volleyball tournament at eight tomorrow morning in Edgerton, thirty-five miles from Burlington, where Amy had lived and worked for the past seven years. She was looking forward to seeing her brother, sister-in-law, and niece, but not getting more of her mom's third degree about 'Well, ya know you're not getting any younger' lack-of-a-boyfriend nagging.

A moonless night with stars blazing across the horizon and some Katy Perry tunes kept her company. She drove just at the posted limit, not wanting to elicit any troopers to give her a speeding ticket. The Blakeshire Memorial Tunnel loomed just ahead, a favorite speed trap of the local sheriff. As she entered the tunnel, a bright light flashed above and ahead of her.

*

Rick Nichols pushed his rented car as fast as it would go on this twisty, forested country road. He had to get to Burlington. He'd finally gotten out of a huge backup caused by an accident on the nearby interstate, but he still had to be in Burlington for his eight a.m. interview with Coffers' Commodities. He'd aced the phone interview and now, fresh out of college, this would be his first real job. He had to get there first, though, despite the backup and having lost more than an hour to fix a stupid flat tire.

He'd grown up in Lincoln, Nebraska, where he'd gone to the university, and was uncertain about this coastal, small town, woodsy territory he'd come to. But his second thoughts would have to wait. This job sounded right up his alley. He needed only a few hours' sleep in the motel in Burlington before his interview. He'd just come to the end of a short tunnel cut through a high hillside. A car was coming the other way, just entering the tunnel when a blinding light lit up everything from above.

*

Amy couldn't see. Her twenty-six-year-old instincts reacted, slamming the brakes and veering right, away from the oncoming car she knew was going to slam into her.

"Damn!" The expletive slipped out. She hated swearing. Then ... nothing.

*

Rick winced, believing a street light shining down from this side of the tunnel entrance may have shorted out. "Damn thing sure is bright. What the ..." He lost all awareness of road vibration, of sounds, of even which way was up. Then ... nothing.

*

It felt just like waking up. A general sense of body position, touch, light, and sound. Everything seemed normal, but it wasn't. It was too warm, for one thing. And the sounds ... rather the lack of it, was totally out of place. No traffic, no birds.

Amy's first thought was a hospital. She opened her eyes to see a featureless wall in front of her. It was lit. It was the source of light around her. The area she'd sensed as a room shifted in her perceptions and she realized she was strapped to a platform and her "room" was little more than the size of a closet. The lighted wall was her ceiling.

Am I dead? she wondered, although all her sensations were noticeably there. *Not the pain I think I'd be experiencing from being in a car crash.*

Then she heard a more distinguishable sound, a muffled scream. *Sounds male.* Still groggy, she drifted back to sleep.

*

Rick woke in a struggle. He pulled against some kind of strap, something holding his wrists down. His nose itched and he needed to scratch it. In his dream, or waking up, Rick strained against his bondage, imagined or not.

He stopped, grunting in total frustration. He came fully awake, his worst nightmare realized. He was lashed to whatever he laid upon. Faint images of the past ... of his brother holding him down thrust into his mind, his sister tickling him. He couldn't fight them, or this. He screamed from the depths of his soul.

A soft hum reached into his consciousness. His panting lessened as a light mist filled his chamber. He relaxed and he slept.

His reactions and responses had been noted and recorded.

*

Amy lay still, every nerve tensed. She was pretty much convinced she was alive, although not sure how. The entrance to the tunnel ... oncoming headlights ... a blast of light ... and then nothing. She thought back. *No crash, no impact, no jarring or pain. In fact, there was nothing at all after the flash. No sensations or memories of how she got from her car to wherever she was right now.*

My phone! Where ... She tried to move and found herself bound. She could turn her head, but lifting it didn't work. Her arms and legs and torso were similarly somehow strapped down. She couldn't reach her leg with her hands to check a pocket, yet something about the touch of her skin to whatever she was strapped to told her she had lost her clothes.

"Oh, my God," she whimpered. "Am I dead? In a morgue? What's happening?" She worked to control her breathing. *Breathing? Shouldn't be breathing if I'm dead.* "Hello? Is anyone there?" she said aloud. Nothing. *But I know I heard something before.* Amy thought for but a second, filled her lungs, and filled the air with a scream of her own. Then she too breathed in a mist and drifted back to sleep.

*

Rick awoke laying upon a soft mat on a platform that jutted out from a wall about two feet above the floor of an oval-shaped room. The smell struck him first. Pine. He looked around, totally confused in the dimly lit chamber, unsure of where he was. He moved and glanced down at himself. No bindings and buck naked.

175

"What the f ...?" He swung onto the floor and stood, bewildered and self-conscious. "Hey!" he called out. "What's going on?" He turned slowly, peering at his surroundings. "What is going on?" he repeated. "C'mon?" his voice dwindling at the end. He saw little and heard nothing.

The oval chamber looked to be domed, about twelve feet high where some lighting was. But he couldn't really see a ceiling above the lights. *About fifteen feet wide, maybe twenty-five long.* There was nothing in the room that wasn't part of it. No furniture, no windows. Just the overhead lighting, and the ledge he'd awoken on.

I am at a frickin' loss. "What is this place?" he yelled out. "Where are my clothes?" No response to his questions. "Hey, can I at least get a cup of coffee? I have to ... Oh, crap, my interview!" he slapped his forehead and became agitated, pacing near the ledge.

Rick's volume increased. "Look, I've got no idea what the hell is going on here, but, I have a really important job interview ..." He slapped the edge of the ledge and propped himself against it. "Damn," was all he could muster.

*

Amy woke, curled into a fetal position on a soft, warm, padded platform. In her sleep, she'd tucked herself against the gentle curve of its wall. But now, she had to pee. Sitting up, her gaze crossed the room she occupied, but no doors or plumbing could be seen.

"Damn," she muttered. *Where in the world am I?* Still not certain she wasn't dead from the car accident she couldn't recall, she consciously took stock of her condition. *No injuries, no pain. Everything's attached but not covered. I could use a stack of pancakes with bacon, and I still have to pee.*

She studied her room. Basically colorless, but the lighting gave it all a soft greenish hue. The room smelled of pine with maybe a hint of mustiness. *Loam or mossy,* she decided. The temperature was warm, maybe seventy-five, eighty degrees, and there seemed to be a flow to the air, but very, very slight, almost just a suggestion of a breeze. Despite being in an obvious room, there was nothing artificial about the air. No mechanical sounds, either.

The mat she sat on drew her attention. Soft and warm, it felt like a high-quality down, but she couldn't find anything fibrous about it after plucking at it a few times. Neither could she find an edge. She felt along the wall, digging into where it blended with the wall, but couldn't pull it out of place.

So, she sat, sans clothing, and began crying. Not having answers was her worst nightmare. As physically comfortable as she was, the gaps in her memory and no apparent answers terrified her. This was horrid.

*

Rick panted, completely spent with the angst of being somewhere he couldn't define and from his efforts to rip the bedding apart. Soft, yes; but he still couldn't get a handful of it to try ripping it out. *Wherever this place is, whoever put me here has got some serious explaining to do!* His logic was to cause damage to get some response from whoever owned this place.

"I got to use it," he said, loud enough for anyone who might be listening. So again, he padded around the perimeter of his confines, this time searching for anything that might be plumbing.

In the far corner, he ran out of patience. "Time to pee!" he exclaimed and proceeded to urinate into the rounded corner. He watched in disbelief as his stream disappeared into the flooring material. Challenging as it was, he checked out the area when done. No odor, not even wet. His fingers didn't smell either after wiping over it, too. Rick sat down, emotionally and cognitively numb. "Maybe I am dead. But then, is this Heaven, or ..."

"No. Nope ... not going there. Time to check out the rest of this place. He stood and headed directly across the room to the far side.

He made it just halfway.

THUD! His head and right knee thunked off something. His chest and torso also recoiled back after contacting an unseen ... something. After a soothing rub to his forehead, he approached again with his arms waving in front of him and touched a barrier his eyes refused to acknowledge.

*

She couldn't believe her eyes. Still propped against the wall after peeing, there was no trace of what, just moments before, had pressed so insistently in her bladder. *Everything went into the floor.* That was her first pee since entering the tunnel on her way to her mom's. *God! She's going to be worried to death!*

Her regularity was striking. Every four and a half hours. That would put the time at about seven in the morning having gone before she left the bar. She didn't need to, but she scanned the room for any wayward window to verify a sunrise. *No, didn't think one would just show up, eh?*

Her nostrils flared. "What's that?" Amy sniffed the air. *Food?* She looked about the room and saw a clump of something steaming on the side of the ledge. Within seconds, a warm, wrapped enchilada-kind-of-thing made her empty stomach growl.

No fear of danger entered her thoughts as she sniffed, then licked, then bit into the wrap. A steamy, almost cheesy mix oozed into her mouth. She tested and tasted her fare and nodded silent approval. "Pretty good, actually. Not sure what's in it, but decent. I could sell this at Duffy's. Always can use a new munchie to sell 'em. Wonder what's in it?"

Oh, hell ... what am I thinking? I've no idea where I am. Still not convinced if I even am anymore. She bit down on the inside of her lower lip. *Ouch! That works.* A second later she tasted her blood. "Okay, I'm going with the idea that I am alive."

She stiffened when she heard a muted thud. Automatically, she turned to face the direction the sound came from. "What now?" Nothing answered. The center of the room. She busily finished her breakfast and headed over to see what could be seen.

*

Rick pressed his hands, then his face against the barrier. From the floor to beyond his jumping reach and from wall to wall it stood invisibly defiant. He kicked at it ala martial arts movies-style and hurt his foot. He slapped and punched at it, tenderizing his palms and knuckles.

Then he stopped and stared. Out of his mind? Maybe, who wouldn't be if they'd been driving down the road one minute and being here the next. Yet ... what's that? A glimpse of something moving ... a hint of a shadow within the wall he couldn't see.

He reached out, but it was gone. Too little, too quickly to even guess if it was real, let alone what it could've been.

Rice? The aroma could not be denied. He wheeled around and spied a packet of something near the ledge. *How the hell did this get here?* He sniffed it. *Yessirree Bob!—Grandpa's favorite quip—food! Great taste!*

Could use some tabasco sauce. It was gone inside of a minute. He returned to the invisible wall.

Rick was far from colorblind, unlike his brother Hank. Poor guy, couldn't tell orange from purple. The wall seemed less transparent ... almost having a hint of depth. Sitting there, literally, was a shape. His first impression was of a Buddha or yogi.

*

After looking at nothing for several minutes, she realized she had a headache. Anytime her senses conflicted, that's what happened. *Can't see anything, but I can feel a wall here.* With no meds, she relied on her meditation as a way to relax. Amy loved to meditate. She sat crosslegged and stretched her back and core. Then, her mantra played in her memory and she sat with eyes closed.

While her headache lessened, her zen remained elusive. *Not negative energy, but something is messing things up.* She opened her eyes and couldn't help but stare, not believing what she thought she saw seemingly floating in midair.

A butt crack? What the hell? Oops! Stop cussin'.

Within the invisible wall she'd discovered when investigating the "thud" she'd heard, was a distinct opaque spot. And it looked exactly like a butt crack. Then it was gone. The lights dimmed three times. A minute later, they went off and stayed off. Amy crawled her way back to the ledge and curled up, but couldn't sleep.

"Where am I, Lord? Can I please know? I'm scared. Please help me." She lay awake for a long time before sleep came.

*

Rick lay awake, having found his way to the ledge after the lights went out. Confusion about the day centered on his surroundings and the damned wall. This invisible thing, except for the moment or two when he thought he saw a shape defied all measuring, all reason. Even with his back against it, pushing with all his might resulted in nothing.

Then there was the burrito. What it was didn't bother him as much as the fact that it had just showed up. Someone is definitely keeping him here a captive. This place, the food ... everything had an answer. He was bound and determined to find those answers. More to the fact that he was also willing to batter the life out of whoever was responsible.

He drifted off to sleep with that thought in mind.

*

The next four days proved to be tedious. A routine was established. Amy preferred to go to the bathroom in about the same place, not wanting to take a chance that anywhere else might not work. She'd always had a good time sense, and came to expect her food to appear at what she anticipated to be about four in the afternoon, if it was about seven in the morning when the lights went on.

She seemed drawn to the room's center. "Butt Crack Central." Her routine included a meditation time. Not to see the infamous butt again, whatever it could be, but to try to see what might have been its cause. Each day, the wall seemed more opaque and less invisible. Even so, more than once she thought she saw a shape passing behind it. She'd even shouted out, stood and pounded on the wall. Nothing resulted from those efforts. Nothing.

*

Contrary to his intent to mutilate his captors, Rick stood in shock when the muted shape in the wall thudded back at him. His mind instantly challenged his perceptions of what the person (thing?) could be. It looked bipedal, but then so was Worf, the Klingon from Star Trek®. He was suddenly unsure.

If whoever had the smarts to trap him and do all the things that resulted in this imprisonment, maybe he was smarter to not charge in. He stood still and watched, content in his isolation, given any of his imagined options. Come to think of it, it was easier to see the shape through the wall today.

*

On the sixth day of her captivity, Amy had had enough. She was determined to be recognized. A plan had developed. Okay, an idea at least.

At a time when the shape seemed close to the wall, if it was somehow another person, she pressed herself against it and pounded on it with raised fists. She very suddenly became aware of the shape's proximity to her, could almost feel a touch against her cheek.

*

There! As clear as it had ever been, the shaded figure looked more human than ever before. So close, he couldn't help reach out and touch the face area. The head actually, maybe he should have taken a practice punch at it, but then ...

A thought struck him instead. What if this was someone else ... some poor person who'd been taken prisoner too. *Just like me.* That changed everything he'd been thinking. His animosity tempered and he became almost compassionate in his perception. *Who knows, two of us can gang up on whoever did this!*

The lights dimmed. *Guess it'll have to wait 'til tomorrow.* He headed over to the bedding area and laid down as the lights went out.

*

When she woke, Amy knew she'd made significant progress yesterday. What would today bring? She rolled over and startled. It was different ... all different. The room had changed. Ten days it had been the same. How is it changed?

From the relative safety of her sleeping area, she looked out and saw the room actually filled the available space. Amy had come to realize that, like a mirror, it somehow reflected the part of the chamber she occupied while somehow not reflecting her. Confusing. The shape's randomness suggested something behind the wall rather than within it or against it.

The lights came on and satisfied her suspicions. The rest of the room mirrored her own. Complete with another bedding area. Complete with another body, facing away from her. With some trepidation she slid off onto the floor and tiptoed across, almost unaware when she crossed the line where the wall had been. She slowed as she neared the other, peering over her shoulder and ... screaming.

Rick startled awake. He rolled across the bed and perched on all fours, ready to spring. He hadn't been prepared for a naked woman who suddenly covered herself and went running back to another sleeping area.

"What the hell? Hey! Wait! Who are you? How'd you get here? He was up and running before even thinking about it.

The woman leaped onto her bedding and huddled in the corner against the wall. She screamed, "Don't come near me! Stay away!"

Rick stopped and backed up, turning when he realized there was no more wall. He then

181

remembered he too was naked. "I don't know who you are or how you got here. Hell, I don't even know how I got here or even where here is."

He stopped and turned to face her. "My name is Rick, Rick Everson.

She looked away from him, even though he was kinda cute. "I don't need to see you naked. What have you done to me? Why am I here?"

"Look lady, you got this all wrong. I was driving to get to Burlington for an interview when ..."

"Wait! Burlington? That's where I live." She sighed and settled her mind. "What's the last thing you remember about that night?"

*

She sat on the bed, he on the floor, but they faced each other. After more than two hours of discussion, comparing their nighttime drive to waking up and dealing with their captivities, they were much calmer. The realization that they were both victims put them on an even keel, but left disturbing questions about their captors and futures.

That day, one of the bedding areas disappeared. Amy discovered the fact and marched to her bed and declared, "No way are you sleeping here! This is mine." Her defiance was clear and Rick simply said that it was all right with him.

The next morning, Rick awoke getting pushed off the bed. Amy told him as he rolled onto the floor, "No way! Get off! I know how to hurt a man so he'll limp for at least a month."

Before Rick could respond, a voice filled their chamber. It sounded near and large.

"You will be together. You are humans from Earth, as you call it. You have been selected to represent part of your planet's life systems.

"We have taken you from there to be part of our collection from your planet. In time you will join others from there as part of our display for the reasoning species of our collective star systems.

"We near our destination. For most of this journey, you have been kept dormant. Decades have passed on your planet since we took you. Your planet is no longer available to you. You are a millennia away. Resolve yourself to never seeing it again. Be warned, there is no escape. We know your kind and we know you will try. You will be cared for and your needs met. Now, look up and see your captor."

The lighting went out and a larger room appeared lit from beyond their walls. Coming into view above them was a monstrously large creature about the size of a building. Tentacles snaked from the sides of its purplish head. They could clearly see multiple sets of blinking eyes and a gaping hole that could be for breathing or eating or God knows what. Mercifully, that light went out and their lighting resumed. They found themselves holding each other tightly.

*

By Amy's count, 158 days later, their room changed again. She and Rick had expected it sooner. But, not only would it have space for the baby they were now expecting, but the new wall separated them from what they suspected was an even larger space. Space enough to hold more humans as well as the other specimens from home. All to be part of the new Earth exhibit of a galactic zoo.

***

Shock and Awww!
By Paul K. Metheney

Attack

So their starship was in the process of eating our starship. A situation I do not think of fondly. We were cruising through the galaxy, minding our own business (that business being to politely subjugate non-space-faring worlds into our coalition of planets) when a crystalline ship in the shape of a giant pyramid pops out of nowhere, extends a giant tube of some sort and starts blasting away at us. Before our bridge crew could respond, the aliens sucked in some debris, and disappeared again. I only assume it was before our bridge crew could respond because I am far, far away from the bridge. As far away as my superior officer could keep me. In all honesty, I am okay with that. If I were in charge of an alien attack, I would aim for the engines, the weapons, and the bridge; not necessarily in that order. I was happy to not be in any of those places. Truth be told, given the sections of the ship that had just been vaporized, I was happy to be anywhere. But particularly not in a high-value target area.

Now, despite the fact that I think our ship is enormous, when drawing up a space-faring starship, crew quarters are the least of the designers' considerations. I shared my quarters with two other crewmen with bunks that folded themselves into the walls and a single computer station. Located down the hall, the head and shower facilities we shared with an unknown number of other crewmen. Better than a prison cell, but only marginally.

Over a period of days, the crystalline pyramid kept popping in and out of existence in a new location, dissecting us with some sort of energy weapon, sucking up the debris and dead crew people into that giant tube, and then popping back out of reality. They have pulled this trick several times now. Once, eleven days earlier; again, three days after that. This most recent attack was five days after their second pass. We knew—and by "we," I mean the bridge crew—that they weren't just cloaking themselves, because our tactical officer would put a couple of missiles right where they popped away, a half second too late. Us lowly crewmen were getting all this third or fourth hand via a hidden channel on our neural networks. Some enterprising engi-nerd type coded an untraceable peer-to-peer network that fed us unofficial status reports of the real goings-on aboard, immediately dubbed RumorNet. The command crew turned a blind eye to this unsanctioned channel because it saved them the effort of keeping the crew up to date and gave them plausible deniability for any inaccuracies and informational security breaches. Plus, it was free and didn't cost them anything to maintain. Say what you will about SpaceForce, but they keep an eye on the budget.

RumorNet spewed out information by the metric tonne about the destruction areas, lives lost in the attack, and the general status of the conflict. Even as an explosion rocked our room and the blast disrupted life support and gravity.

*

One Week Earlier

"So, Lewis, first posting on a starship?" the ship's doctor, Stevenson, asked.

"My first posting ANYWHERE," I said. "I finished boot a while back and deadheaded here from Alpha Centauri 6 on the DeGrassi. It took a bit to get here, wherever here is."

"How do you like it so far?" Stevenson asked as he adjusted the sensors on the diagnostic couch.

"It's very different from boot camp. There, we had days and hours to formulate plans and make decisions. Out here, we have fractions of a second. And the technology! In boot camp, they focused on critical thinking, loyalty, and character. Basically, breaking down our individuality and personality. You know, the usual stuff. Not so much the latest techno-toys. There are things here people on Earth never imagined."

"Actually, they probably did imagine them there," Stevenson said. "We just use them out in the field. As for split-second decision making, don't worry too much about that. Our captain takes credit for all that. I want you to lay there and relax a bit. I'm going to take some of your blood and store it."

"Why?"

"In case of emergency."

"What kind of emergency?" I asked, suddenly concerned.

"One in which you would need some of your own blood, of course. While we wait, tell me a little bit about yourself. I haven't had a chance to read your file. How did you land your envious position on the *Hawking*?"

"Probably nothing you haven't heard a hundred times, Doc."

*

Six Months Earlier

I was arrested for having sex with a minor. Now before you get all "What-a-pig!" I am not a pedophile ... or an idiot. I asked her her age. I even asked her for her ID card first. It said she was twenty-two. How should I have known that the years on Alpha Centauri 6 are only nine months long? When checking her ID, I *may* have neglected, in my heightened emotional state, to notice that she had the same last name as the territorial governor. Okay, maybe I am an idiot.

The magistrate I found myself in front of, did not find "Nuh-uh!" as a legal defense. His honor gave me the choice between ten years as a guest of the territorial corrections facility, or "Tell him what's behind door number two, Johnny:" five years in the space service. I made the choice that any intelligent fellow would, I ran. When they caught me two days later, I chose ten years in the space service as opposed to three times that amount in a slightly less hospitable environment. Five extra years for two days of hiding in a bus locker seems a bit excessive. Looking ahead at my upcoming ten-year career as a crewman third class, I may have made the wrong choice.

*

Induction

As you probably know, one of the first things they do after basic training strips away your will to live, is implant a military grade neural

187

implant at the base of your skull. "Military grade" means "mass manufactured by the lowest bidder." The communications function theoretically may operate more securely, but it itched like the devil. They don't implant them earlier because if you die during boot camp, they would have wasted an implant.

"Is that gonna hurt?—OWWW!"

"Yes."

"You could give a fellow a little warning, you know."

"Why?"

I may have thought long and hard about the corpsman's ancestry and his relationship to his mother in those last few seconds of being off the grid. I may not have, but that's not where the smart money played.

He explained the neural network implant with all the bedside manner you would expect from a low-level military medic.

"The neural implant releases nanobytes that insert themselves into the proper areas of your cerebellum to facilitate communications, tracking, computer interfacing, and provide unique access to technology, areas of your postings, and data storage. It also tells time."

I quit listening after "nanobytes that insert themselves into the proper areas of your cerebellum." I don't remember volunteering to have microscopic machines crawling through my skull. I also don't remember the judge asking.

For the most part, when the implant works properly, it's pretty ingenious. It locks you out of doors you are not allowed to enter, keeps you from accessing the computer functions and data you shouldn't access, enables you to send and receive (what I would consider less than) "secure" communications just by thinking them a certain way, and allows the space service to track you anywhere. Anywhere. All things I am not a big proponent of. Of course, if I were in charge of a large space service that recruits a great deal of its lower ranks through the judicial process, it's exactly what I would do. Some of those people are incorrigible.

Armed with an itching spot on the back of my neck, I left the B.I.T.C.H. (Basic Induction Transition Center—quit worrying about where the H went) to report to my temporary quarters while awaiting a posting. My posting was on the *U.S.S. Hawking*, which I finally made it to three months later.

*

I, Vacuum

In case some other species finds this journal, I guess I should give them a heads up about us. We are basically humanoid in nature. Every school kid knows the theory that humans were "seeded," along with thousands of other worlds, from a star-spanning race long lost to history. Two arms, two legs, ten fingers, and ten toes (more unique than you might imagine among the stars), and a head that contains our faces and what our drill sergeants laughingly referred to as our brains. An endoskeleton of very breakable bone material surrounded by musculature and nerve endings contains the whole enchilada. We consider ourselves "human." And not just human, but The Humans. A perception that several thousand other systems might disagree with. Scientists believe that there are more than one hundred billion planets in the Milky Way Galaxy. And over one hundred billion galaxies.

I said all that to say this: in my humble opinion, there is only ONE Lewis Haversham III in all the universe. My drill sergeant said he was very thankful for that.

I think of myself as a survivor. Survivors do what they can to continue their basic functions in life. I've gotten used to eating ... and breathing. I'm real fond of breathing. Your species may not need to, but it's tops of my seven essential functions. Numbers three through seven include: eating, drinking, sleeping, smoking cigars, and disposing of bodily wastes. Number two should go without saying.

My new superior (do NOT call him an officer) on the *Hawking*, Sergeant M'Bari, at our first meeting, made my former drill sergeant seem warm and cuddly by comparison. He loved me. That's what I took away from our first interaction. He may have said something along the lines of "bending me over and using me like a two-credit station trollop if I got out of line." I took that as "he loved me." Our second meeting was not quite as heart-warming. I was sitting in my quarters with one of my two "roomies" about to light up a cigar when he exploded into the room. Note: Sergeants do not enter a room, they impact it. Sgt. M'Bari stands about half my height again, twice my width, and about five times my physical fitness. The man is the size of a shuttle craft.

"Son, if you light up that cigar, I'm going to arrange it so you can smoke the whole thing ... Outside."

Now I'm down to six basic functions.

On a ship with a compliment of about forty people (I use that term species-neutral), everyone wears multiple hats. Based on my aptitude tests and Sgt. M'Bari's recommendation, I earned a fairly prestigious posting: janitorial, maintenance, security, and generally anything anyone in rank above me wants me to do. Everyone is above me in rank. All that may not sound important, but Sgt. M'Bari says "those toilets won't clean themselves!" Actually, they do, but I didn't think it prudent to correct him at that time. See the part about where I really like to breathe. I scored a prestigious security team post. "Prestigious" because if there is ever anything dangerous onboard, I am part of the elite team that is in the front lines. There was no counting my joy.

So my career as a crewman third class launched. I maintained a fairly low profile since I noticed that showing any kind of initiative may end up with you on an away mission to a sometimes hostile planet. Many of my fellow crewmen did not return from those missions. And yet, the bridge crew always did. Coincidence? I think not. There was a brief conspiracy theory about what color shirts they wore, but since all crewmen wear a bland coverall-like jumpsuit, it quickly dissipated. The current rumor is that the bridge crew uses them as human shields. No one has come back from an away mission that will disprove that story.

Security duty involves breaking up an occasional crew fight and repelling boarders. Since no one has ever boarded a StarForce ship, I janitor. And I try not to be exceptional at it. Who knows? Maybe there will be a need for an exceptional janitor on some away mission. I could probably live a long and happy life *without* living as an underachiever, but why take the chance?

I, with a few others, maintain the ship's robotic maintenance staff. We oversee the cleaning, painting, and upkeep. With little robotic boxes doing most of the serious work, I have a lot of downtime. It's a big ship. One could easily lose themselves on it and avoid attracting the attention of the officers quite easily. Since there are almost no crew fights, I often find downtime on one of the cots in an unused cell of the brig. It's a hard job, but someone has to do it. After all, if the bridge crew is the best and the brightest, they have to be superior to someone. I found my niche.

*

"Lewis, your personality encompasses the three C's: cowardly, cheap, and conceited." That was Mom.

First of all, Mom, I am not a coward. I think of myself as very brave. It takes a certain type of courage to not worry what other people will think when you bravely extricate yourself from situations in which you might come to physically harm.

And another thing: I am not cheap. Just six years ago, I bought you a Mother's Day gift. Granted, I bought her a ball cap at a spaceport gift shop, but I still paid real credits for it.

In addition, I do not think of myself as conceited. I believe that I am very humble despite my video star handsomeness. You're just jealous.

Fortunately, my dear old dad, during one of his more sober and lucid moments, thought more of his oldest child.

"Son, with a mind like yours, you are going to go places. Big places." I didn't know he meant the territorial corrections facility. Dad never was my biggest fan. Turns out he was right. I've been to enormous planetary systems. Well, I was in the *ship* that went to them. Except for one furlough, I haven't been off a ship in ages. But the ships are pretty big. So, the old man was right on the money about me.

*

Invitation to Evacuate

I was only floating for a moment when the explosive decompression blew out the bulkhead wall. As the oxygen blasted into empty space, that black maw in the hull pulled me toward it. I gripped the edge of the bunk and held on for dear life. I don't want to die. It's a big thing with me. I don't have any regrets, but if I had the chance to live my life over again ... well ... it makes me tired just thinking about it. I know it's unlikely, but it's still worth giving it a shot. I held on to the bunk as I watched one of my roommates sucked into the void. I never did learn his name. He will always be "Unnamed Roommate Number Two" to me. A fraction of a second after he fell forever into space, an invisible energy field sealed the room and automatic systems re-pressurized the area. A second too late for Unnamed Roommate Number Two, but right on time for me. With gravity restored, I fell to the flooring in a heap of tan uniform and flop sweat.

Oh for those glorious moments when the beautiful Lieutenant Wa was treating me like a leper. Good times.

*

Turns out that the damage control team had more to concern themselves with than the cabin of three minor crewmen. They clearly did not place as much value on my health as I did. Holding my head, as if to nurse the universe's worst hangover, I managed to get to my feet, happy to see them still attached. The energy barrier still held in the atmosphere, but since lowest bidder manufactured that emergency field generator as well, I wanted out of that room ASAP.

As I watched the alien craft disappear from view, I concentrated on my neural implant's main communication channels, trying to contact the first response team (or anyone really), but all I could "hear" was a blast of high-pitched screaming static from the direction of the hole in my wall. I fell to the bottom bunk, the blanket and pillow long lost into space.

*

Six Hours Ago

I had spent months successfully avoiding the watchful eye of any officer on whatever ship I happened to be on and was happily trying to remain invisible. I had set up several small underground gambling operations, a bootleg porn streaming vid rental network, and a morally ambiguous massage service onboard. I narrowly avoided being caught at any of these, sometimes only just, and surprisingly earned very few extra credits. It turned out to be a lot of hard work avoiding hard work. Whoever said "crime doesn't pay" must have been following my lead. I look back at all the schemes I involved myself in over the course of my life: some were profitable and some were mine.

I was just coming back from failing to collect a debt that a crewman owed me for some interactive adult vid feeds via his neural net when I ran into the curvaceous Lt. Wa. Literally ran into her. Best part of my day. Considering the way my day turned out, that was not saying much.

Lt. Wa is also Human, but from a curious bloodline that gave her the most exotic features and a body that most lower deck crewmen only dreamed of. For some reason, she did not find it amusing that someone had nicknamed her "Lt. Wow." Whoever created that sexist pronunciation should go to the brig instead of running several small underground gambling operations, a bootleg porn vid rental network, and a morally ambiguous massage service. The bottom line was: she was very sexy. We had a lot in common.

"Excuse me, Lieutenant." Doing my best to *not* extricate my limbs from hers, after rounding a corner and bumping into her chest first.

"It's quite all right. If you would step back, that is." I could tell she was really partial to me.

"My pleasure." Who says single entendre is dead?

"Crewman, do I know you?" Trying to stay hidden from the bridge crew was now biting me in the ass.

"Haversham, ma'am ... er ... sir. Crewman Lewis Haversham III, at your service."

"Well, Crewman Lewis Haversham III, do you always accost senior officers in such a manner in the hallway?"

"No ma'am. Just the attractive ones." Wit, thy name is Lewis.

You heard it. I said she was attractive. She said I was drop dead gorgeous. Well, not exactly those words, but "drop dead" was in there somewhere.

"Don't you have duties to attend to, Crewman Lewis Haversham III? If not, I am sure some can be arranged."

"No, Lieutenant ... I mean yes, Lieutenant. I have duties to attend to." I am positively ingenious in my small talk. "Is there anything I can do to you? Uh ... for you?"

"You can step off and not accost me in the future."

"I don't want you to go away thinking I'm an idiot." I truly wanted her to think as much of me as I did.

"Why not? That's the way I started."

I backed away, knowing I had made a lasting impression. I was practically floating on air right up until the moment six hours later when I was literally floating on air.

*

Rescued?

The damage control team did eventually rescue me. Tears of joy streamed down my face and I'm sticking to that story.

"Crewman, report to the bridge!" the sergeant in charge of damage and rescue ordered.

"Why? This is NOT my fault." That last sentence I was thinking of having tattooed on my forehead.

"Captain's orders. Now move."

The good news: turns out that I, specifically, had been not ordered to the bridge, but the entire security contingent had. The bad news: I am the entire (surviving) security team. Seems Security was having a birthday party for one of the members in the galley when a blast from the invading ship either vaporized them instantly, removed all their oxygen, or sucked them into space through the resulting hole in the bulkhead. It seems outrageously unfair. They didn't invite me.

*

The scene on the bridge was a singular voice of chaos. The captain was barking orders. Everyone else was staring off into space, communicating via their implants, totally ignoring him.

"Lt. Wa! Report!" the captain snapped out.

"So far, we have fifteen casualties or unaccounted for, six injured, two of those critically. Dr. Stephenson has co-opted a xeno-botanist and a cook, both with medical cross training as assistants. Repairs are commencing on all affected decks. Environmental fields are holding until permanent hull plating can be replaced."

"What is happening with our friends out there?" the captain asked.

"The attack has subsided," Lt. Wa reported. "We were unable to effectively counter-attack so the decision to retreat was entirely theirs. We have no idea how they are able to phase in and out of normal space so readily. However they do it, leaves no energy signature behind. Our best guess: they have headed toward the closest system."

"What is our engine status?" the captain asked.

"Slider Drive is still viable, but not recommended with huge portions of the hull missing," Lt. Wa said.

"Yeah, well I don't recommend getting sliced and diced by a crystal pyramid, but we don't always get what we want. Lieutenant Davis, set course for that system at flank speed," the captain ordered the navigator/pilot. "What's our ETA for that system?

"At top speed, sir," Davis stated, "about twelve days."

"Twelve days?" I blurted out before thinking. I do that a lot. "I thought the ship's Slider Drive was faster than light. Why does it take so long? That system is right there."

"Who is this idiot?" the captain barked.

"Crewman Lewis Haversham III. Currently our entire security detachment," Lt. Wa said cooly.

"We are so screwed," the captain said under his breath. "Well, Crewman Lewis Haversham III, the reason it will take so long to travel such a relatively short distance is: it will take the computer four days to

194

calculate our jump to faster than lightspeed, unless of course you would like to try it without exact calculations. It will take four days for us to gradually work our way up to that speed, unless you would like to be smashed to a jelly-like goo on the back bulkheads by the G-forces. From there, we travel a few hours at supra-lightspeed. Then it will take us four days to slow to a survivable speed, unless you would like to be smashed into a jelly-like goo on the forward bulkheads. So twelve days is not so bad for a three quarters of a light-year trip, wouldn't you say?"

"No, sir," I stammered. "I always prefer the goo-free option."

"Lt. Wa, tell the engineering team they have four days to get this bucket ship shape. I want us battle ready by the time we hit that system. And get that ... guy (indicating the entirety of the security team whose name he didn't bother to remember) and whoever else you can round up down to the SLIP room and get them up to speed as quickly as possible."

Lt. Wow grabbed me by the arm and dragged me out the door of the bridge. We met Sgt. M'Bari headed for the bridge.

"M'Bari, you're with us," she ordered.

With a single "hmph," he did an about-face and followed us to the SLIP chamber. I'm sure he was scowling at the back of my head the whole way. Turns out I was not the only member of the security team left alive. He didn't make the birthday party invitation list either.

"Lieutenant? I'm not being purposefully dense, but what is a SLIP?" I asked.

"Good thing it's not on purpose."

*

Technical Specs for Dummies

Turns out SLIP stands for "Solid Light Image Projection." Quite brilliant, actually. It was meant for away parties to do planetary exploration without having to leave the safety of the ship.

We fire a SLIP missile down to the planet. It pops open and ejects SLIP backpacks. Solid light holograms of crew members who remotely "pilot" them from casket-like pods onboard. They are actually manipulating human shaped force fields with holograms projected over top of them to give themselves the appearance they would normally have. That's for psychological and ease of use reasons. They could program it so you would look like an Antarean, but who would want to? Except Antareans, I mean. The crews' holograms wear the devices on their holographic backs to maintain their density and communicate with each other and the ship. The landing party doesn't have to worry about atmosphere, bio-hazards, or radiation. They control their holograms and communicate with each other through "quantum comms" which seems to me like telepathy, but let the engi-nerds explain the science. Distance is not an issue for quantum comms which also transmits and records 3D images and data back to ship.

"We may not have time for a proper training session," Lt. Wa said. "You'll just have to learn very quickly. On-the-job training as it were."

"Hey! There's no call for that sort of language," I protested. "Learn" and "job" are two of my least favorite words. Also not a big fan of "responsible," "earn," and "volunteer."

"Get in the pod," Sgt. M'Bari growled.

*

On The Job Training

Sgt. M'Bari did not get into a pod as he had plenty of experience piloting a SLIP. Instead, he joined the two technicians who monitored our life signs and data flow. An important job because if you die in a pod, you're ... you know ... dead. While we waited for the SLIP missile to launch, the technicians scanned us for stress factors.

"Crewman Haversham, while your SLIP personae cannot be harmed during the exploration, your physical body, here, can be impacted by an unforeseen event. This is one of the reasons we do not allow anyone with a cardiac history to pilot SLIPs," the technician explained. "Under adverse conditions, it harms the driver."

What could be stressful about facing off with alien warriors? I'm just a janitor. How did I get into this mess?

"But it's safe, right?" I said while attempting to climb back out of the pod.

"Oh yes. We almost never lose anyone."

"Almost?" I said, as he gently pushed me back into the pod with a smile on his face.

"Those hardly count. Just ask the bridge crew."

"Relax, Haversham," I heard Lt. Wow say inside my head. "You're as safe here as your mother's womb."

"What if Mom was an alcoholic, drugged-out, suicidal cliff-diver?"

"Then you're safer here."

196

"Just lay back and relax," the technician said. "Clear your head of all thoughts."

"Shouldn't be a problem for him," Sgt. M'Bari transmitted.

*

It took them few minutes to target a nearby largish asteroid and fire the SLIP missile at it. Lt. Wow and I laid together quietly. Well, in separate pods with several technicians and Sgt. M'Bari standing over us. It could have been more romantic. The missile must have ejected our backpacks properly because the next thing I know, I am standing on the surface of the asteroid with Lt. Wow giving me instruction in piloting the SLIP.

"As you can see, the image looks just like you. Unfortunately. With more time, we can program it to project a more physically fit, more handsome, version of you. It doesn't change your holograms ability, but it's psychologically more effective."

"You mean I perform better if I look better?" I asked.

"No, it makes me less nauseous," Lt. Wa said with a straight face. I looked at her holographic avatar. It looked very much like her. Dark hair, tied in a StarForce-approved ponytail. Lean body with ample curves. Her eyes, lips, and cheekbones in competition for Most Exotic Feature. Either she didn't feel the need to enhance her holographic image or I always see her in an optimized form in my mind. It was weird seeing her in her somewhat form-fitting tan uniform, with just a slim backpack and no space suit, considering we were standing on an asteroid hurtling through the vacuum of space.

"Just move as you always do," Lt. Wa continued with her training lecture. "The computer onboard translates your synaptic impulses to the SLIP at quantum speed so there is no noticeable lag. The force field skinning your holograph enables you to interact with physical objects. You cannot reduce your image's density or the backpack would have nothing to hang on to. It would also screw up the computer that allows us to simulate gravity in this form."

"There's gravity here?"

"No. The computer and backpacks just simulate it to make it easier for you to navigate. With a few mental commands through your neural interface, you can adjust your strength, stamina, and various physical reactions to have your holograph perform amazing feats. I don't recommend it while in training. It's hard enough teaching you how to walk without falling, let alone leaping ten stories."

197

"So most new trainees have a hard time just walking in their SLIP units?" I asked.

"No, I am just banking on your usual coordination and intelligence," Lt. Wa said.

"The SLIP fields are impervious to physical damage, but I don't recommend testing that theory as your backpack is not. You aren't really here or breathing, so a hostile atmosphere or biological agents such as viruses or diseases are no problem," Lt. Wa continued. "There are a few limitations. While the sensors in the backpacks record and transmit gaseous chemical data, the holograms have no sense of smell. On some of the planets I have been to, that would be a blessing." I think that may have been her first attempt at humor. Ever.

"The SLIPs also can't carry any weapons," she explained as we jogged across the surface of the asteroid. "No need to defend ourselves since these are just force fields covered in holograms. We normally just use these exploring new worlds. SLIPs can't project beams like energy weapons."

Oh, come on now! We are talking about the possibility of encountering a hostile force, a blaster wouldn't suck, hologram or no hologram. Did no one think about strapping one onto a backpack before loading the missile?

After about three hours of running, scanning, and throwing bigger and bigger rocks, I transmitted to Lt. Wa: "If I'm just a hologram, why do I feel so thirsty?"

"That's your real body. You have a bit of cotton mouth and may be a little dehydrated. One more lesson and we will take a break," the lieutenant said. "Epsilon."

"What's 'epsilon'?" I asked. Turns out she was transmitting to M'Bari.

Right where the lieutenant was standing, a gigantic creature of rock, scales, and teeth appeared, snarling at its next potential meal.

I looked around for the lieutenant, and not finding her, followed my instincts. I ran. I was nearly a half a kilometer away when I realized that I was a hologram and the creature couldn't really hurt me. I also realized the lieutenant hadn't followed my very intelligent lead. I turned, ran back to the beast, and in my most arrogant stance, flipped it the bird. "WHERE'S LT. WA?"

The gigantic hand-like fist seemed to move in slow motion as it backhanded me into a boulder. As my eyelids fluttered and I blacked out, I noticed the backpack on the shoulders of the monster. And here I thought she was starting to like me.

*

Epiphany

"He's going into shock!" the engi-nerd shrieked. I couldn't see him, but even through the darkness around me, I could hear him. Barely.

"Leave him in the pod, but get his feet up."

"Wrap this stimulator blanket around him."

"Get an IV started and let's get some fluids in him."

"Slap that cardiac regulator on his chest."

"It's always the newbies."

An hour later, they lifted me from the SLIP pod. Even Sgt. M'Bari was gentler. Well, by his standards anyway.

"I swear I slowed that punch down. Why didn't he accelerate his SLIP and evade?" Lt. Wa was asking no one in general.

"The little idiot probably didn't know you could do that." Sgt. M'Bari's gravel-like voice.

"The 'little idiot' is right here, and NO, I didn't know you could do that," I croaked.

"You mean, you came back for me, thinking that Andromedan Rock Beast had me, and you didn't know you could accelerate your speed?" Lt. Wa asked in amazement.

"Yeah."

"That ... that ... that is the ... dumbest thing I have ever heard in my life!" Lt. Wa snarled. "The smart move would have been to realize you could dodge the blow. No. Scratch that. The smart move would have been to run away as fast as you could and protect your SLIP."

"I thought it as incredibly brave."

"You *thinking* is highly unlikely. You managed to destroy a very expensive piece of equipment," the lieutenant said. Then in a quieter voice, "And you could have been killed, you moron."

"So, not brave?"

"Not smart," she said a little more gently.

We sat there in silence. The SLIP engi-nerd fussed over my readings and IV. Lt. Wa fumed. Sgt. M'Bari grinned. And me ... I had an epiphany.

It's not that the bridge officers use the crew as human shields during away missions, it's that the crew doesn't have enough experience in the SLIPs and get themselves killed. Wait till this hits the RumorNet. It's possible to survive an away mission. I am living proof.

"I wanna go back!"

The engi-nerd was the first to regain his voice. "Are you insane? You just barely survived *that* attempt."

"The more SLIP missions I survive, the more likely I will survive a SLIP mission." I swear it made more sense when I said it in my head.

Sgt. M'Bari raised an eyebrow. Lt. Wa just stared at me as if I had grown another head. Maybe I had.

The technician insisted that we eat, had plenty to drink, and a quick nap before we returned to SLIP pods. This time Sgt. M'Bari accompanied us to the asteroid. There were plenty of SLIPs to allow him to do so, I just think he wanted to see it to believe it. I insisted that he and Lt. Wa give me advanced SLIP training. Mental note: Do *not* insist on anything ever again.

*

Change in Plans

Nearly four days later, we stepped back on to the bridge together. This marked my first time back since starting SLIPs training.

"Lt. Davis, prepare to initiate Slider Drive," the captain ordered.

"Sir. If I may. I think we should wait," Lt. Wa interjected.

"Why in the universe should we do that, Lieutenant?" the captain growled.

"Sir, while we were in SLIPs training, I was wondering why the aliens didn't attack us again."

She had time to think about *that* while I was fighting for my life against her and M'Bari's holographic horrors?

"Go on."

"I think we could save considerable energy just waiting for them to come to us. They only seem to be attacking on prime number days. I checked some historical records and a few centuries ago, there were some reports of a similar incident back on Earth that confirms that theory. If I'm right," the lieutenant continued, "we will only have to wait seven more days."

"So, we just wait around for them to destroy us? Is that your plan, Lieutenant?" the captain said, somewhat less than convinced. "Just *exactly* how did they defeat them once upon a time?"

"Trickery, sir," Lt. Wa said.

Then I did something that surprised everyone. No one moreso than I.

"I might have an idea about that sir."

"The idiot speaks," the captain said, clearly enamored with me.

"Sir, it may be worth listening to Lewi ... Crewman Haversham, he has some experience with ... deceit," Lt. Wa added. She had taken the time to look up my record. I was touched.

"Hmph." I'm not sure, but I think that was Sgt. M'Bari agreeing.

"All right, Haversham, what is this plan?"

"Sir, have you ever heard of Three Card Monte?"

It took me the better part of an hour to explain what I had in mind. It actually would have been less, but Lt. Wa and even Sgt. M'Bari kept interjecting tactical suggestions. Okay, maybe they *did* improve the plan. It wasn't so much a plan really. More of an idea. At the end of it, I wasn't being ordered into an airlock, an upgrade from my usual schemes.

"This is potentially the dumbest thing I have ever heard."

Tell us how you really feel, Captain.

"Sir, with all due respect," Lt. Wa said, "do we have another plan?"

The captain mulled that over for a second or two.

"Fine. What are you waiting for? This dumbass plan won't do it itself."

Lt. Wa, after a glance at me, fairly ran away. Toward the SLIPs lab. Sgt. M'Bari barrelled toward the armory. Lt. Davis immediately crawled under the control panels for the communication and sensor arrays.

I spent some time on the RumorNet with the crew, then headed to sickbay.

It took me several minutes of arguing with Dr. Stephenson to get him to part with his beloved hemoglobin reserves, but I finally found the right logic.

"If this doesn't work, we won't need them anyway." Hardly an encouraging argument, but effective.

*

Seven days later, we were as ready as we could be in that amount of time. I stood on the bridge brimming with false confidence, secure in the knowledge that similar to what I had told the doctor, if this didn't work, I would never see the court martial coming.

*

Run Silent, Run Monte

True to Lt. Wa's calculations, exactly eleven days after the last attack, the crystalline pyramid appeared in space, tube extended to resume it's duties.

Our ship listed in space, seemingly dead, with tons of debris floating around it.

The pyramid did not expect that.

A half dozen pieces of debris blinked from sight.

Without warning, seventy-two starships, appeared in space, all aimed in the direction of the pyramid.

The pyramid did not expect that either.

One second later, the ships disappeared and reappeared in a different position.

Yep, you guessed it: The pyramid did not expect that. It was a day of surprises for them.

Seconds later, miraculously, the pyramid exploded from the inside.

Even more miraculously, I was still alive to watch it. Though part of me wished for a quick, clean death.

*

Behind the Scenes

I know you are dying to know how I did this. Well, I didn't. Everyone did. It was just my ingenious idea that inspired our survival and the total annihilation of our enemies. In my humble opinion.

The lovely Lt. Wa wrangled the engi-nerds to program a dozen SLIP missiles to eject a half dozen backpacks as usual, except now, each which would generate holograms of StarForce ships on a signaled command. Tons of debris from earlier run-ins collected by the crew, which yours truly coordinated via RumorNet, deposited the wreckage into the airlocks, along with the SLIP missiles. The blown-out debris also contained large quantities of bio matter thanks to Dr. Stephenson's blood banks and the few remaining bodies left on board after the first attacks.

We knew approximately where the alien vessel would appear thanks to Lt. Davis configuring the communications and sensor arrays

202

to detect the static the pyramids generate when phasing. The computer used that data to aim all the holographic ships generally in that direction.

Sgt. M'Bari only had time to re-engineer six missiles with tactical warheads, near-lightspeed power plants, and instantaneous and automatic guidance for the tube openings. He is *such* a slacker.

The nanosecond the pyramid arrived, the six warheads took advantage of the aliens' shock of both seeing us incapacitated and then finding themselves surrounded by StarForce ships. Being unmanned, the missiles didn't have to worry about G-forces turning anyone into goo. Their speed was almost instantaneous and they seemed to blink out of sight, traveling at near-lightspeed into the tube.

As soon as the warheads disappeared, our ship took off at its highest sub-lightspeed on a random course, zigzagging away from the blast area. The timing and coordination of all this was so critical that the preprogramed computer executed it. That includes the sudden course changes, which as much as it shames me to say, enabled me to repaint a corner of the bridge with motion sickness.

*

Aftermath

"Good job, every—WHAT IS THAT SMELL?" the captain bellowed, turning in my direction.

"My stomach may not have reacted as well as it could have during the sudden course corrections," I said weakly.

Lt. Davis snickered. Sgt. M'Bari provided his usual "Hmph."

"Be that as it may, your plan seemed to work, Ensign Haversham," the captain said.

"*Ensign* Haversham?" I asked, somewhat surprised.

"What's the point of being captain if I can't give battlefield commissions?"

"But—"

"Lt. Wa will supervise your officer training, upgrade your implant, and as soon as she thinks you're able, you will assume your duties as tactical and security chief."

"Thank you, sir," unable to keep the shock from my voice. Then it hit me. "Does that mean I would be Sgt. M'Bari's supervising officer?"

"I guess it would."

"Hmph." That was me.

Lt. Wa smiled. Sgt. M'Bari did not.

***

Sailor's Saga
by Steve Rouse

I stabbed at them, slashed at them all throughout the star-filled night. They kept coming. I screamed and muttered and growled with every slash and thrust, "Damn you all!"

Fishing the waters even this far out into the Gulf Stream had been my life the past sixty-two years. I knew much. But of late, I'd gone too long without a catch. That drove me farther out into deeper waters seeking a monster to claim. On the second day one took my bait and the battle began. For three days we wrestled. He from his world and me from mine. During the day, the merciless sun burned 'til even my weathered hide was tender and my eyes could only squint. At night the tickling winds and cold moon mocked my plight. My hands ached and bled.

But I prevailed and the great beast I had grown to respect died on the end of my spear. Alas, my success proved to be my foil. Such a fish! So large it would have swamped my boat. To cut it up would destroy too much meat. So, I opted to lash it to the side to better protect it. Protect it from the sharks I knew would come. I set my sail and prayed the Creator would guide me swiftly home. Night settled in.

They came. With dorsals streaking across the surface, they seemed to number in the hundreds. Mouths gaped and the moonlight reflected from thousands of flashing teeth seeking to shred my treasure. My boat shuddered and lurched with each hit, each tug. I drove my harpoon into scores of writhing, biting sharks. I thrust it down on a huge dusky, piercing her through the gills. Her eyes widened and she rolled, yanking the spear from my numb hands, then she slipped beneath the carnage.

I threw myself down across the gunwale and half on what was left of my marlin, my knife slashing at every mouth near enough. The blood from gashes on my hands added to their lust.

Saltwater soaked me, yet I knew my tears mixed with it, stricken with the loss of my treasure. He'd fought me so admirably and did not deserve to be so savagely ripped asunder.

Another shark surged up, landing against my side, still flopping. Another rose and bit down behind the marlin's dorsal fin, its nose pushing my thigh out of the way or surely I'd be missing a huge part of my leg if not dragged under and likewise torn apart.

As the shark sunk back into the sea, my small boat listed severely, shaking violently from the beast's tearing its bite free. Water rushed over the marlin and me and began filling the boat. I drove my knife into the side of the shark atop me and used it to pull myself toward standing. It thrashed and tumbled in the boat, almost tossing me into the mouths below. I reached for the mast but the beast's tail took my legs out from under me. I toppled onto it, but closer to the mast. I stretched again, managing only to snag the draw line. It was enough.

My boat swamped. As it filled, the shark wiggled out over the gunwale toward the bow, its tail dislodging and scattering my possessions. Other sharks remained and continued their rampage, pulling at what was left of the marlin's carcass. I gave up the fight, wedged myself against the higher gunwale and mast and waited for the inevitable.

The boat finally rolled despite my efforts, its sail slapping the waves, fatally wet. I crawled out and straddled the hull. The demons of the deep had finished their feast and moved on. The lightening eastern sky helped ease my tension, but allowed a deep, aching exhaustion to manifest itself. I slept.

The sun had almost reached its zenith when I stirred, sore and thirsty. The sea was calm. I had to chuckle at the irony. So tranquil today unlike last night. A frightening mask that hid so much raw terror in the jaws of sharks and other beasts of the deep.

With no sign of sharks, I dropped into the water to inspect what remained of the marlin. There was little left of my treasure but skull, rapier, fin, and bones, save a piece of meat behind a gill, too small for sharks to get to. I rose up a bit and groped about inside the boat and gunwale hoping to find the knife. Nothing. I returned to the carcass with straining lungs, but paused when I saw a massive pale marine giant or perhaps a school of tarpon pass deep beneath me. I tore off the meat and surfaced. Those two bites of raw fish would be my only meal. I also rested well knowing that whatever residents of the sea had passed under me, I was no longer of interest.

Near noon the next day, I raised my head and looked about. I did that as often as I thought of it. A blur on the horizon caught my dry eyes. Squinting, I watched as it became the sails of a three-master bearing down on me from the nor 'east. I could no longer call out, but did manage to wave and slap the hull. They lowered a boat.

I was saved!

*

"Hey, uhm, what's your name again?" the sailor asked as he stood in the doorway.

"Santiago, *senor.* Santiago Gallardo," I told him as I knew good English and understood his question. "And you?"

"I's Michael," he said grinning with some teeth missing. "I's come to take you to see the captain, if'n you're up to it."

"That is good. I've rested in the care of your ship's crew for three days. I can thank him and find out how I may serve his ship to pay back his kindness."

"His kindness?" Michael chuckled and shook his head. "I been with Captain Peckab since the whale took his leg and I's kin tell ya dat man, he ain't got a speck o'kindness in him. Nuthin' but revenge, dat one."

We left my quarters and climbed up several stairways and through four hatchways before I was finally blinded by the sun. Its familiar power felt instantly good against my skin, warming me to the point that I hadn't realized I'd been cold. But it was my eyes that had a difficult time taking in what was before me.

I'd lived my life on the sea and knew most of its denizens. We killed for food or to sell, but what I saw spoke of pure killing for its own sake. The deck of this ship was adorned with bones, jawbones, and teeth—thousands of white teeth all worked into the gunwales, the railings, the planking, and the rigging. Not shark teeth, no. Whale teeth. Stretched in the rigging, too, were strips of baleen humming in the wind. This ship sang of death.

Of course I'd heard of and seen my share of whaling ships. They hunted them down for whale meat, yes, but more for their blubber which they boiled down for whale oil. Lots of money to be made for all of them on the mainland who loved to buy their whale oil. Nature ought to be respected because we all depend on it. But I am no expert on whales. I've seen lots of them. They're too big for my boat. Too big for all the boats in my village.

Michael and I made our way across the mid decks toward the poop deck where the wheel was. I saw him in all his naval splendor even before I climbed the steps. About my size, but looking much bigger with his uniform which was a long coat with many layers and a large-brimmed hat, complete with a big feather. His pantaloons billowed in the wind. He had a single black high-top boot on his right leg. His left leg ended above his knee, but he wore a carved whale bone, probably from a jaw, to be the lower half of his leg. It was all tied into something leathery pretending to be a shoe. If I was him, I'd not crop the pant leg and let it hang down. He looked like he could fall over with just a bit stiffer breeze.

He musta seen us coming because he pivoted on his peg leg to face me. "Argh, an' this must be our sailor guest, the half-dead old fisherman. I'm Captain Gregory Peckab of the good ship *Factotum Mortua*. We sail for the Northeast Company out of Boston Harbor securing whale products, oil, blubber and the like." The man hopped a bit as he walked around the two of us. "So what's your name, old man?" He turned quickly to Michael saying, "He does speak the King's English, eh?"

"I do, good Captain. I thank you for your rescue, good sir." With that I bowed like I'd seen them all do when visiting our village. "If there is any help that I may render that would in some small way repay your kindness and generosity in saving my life, it is yours."

"Well, uhm, yes, of course, uhm ... What was your name again?" he asked.

"I am known as Santiago Gallardo. I am a fisherman from Anguilla." I held out my hand in greeting, also learned from the white men in their tall ships.

The captain ignored my hand and, instead, wheeled around, gesturing across the span of his vessel. "You were a far bit from home when we hauled you aboard, old man. I'd say a good two hundred leagues. This fine ship can't take you back home until we finish a mission, a task given me by God the Creator, I dare say.

"You may have noticed, old man, that this ship is festooned with the remnants of the dead, those denizens of the deep as large as this ship, or even bigger!" Peckab pointed a gnarly finger at my nose as he spoke with rising enthusiasm and grit. "We are hunters. Hunters of the most God-forsaken creatures ever found on this Earth.

"Did you ever think why such a creature exists, old man? A creature that size, destined to be an ocean dweller, and not able to breathe in it? No! They must rise to breathe the air! They are tied to the surface just to live! And it is here we will be waiting for them armed with harpoons to take them to serve all of mankind.

"'Course, it is a fair share of work, but these men," he added, still gesturing, "these men are the best strippers and flensers afloat. They can strip a whale clean of its skin in two hours. From there, see over to the mizzen mast? Those be the try-pots to pull the oil from the blubber. The meat either goes to the hold and casked in salt or to the galley. We've more'n a hundred barrels of whale oil in our hold. A fine crew indeed."

He stood with both hands on the fore poop rail, breathing like he'd just run a race. Truly his heart was in his calling. "I've no experience with whale, Captain. But I assure you that I am well qualified to render any fish into meat pieces. I would assume that could include a whale, with some guidance. If that pleases you, sir."

Again he turned quickly and took two hobbles to stand before me. "What would please me, old man, is that you would tell me of any sightings you have had or heard of a whale, a damnable abomination of a whale. A sperm whale with white skin? Any such encounter, my good man?"

"I have had none, Captain. Never heard of such a whale in my time at sea," I answered.

"Are you calling me a liar?" he screamed so loud that even the men in the rigging paused and gawked down to see what had tindered their captain.

"Ahh, ah, oh, of course not, C-Captain, sir. I m-m-merely said I had no knowledge of such a beast," I stammered, taken aback at his ferocity.

"Good. Damn good, old man. Because I have proof. Proof that such a devil exists." He leaned back and raised his peg leg and slammed it down atop his chart table. "This damnable curse is proof of the white devil, Moby Dick! Near two years ago we had the monster surfaced and speared. I was moments away from throwing the fatal harpoon into its lungs when it dove, dragging both boats and twenty good men under with it.

"An' if we thought it meant to escape us, we were sadly mistaken. The monster turned and rammed into our midst as we struggled to the surface. I'd just taken fresh air into me lungs when it breached beneath me, lifting me high up upon his snout. As I slid off, he took me into his gaping maw and snapped it closed, cutting me leg clean off. If'n I hadn't lost the leg, it'd have dragged me down to meet Davey Jones hisself.

"So, we hunt this demon on each and every voyage. 'Tis the third trip since its attack and we've seen him spout yesterday! But he's wary, that one. Kin probably smell us comin' and knows I won't rest 'til he's bloated 'n belly up. Eh, Wha? Hey hey hey."

He had a cynical laugh, like a child on the beach when torturing crabs. Then he looked at me and I felt naked, completely at his beckoning.

He shrugged and said to Michael, "Put 'im to work in the galley. Old Crusty'll keep 'im busy." He pulled his glass up to his eye, and began scanning the horizon.

I'd been dismissed. Michael and I made our way below decks to the galley. Old Crusty was the galley's master, a soggy fat man, about half my age. He spoke only French and I didn't. He showed me what to do, grunting as he demonstrated. I motioned to him that the knife he gave me needed sharpening. He just grunted more and pointed to the filthy cutting board. I set to task with only a few corrections. Then he nodded, patted me on the head, and went to the other side to tend his boiling pots.

I spent five days in the galley when a general excitement permeated the ship. Michael came to the hatchway, breathless. "Santiago! The captain says to come on deck. We've sighted Moby Dick!" We bounced between the bulkheads heading topside as the ship veered into the wind.

As I got to the main deck, all was chaos. Every sail had been set and the wind had found each of them. The billowing and popping of the canvas as it trapped the wind brought more popping and creaking to the wooden deck. The *Factotum Mortua*'s bow dug deep into the sea as it picked up speed.

Crew members ran about with lines and floats, all heading to the boats. Grand vessels they were too. Each a full thirty feet long and wide enough to lay on a bench. Ten thick oars eight to ten feet long, and a supply of harpoons lashed to its decking.

All four of these were being loaded for the grand chase that would end the life of this monster white whale and avenge the captain's leg. I stayed next to the gunwales near the hatch by the mizzen mast, aside an already attended try-pot.

Peckab slid down the poop deck stairs, landed, and scanned the ruckus. He saw me and screamed out, "Watch, old man, and you will witness the justice of the Creator as I pierce the life out of this white demon!" He ran headlong to the nearest boat and was pulled aboard. The boat, laden with fourteen men, most at the oars, was swung out and lowered into the sea. Within minutes, all four were racing toward the port horizon. The captain's whaler stood out, decked with the same teeth as the ship and a baleen pole flying a red and yellow banderol.

From atop the main mast, I heard the call, "Thar she blows! Hard a port." We all looked and I clearly saw a whale breaching. An odd giant. A white sperm whale bigger than the ship when only half out of the water and rolling to land on its back. Its splash seemed large enough to swamp the ship on which I stood. I'd felt the captain was crazy and now I feared the crew must be as well. To be so driven to kill ... It made so little sense to me, and yet I knew I'd fished, I'd killed for my own for survival, not a vengeance-ridden madman's quest against Nature.

I stayed on deck to watch. The whaling boats spread out creating an arc. The sun was half passed the meridian and the hunt was to our west, so some glare distorted my view.

This creature, Moby Dick they'd named it, spouted again well ahead of the whalers, its white skin shimmering in the sunlight. As beautiful a creature as I'd encountered. I could even see its pale skin under the water. I stopped, suddenly remembering a large pale mass swimming beneath my overturned boat the day after the sharks' carnage. *Could it have been this same whale?*

My eyes followed its form moving fast just below the surface, quickly creating a wave ahead of it. The whalers saw it too and each boat turned to counter the whale's approach. Cries from the deckhands all around me showed that they understood what was happening.

The whale had come about and seemed intent on ramming into the whaling craft. As it passed between them, one boat loosed harpoons at it. As if in response, the beast circled and came up a full half of its length out of the water and laid back directly onto the boat that had attacked it. I could hear the splintering of the boat even over the cries of its crew.

The second boat on that side picked up speed and turned toward the whale. One brave harpooner stood at the bow, his lance at the ready. He never threw it. The whale burst from the sea at their starboard and brought the whaler under with its jaw crushing their tiny craft.

All went silent. The crew of the *Factotum Mortua* stood stunned. Rowing sounds reached us as the battle had taken place just less than half a league distant. Even the wind had paused as if to witness the duel. A minute, perhaps more, passed. The only movement, the small waves and the remaining whalers. I was amazed as Peckab's boat moved farther away from the ship, no doubt hell-bent to exact his revenge.

I lost my footing when the ship rocked with a dull thud. One crew from the rigging was knocked loose, hitting the decking with a sickening crunch. Several attended him, but I ran to the opposite side, prompted by shouts from others. I peered down and saw swirling waters and some splintered boards of the hull and the fading shape of the whale that attacked us!

Another jolt shook the ship and I saw the submerged shape of the beast swimming away behind us. The strike caused the heated try-pot to splash and the poor sailor next to it was drenched in hot oil. His screams lasted only long enough for two fellow sailors to throw him overboard. I stood aghast.

Moments later, another hit with the sound of more splintering. A large section of wood surfaced behind the ship. Someone cried out that it was the ship's rudder.

Another shouted immediately after. "Avast! Thar she blows. Astern." I looked out over the aft rail and saw the top of the white whale now swimming directly for the two remaining whalers. They must have witnessed its attack on the ship as they were now rowing toward us.

I lost sight of the whaler directly in line with the whale until it dove once more. The harpooner threw hard directly beneath his boat which then rose up, riding on the whale's back, the harpoon clearly embedded just behind its dorsal fin. With a flick of its flukes, the boat sailed into the air, spilling everyone. The monster then returned and, with those same flukes, battered the sea until the water turned a frothy red. Only Captain Peckab's whaler was left.

That boat stayed adrift, oars raised, waiting.

Moby Dick surfaced, spouting defiantly, and faced the captain. They were maybe four to five hundred feet apart. Simultaneously, all oars bit into the water and the captain's whaler lurched ahead. The whale did not react, but floated as if just sunning itself. Peckab's boat quickly closed the gap between them. At about fifty feet, the captain, standing at the bow and brandishing a harpoon, threw.

The weapon struck true, driving in high on the whale's snout. It snorted again and lunged, hitting the whaling boat with its mouth wide. The whaler, caught beneath its jaw, was pushed down beneath it. Again I heard the crunching of wood as the boat shattered, men and pieces of boat spilling from the sides. The monster shook its massive head and turned away, a red trail dripping down its front. It slowly returned below the waves.

A collective breath escaped from the ship's crew, part sigh and part fateful moan. The first officer called muster on the main aft deck. He said a heartfelt prayer for the deceased and then quickly dispersed crews to assess the damage and execute repairs. No other boats were aboard, so rescue had not been an option. Until it grew too dark, the sailors in the crow's nest had seen no survivors.

I was tasked to help keep the broken rudder from drifting from the ship. Five of us jumped in and swam it back to the ship's stern. We then began lashing lines to it that were fed to us through the stern rail and tied off to the mizzen mast. Each of us had a short axe to cut off sharp wood chunks and excess line.

I had lashed the final line by lantern light while the others climbed back aboard and stood ready for my turn. Michael stood at the rail and suddenly screamed, "Look out!" just as I became aware of a low, throbbing sound behind me. As I turned to see, without waiting for another heartbeat, the ship was hammered by a massive tremor almost tipping it. The rudder I stood on rose on a swell and slid to port, breaking three of our lines. I managed to hold on, almost losing the lantern. From inside the ship came a second shudder, but this one due to an explosion.

I guessed the stored whale oil had caught fire from whatever caused the first shock. Smoke billowed from hatchways on deck and from portholes in the hull. A third blast knocked me off the rudder. By the time I'd climbed back onto the rudder, the entire ship was ablaze. Even the sails and rigging were afire, burning shards dripping onto the decking.

I spotted one of the axes dug into the rudder and quickly cut the lines we'd spent hours securing. The ship would sink, of that I was certain. I needed some distance so not to be dragged down with it. I called out hoping to draw attention for any others to save themselves and join me. Once loose, I dove in and began pushing the rudder, now my raft, away from the ship.

*

I sat at dawn amidst the flotsam, adrift on an oily ocean. Alone. All were gone, sad victims of an angry whale. The ship and all its stores lost. All to appease the cravings of a vengeful soul. I felt so sad for all, even Peckab. What a horrible way to die, digested in the whale's bowels. Even he didn't deserve such a fate.

But now I had to face my own. For the second time in less than two weeks, I lay upon the open sea with no craft under me. Now only broken, soaked timbers. I had no water, no food, and no idea which sea I inhabited. Being within the depths of the ship, I'd no clue the direction we'd sailed following my first rescue. We could be hundreds of leagues from a coast, or an island could be just beyond the horizon. But which direction? If only I'd asked. Michael would have known.

But none of this pity could help me. By noon, I'd a plan. With the axe, I cut my leg and bled into the water in the hopes of drawing a predator. Meat is meat and I could sink the axe blade deep into a shark or whatever swam too near to investigate.

By evening nothing had swum close. Only the sounds of the sea and a breeze that tickled my ears reached me, until a faint cough caught my attention. I stood and gazed intently toward some debris floating nearby. That seemed to be the most likely source, save that I might be losing my mind. I dove in and swam about one hundred feet or so, listening and calling out. Finally, with his obviously broken arm wedged in the remains of his whaling boat was Peckab, badly broken.

I whispered in his ear that I'd come for him. He shifted his gaze toward me, but I could tell he saw me not.

"Who's there? Is that you, Herman?" he gasped.

"No, it is Santiago. You rescued me," I explained. A motion in the waves, just past him ... I saw a fin break the surface, heading toward us. *Shark!*

"Who?" he asked again.

"The old man you saved," I said. "We must hurry to my raft. Your ship is sunk." I spoke as I examined his arm to see if I could be gentle dislodging it. I didn't think so. "Captain, this is going to hurt, but I have no choice. There are sharks in the water." I fastened a firm grip on his arm.

He panted, "No, let me die. The white demon has won." He began to sob. "Let me die, old man. Let me die."

I yanked his arm free of the wreckage. He screamed long and loud. I wasted no time and swam him back to the raft. He made no sounds and I focused on the shark fin, meandering ever closer.

At the raft, I tried to raise him from beneath, but could not. So, I climbed onto its timbers while grasping his collar. I was suddenly pulled off the raft and lost my grip of Peckab. Righting myself underwater, I could see only his receding shape flopping in the mouth of a large shark. Nature had been avenged.

I sat down and sang. It was the only thing I could think of doing. Again, from my youth, both *mi madre* and *mi abuela* sang to us when we were sad. I sang until the sun hung just above the western horizon, then I cut my other leg and sought some food.

The waters were gentle and, with the lessening light, I scanned them intently for I was starving. After some minutes, a movement under the raft caught my eyes. I pulled my leg up and raised the axe, anxious to eat.

A massive shape neared the surface just beyond my reach. It seemed wrong ... lighter than any fish and immense. *The whale!* My heart suddenly beat twice as fast and my breathing was shallow and as quick as a spent lover. The way it attacked the boats, leaving Peckab until the last ... I feared it returned to see him, and thus me as well, finished.

A blast of bubbles rose to the surface along with a hissing sound and the thing lifted itself to the surface. Water slid from its metallic sides and there were windows with light shining from within. Then, with a thunk and clicking sounds, a hatch opened from its top like on any ship and a man, completely dry, stepped up and waved to me. "Ahoy, can I help you, old man?"

I stood bewildered and waved back. "*Si, senor. Si.*"

I was twice saved.

*

As I received the man's help to get aboard this metallic ship, another man joined us on the deck. "Mr. Land, what have we found?"

The man helping me to the decking answered. "Aye, Captain. We have one survivor, sir, this gentleman."

"Only one?"

"Aye, sir. He's all we've come across."

"I see, Mr. Land. Launch a boat and scour all this flotsam for possible survivors. And be quick, sir." He added glancing to the west. "There's less than an hour's light to be had."

"Aye, sir." He answered. Then to me he said, "Glad we came back. If you go down that hatch, there are others to take care of you."

I walked toward the hatch and the man identified as the captain. "Thank you, sir. You have a miraculous vessel. I am Santiago Gallardo, sir. I ..."

He waved me silent. "You and I will talk after you are fed and have had a chance to clean up, my good man. Plenty of time to talk later."

"Thank you, sir. Thank you." I followed another man down the hatchway and through several hallways of metal and was delivered to a room in which I bathed and ate. New clothing awaited me in my quarters, a different room. I donned these and laid on a bed. Sleep came quickly.

*

After breakfast, I was taken by the same man I first saw, Mr. Land, to another part of this strange ship and told to sit and wait for their captain. I have never been in a finer room in a house on land as I was in now. It had no windows that I could see. A thick, green carpet, rich-looking wall hangings and dark wooden furniture filled the room. The walls looked papered with fancy paintings all through the room. One

216

section held a shelving full of many, many books. Three hundred forty-eight, since I had both the curiosity and time to count them. Lamps lit the room, but not oil or candles. Their light was constant and left no soot I could see.

This room was all very different from the metal walls and floors I walked on to get here. Its ambience made me feel its owner was both important and wealthy. I still sat, taking in the atmosphere when an oaken door opened and a man in a smoking jacket entered. The man was older for he sported a trimmed white beard and had a full flock of white hair. His skin was rugged but pale. He approached me with hand extended.

"Hello, hello my good man. Welcome to my ship! Such a wonder that you survived the destruction of the whaling ship. I am Mason Dakkar, captain of this ship, the submarine *Cachalot*. It is a word that means sperm whale, a one-of-a-kind wonder. I would be honored to give you a tour of her, after we've had a chance to get to know each other. Tell me of yourself." He sat down in an overstuffed chair and gave me his full attention.

"Yes, sir, thank you," I said. "My name is Santiago Gallardo. I am a fisherman from Anguilla. It is an island near the ..."

"Oh yes, yes. I know Eel Island well," he interrupted.

I spent the next half an hour telling my saga of the marlin, the sharks, and my time on the *Factotum Mortua* until its demise by the white whale, Moby Dick. Captain Dakkar sat comfortably during most of the story, but seemed on edge as I described the battle with the whale.

"And what of your captain, senor?" he asked.

"Captain of the *Factotum Mortua,* not a captain of mine. He survived his battle with Moby Dick, but was badly hurt. I found him amidst the wreckage but he died, taken by a shark, before I could rescue him."

"Thank you, Senor Gallardo," he offered. "It is good to know what happened. As I am a man of honor, it behoves me to tell you that part of the story you do not know."

I looked at him quizzically.

He continued. "We shall talk of it at dinner tonight. Before I go to attend to my ship, you are welcome to wander about, but please understand that there are areas vital to the submarine's operation and safety that you cannot visit on your own. You are welcome to remain here ..." He stopped and walked to the narrower front wall which opened under some control he fingered, revealing a huge window looking out on the sea. "... and witness the spectacles that only the ocean can show you."

"*Mia madre!*" I heard myself whisper.

He smiled as I gawked and added, "I'll return to you shortly."

I stood in awe that the room was not flooded, it seemed so close. The thick window spanned the floor to the ceiling, about seven feet, and a good twelve feet across.

I have no idea how much time elapsed as I spent it all seeing the ocean from beneath the waves. It was one and the same sea I'd spent my life upon, venturing into it as needed. But the expanse of water shocked me. So much, so deep, and so sparsely scattered was the life I saw. And I witnessed much! Schools of hundreds of tarpon each the size of a man or bigger, lone fish I did not know, sharks swimming with many other sharks alongside other fish I'd assumed they'd all eat, and whales beautifully arching and twisting with calves matching their moves. I even saw marlin, so peacefully swimming I came to tears.

We must have been sailing—do I call it that without sails?—closer to the surface as, despite my efforts so much so that my eyes ached, I could not spy the bottom. The greenish blues, though, streaked with wavering sunlight, were nearly hypnotic. I came to see when some cloud passed overhead that the light beams dissolved into greyness, only to reappear with breathtaking brilliance.

Sometime later, I heard the door open behind me. "It is a wonder, is it not?" Dakkar faced the window, hands on his hips. "But this is only one of the magnificent wonders of the *Cachalot*. Come! I'll show you."

For the next two hours we went from bow to stern on all three of its levels. The ship held more art than some museums, all formerly owned by Dakkar's family. It also was a trove of scientific wonders giving the ship, this underwater vessel, the ability to rise and fall in the oceans like a plane in the air. It used a fuel based on electricity that also lights the interior and can shine lights around it. The air is filtered by it, too.

Since it sails beneath the surface, it is not limited to windage and can travel where its crew wants to go. The captain told me they were heading toward their island, but did not provide details of which one or its location. We'd be sailing for another three days to reach it. Once done there, he then promised to return me home.

I'd been gone for weeks and almost had given up thinking of returning to my modest home on the northern beaches of Anguilla. I missed those sands, my neighbors, the forests, and even the rocky shoals of the eastern coast where the fishing was always an adventure.

Nothing like I'd lived since the marlin. But then, I'm sure my friends must suspect me dead by now, some accident or Nature herself claiming my life.

My face must have shown my sudden mood swing.

"Santiago? Are you all right?" my host asked.

"*Si*. Yes, I am fine. Your offer to return me to my home touched me and I realized how much I'd missed it. I am in your debt, sir, yet again."

We were interrupted by Mr. Land, Ned was his first name. He spoke quietly in Dakkar's ear, who then nodded. Land left. Dakkar told me a problem had arisen that he needed to attend to immediately. He made to leave, but then paused, and asked if I valued life, all life.

"Of course," I answered.

"What of a life that threatens other lives?"

"If possible, it must be stopped."

"Then, you are welcome to come with me." We walked to a larger room with many, many gauges and pipes and controls. I saw it earlier on his tour. He'd called it the control room. A gush of water spilled from the overhead hatch and Dakkar motioned me to follow.

We came up on deck. Ned Land stood peering through a telescope, which he then handed to Dakkar. When the Captain had looked, he handed it to me.

"Have you used one of these before?" he asked.

"I have, sir. A sailor from a ship that visited my island let us look through his," I explained.

"Good. Close your one eye and look toward the horizon, there," he said, pointing.

"No! It is attacking the other ship!" I exclaimed. "Why?"

"Piracy is a popular trade at sea. It flies the skull and crossbones, the pirate flag. Come, we will stop them." He took the telescope and we returned below.

I waited in the front parlor with the big window. I both saw and felt the increasing speed of the submarine. We were quite near the surface and I felt a sudden and profound vibration to the ship along with a distinct low, almost growling sound.

In the near distance, the keel of a ship appeared. Within seconds, as I realized we would, we struck the underside of that ship, sending a tremendous jolt through the *Cachalot*. The vibrations ceased and the ship turned sharply, causing me to brace myself with the wall.

I ran to the door to offer help should any be needed because of the collision and found the parlor door locked. After several minutes of pounding and calling out, I realized I'd been kept here deliberately.

*

Two hours later, Dakkar came in. I sat staring out the window, unsure of what to say.

He sat quietly in his chair. "I do apologize for keeping you here. I felt you'd be safest here and, quite frankly, not in the way. Our task was necessary."

"How are we still afloat after striking—what was it, the pirate ship?"

"Yes. The *Cachalot* is equipped with a saw-like lance. We extend it—I'm sure you felt the vibrations caused by the water's friction—and ram a ship, ripping out its keel and sinking her. We only use it to defend ..."

I stood and faced him. "Use it to defend what? A ship being attacked by pirates?"

"Yes."

"And a whaling ship hunting a white whale?"

He paused before saying, "Also yes."

I continued. "How dare you sit and speak of death so calmly! How many sailors died just now at your intervention? Do you want to know how many you killed on the whaler? The white whale killed about fifty. You only killed thirty, thirty-five. It is like you have declared war, but forgot to tell those you would kill."

He sat and barely whispered, "If you are willing to put me on trial, I must be allowed to present my story."

"As you wish." I sat back down intent on hearing his story.

"I'd first seen the albino many years ago along the coast of Brazil. In addition to being all white, it was huge! I felt a special bond to the beast. Both he and I were considered different by the rest of the world. Not a pleasant thing, mark my words. I named this vessel after

220

that sperm whale when it was launched. I've seen him only half a dozen times since.

"Three days ago, we were sailing north and we heard a good deal of noise ahead. One of our scientific instruments listens to the sounds in the sea. We followed them and came across the albino, your Moby Dick, diving passed us with a harpoon in its forehead. We surfaced enough to see the wreckage and surmised what happened. I admit here that I acted out of rage against those who obviously sought to destroy such a rare creature.

"So I ordered the sinking of the whaling ship you were on. I do apologize, but I knew some price must be exacted. I had no idea the albino had damaged your vessel until I heard your story.

"I was surprised when your ship exploded. Most ships just flounder, capsize, and sink. The *Factotum Mortua* must have had a cargo hold of oil barrels that spilled and burned.

"I take full responsibility for the loss of the ship and its crew. And again, I am sorry to you for that necessity and for what you were forced to endure. It was in the hopes of finding any survivors that we returned at all. It was then that we found you."

I sat silently, fists clenched in my lap. I finally managed to ask him, "And how do you propose to account for the deaths of thirty-five sailors and the cost of the ship and its stores?"

He stood up stiffly and inhaled deeply. "Pirates are acknowledged criminals and, having broken mankind's laws and those of God, deserved to die. I spared them the time and cost of a trial. I had hoped you, as a fisherman, would understand the need for the whalers to pay for their crimes against the sea and its creatures.

"Mankind has usurped Nature. They may rule their lands, but they are not the rulers of the oceans! I will not allow them to rape and pillage here. Man is not the master here!

He walked out.

I sat in disbelief. This man I had come to admire murdered two entire ships' crews and sent their vessels to the seabed. The pirates I can understand, but not the *Factotum Mortua*. Only Peckab should be held accountable, unless ... they all ... I had to consider all I heard and saw. How guilty would they be? "The ship sang death" I remember thinking. Perhaps, as radical his means, perhaps Dakkar was justified?

*

I'd eaten in my room. He came to talk and sat uncomfortably on the edge of my bed.

"Santiago, I find I need to apologize to you. My reactions, I fear, were governed by my emotions. I so wanted you to understand the reasons for my admittedly desperate actions. I failed to convince you and you now must think me a murderer. I have felt comfortable with you and I felt I could confide in you, bare my deepest, darkest secret."

I sat at the chair at my table. "You did what your heart told you must be done. But it was a drastic and dastardly thing, killing innocent sailors. Yes, they sailed to kill whales. I have spent my life killing fish. How are we different?"

Dakkar's face distorted and he began to cry. Openly weeping, he laid on the bed and smothered his face in the pillow.

After some minutes, he sat up and collected himself. "I spoke with you about being different and how that has motivated my life and bonded me to the albino. My difference isn't as obvious only because I have hidden it, but it is why my family disowned me and why I killed them for it."

Dakkar stood and loosened the tie on his smoking jacket. He raised his shirt and exposed full breasts as you would find on any woman. "I assure you, Santiago, I am as male as you." He dropped his pants to prove his point. He was.

"Somehow, Nature has branded me as being different. I was considered an aberration by my father, locked away and later disowned. He died by my hand and I took his treasures and burned the family estate. I fled and found an island. We are sailing there now. I then sailed for many years collecting knowledge and science. I returned and, with help, constructed this ship.

"I disavow humanity for its cruelty and wanton greed. I ask you to try to understand, to keep my secret, and to forgive me my sins. I value your friendship." He stepped to the door and paused. "Well?" he asked.

"Your secrets are safe. I will work to understand the rest."

"Understood and accepted."

*

That night, the *Cachalot* surfaced to get fresh air pumped in.

While we stood on the deck, Dakkar's gaze strayed to the heavens. "Beautiful, is it not?" he asked me. But before I could answer, he continued. "So few look at the stars and those that do see only lights. Some even study them, but only a few can use them as others read the topography of the land.

"Sailors do. You and I, eh, *amigo*, we know how to look at the stars. We see a map, a guide to get from where we are to where we want to be. Aristotle and Copernicus, Tycho and Galileo. All of those intellectual giants focused on the stars seeking a better understanding of them. You and I and others making their way in the oceans use what they discovered and deduced.

"Wait until we get home. I have a telescope larger than almost any. I have seen much through that spyglass, looking upon the surfaces of our moon, of Mars, the moons of Jupiter, and have counted the rings in Saturn's necklace. And we will be there in time for Mars's closest orbital point to our Earth. That is the main reason for us to return now. That, and to execute some timely repairs."

Two days later we'd arrived. I saw the mountainous side as we approached, but then we submerged. When the hatch opened, it was like daylight had been banished.

Two men came up the ladderway behind us. Each had a lamp. I looked up but saw no stars.

Dakkar read my actions and said, "We are in a deep cave just beyond the coast a quarter way around the island from the natural lagoon. We had to dig it out a bit to allow the ship to enter underwater. That way no surface ship has access." He shone his lamp ahead of the submarine to a faint glow. "That is our dock and the way up into the residence. A full machine shop is just to our left."

"It is warm in here," I noted.

"Oh yes. The island is volcanic, so I designed the house to take full advantage of the geothermal energies. A turbine is spun by the natural steam. That generates the electricity the shop and the house use. The ship's engines generate their own.

We followed the staircase, hewn from the rock, several stories up. Small gaps, mere inches, were spaced along the way to allow daylight in to illuminate our way. We entered Dakkar's home. I found it to be as elegant as his room on the ship. Thick carpets, wooden accents and doorways, and artwork including some statues filled the rooms and halls.

"This was a series of smaller caves until I moved in here, except for the stairwell. That was nearly the way you just saw it, except for the steps themselves," he explained. The tour continued throughout the complex and ended more than an hour later on an outside covered patio. At its center stood a large device, a long cylinder pointing up and out. The telescope.

"The roof is canvas and painted to match the surrounding rock so, when closed like this, it matches and this patio is hidden, virtually rock to anyone looking. I open it only at night, sometimes stargazing all night. We'll spy on Mars tonight. We are on the southern face of Nemo's Peak, so I get a good range of view."

"Nemo's Peak? Who's Nemo? I asked.

"No one, really. An old friend, long since dead."

I ascertained his reluctance to discuss this "long dead" someone, so I let the issue die. We continued settling in and I was allowed to roam. I returned to the cavern. A series of overhead lights were shining, filling the cave with enough light to find one's way. I watched as sailors unloaded stores of food and crates from the ship, switching on lamps in the shop area which were much closer to sunlight within a smaller area.

Returning to the residence, I passed a doorway as it was opening. Dakkar stepped out and, on seeing me, stopped. He gestured for me to enter, saying only, "Please."

I did. He turned a knob and wall lamps went on as he closed the door. "Thank you for coming in. I want to share something." He walked to a drapery laden wall and pulled a sash across it, opening the thick deep blue, velvet drapery. In a recess were two paintings. Beautiful, rich oils and fancy gold gilded frames on each. One was of a woman, angelic in her beauty with long, dark hair. Very Spanish in her look. The other was of an infant in a cradle. Soft, fair skin and eyes that could see angels. The artist had painted a subtle suggestion of an obscure background figure with wings curved around and supporting the cradle.

"These are the most beautiful paintings I've ever seen," I told him. "Special to you?"

Dakkar turned sad eyes toward me. "My wife, Maria, and our daughter, Gabriela. They were murdered by sailors who stopped here when I was gone. I saw their ship leaving as I approached my island. After discovering their crimes, I followed and sank their ship, being certain that every one of them died."

"Dakkar ..." I began. "My friend, all people are not evil. I understand your anger. I forgive you your sins, my friend. And, I am so very, very sorry for your loss." We embraced.

"After dinner, we will search the skies," he whispered.

That is just what we did. We had dinner as an entire crew, and, when dark enough, I met Mason on the deck. The roof was rolled back and the sky was ablaze with stars. Seeing them, I knew we were south of my Anguilla, but could not say how far. He sat with some papers and notes, positioning the telescope and then announced he had found Mars.

He allowed me to look and described in great detail what I was seeing and that it was the closest to Earth right now. "Perigee" he called it.

I pulled away from the telescope's eyepiece and remarked, "Very interesting. But you didn't mention what the bright flashes were on Mars's surface."

He sat and looked himself for several minutes, consulting his notes. He jotted some additional ones and looked again. "Most interesting," he said mostly to himself. "They look familiar, like a volcano or some kind of gaseous explosion. Almost like seeing a canon firing toward us," he mused aloud.

"Like someone on Mars is shooting at the Earth?" I asked, then chuckled. "Mankind is far too busy fighting itself. I can't imagine a war between worlds."

***

Carefree
by Paul K. Metheney

Carefree. That's how he envisioned bikers as a kid from the back of his parents' station wagon. *Free as the wind, blasting down the highway, swerving in and out of traffic, without a worry in the world.* He longed to be grown up enough to own a motorcycle and experience true freedom. He couldn't wait for such carefree abandonment, with no homework, girls, parents, or ANYTHING to weigh him down. That would be the life!

(Puff!)

He reminisces back to his teens, borrowing his friends' dirt bikes, worrying that if he broke them, he couldn't afford to fix or replace them. Eventually, he struggled and scraped to buy his own, albeit used, Honda 450cc Nighthawk. It was all he could afford, mowing grass and working part-time for a construction contractor after school. As much as he cherished his Nighthawk, it didn't satisfy his needs. He ached for a big bike to transport him and his cares effortlessly down rural byways in a Peter-Fonda-esque blur.

Man, I need to slow it down a bit. This bend is a perfect place for a deer to jump out of the brush. When I crest this hill, what's on the other side: a line of traffic at a standstill or a sudden turn? Do I have enough gas to limp to the next service station? I need to remember to check my chain when I get home. Is it going to rain?

(Puff!)

As he neared high school's end, he sold the 450 to help pay for his upcoming tuition. His father passed away a few years prior, and his mother squirreled away the meager life insurance money available to them, to finance his way through college. He sold anything he owned of any value, including his treasured Nighthawk. It crumbled the edges of his heart to do it, but he needed every nickel to afford school. He continued to labor part time in construction while attending day and evening classes at the local community college, helping his mother as much as possible. His height and size landed him a job on weekends as a bouncer. The contractor work, a yard-sale set of weights, and his father's genes gave him the physique of a bodybuilder. But athletics never interested him. Running with a football never gave him the thrill of straightening the curves of the Blue Ridge Parkway. Not a week passed in which the road warrior in him didn't yearn to put his "knees in the wind" once more.

How can I afford a bike? I need to work at least one or two more jobs per week to afford it. Mom needs even more help with the rent. What if I talk to my boss at the bar about more hours? When I do get a bike, how much will it cost to maintain it?

(Puff!)

With a commercial art degree in hand, he snared a job as an assistant art director for a small ad agency. Although thankful for gainful employment, no one would describe his art director salary as astronomical. Despite his working multiple jobs throughout school and the limited help his mother could provide, he had accumulated what seemed a crushing mountain of debt from tuition and books. To add to his worries, his mother was getting on in years, and he continued to live at home to help her financially and physically around their small, two-bedroom bungalow.

A year out of college, he had scrimped enough to place a down payment on a Harley Davidson Road King. Several years old, but as clean as the day it came off the assembly line, the Harley called to him. It would require working two or three jobs for several years. He became desperate to find regular freelance jobs to help make the nut, but he now owned a REAL bike. His mother pestered him until he agreed to take the AMA motorcycle safety course, with a certain amount of reluctance, even though he already had his motorcycle endorsement from his Nighthawk days. Upon completing the three-day course, he realized it had knocked the rust off of some of his old skills and in truth, he learned a few new things to make him a safer rider.

And ride he did. Without exception, each moment not working or helping out at home, he rode. His co-workers thought of him as *eccentric* for always riding his motorcycle to work. He took every precaution: checking its tires on a regular basis (a blowout at sixty miles per hour could put a real crimp in your day), filling any fluids as needed, inspecting his tires daily for tread depth. He wore a Kevlar-armored jacket and pants, and always wore his helmet, though the state did not require one over the age of twenty-one. He ached for the peace of mind and freedom nothing but the open road could give him.

Whoa! Where did that BMW come from? Oh. Texting while driving. Damned kids will be the death of me. Okay, maybe she is just a few years younger than I am. Checking over my shoulder twice to make sure a semi changing lanes doesn't crush me like a beer can. Triple checking the mirrors. You just can't be too sure. Gotta keep scanning the road for debris.

(Puff!)

He remembers worrying about needing to build a shed large enough to keep his bike out of the elements. Later, when his mother could no longer drive, he held on to their old family car, to ferry her to her treatments and run errands for her, but vowed never to be dependent on four wheels himself.

Is that car going to come to a complete stop at the intersection? Do I have enough tread on my tires to pass inspection? What if a dog ran out in front of me right now?

On his first vacation from the agency, he rode his motorcycle to Sturgis Bike Week in South Dakota. He had pinched pennies for more than a year, skipping lunches and living like a miser to afford the camping trip. The ride itself took up most of his time off, and he spent very little actual time in Sturgis itself. Punctuated with the stress of riding racetrack-like slabs of highway, the heavy traffic he encountered, the threat of running out of gas, the possibility of the bike breaking down, and areas where his cell phone had no signal, the entire trip had exhausted him with a general sense of tension and strain.

Damn! Soccer mom fussing with a van full of kids turned left on me! My front tire is going to need to be replaced soon if I keep locking them up like that. Reminds me of the weekend a biker in Daytona swerved out in front me during Bike Week. Surviving involved a matter of inches, lightning reflexes and good luck.

All these memories flood through him as his mom arrives home, bone tired and weary. Her bus stop is a long walk from their home, and the chemotherapy is poisoning the life out of her. With a weak smile for him and asking about his day, she hangs her coat and starts to prepare his supper.

Do I have enough money for gas? Is some dumbass going to veer off the exit ramp at the last second? Most accidents happen at intersections.

As it always does, The Memory creeps into his forethoughts. The late night at work. Feeling of exhilaration as he mounts his bike to head home. The Cadillac swerving into his path. The split second of flight as he hurtles over the handlebars. The crunching impact of the telephone pole on his back. The weeks of surgery. The endless insurance forms. The fruitless lawsuits.

She moves aside the tube into which he puffs to move his wheelchair, wiping applesauce slipping from his slack mouth. She feeds him another spoonful, and all he thinks is:

"God, I'd give anything for those carefree days again!"

***

Post-19
By Steve Rouse

Jeanne got out of the police car, staring in disbelief. "Just like you said," she muttered. "But, what the hell is it?"

"We were thinking that you might have some idea, Dr. Kinders. At least, that's what we were hoping anyway." A police officer in an unwrinkled uniform stood next to her and extended his hand.

"No! Protocols. I'm sorry, but I forgot my gloves."

"My apologies," he said. A thing ... about the size of an apple, appearing metallic, hovered about five feet above the pavement right in front of the Target store's main entrance. They both stood six feet apart, looking at it. "Anything come to mind? A project, maybe, of an outstanding student of yours?"

Jeanne looked at him. "I teach physics, not science fiction. This is nothing of mine, nor anything anyone has ever mentioned to me. In fact, why the hell am I involved in this again? I mean, I've only been out of the hospital for about a week, just starting to feel human again," she said while adjusting her mask.

"I'm Commander Michaels, Phil Michaels, Metro PD. From what I'm told, this thing just showed up a few hours ago like out of a bad sci fi film in a flash of light. And, according to our officers, whenever someone touches it, it tells them they aren't you and to go get you."

"This is too bizarre. Honestly, Commander, I have no ideas ... just too creepy. May I go now?"

"Please come with me," Michaels said while stepping toward the thing.

"No!" It didn't come out as forceful as she'd intended.

"Not even as a scientist?" he asked.

"I'm an educator." Jeanne Kinders put an emphasis on that last word.

Commander Michaels beckoned with an outstretched arm. "With a doctorate in applied condensed matter physics."

She sighed and walked toward him.

Scientifically, she was curious. It had no lights, nor made any discernable sound. Silvery in color with subtle washes of sky blue and orange radiating from its top and bottom alternately.

"Like some kind of techno-chameleon," he said.

"Whatever that is," Jeanne said.

He cleared his throat. "Now watch."

With his hand still gloved, he touched the device. It did not react. He pushed against it. It did not move. "Now, the interesting part."

He removed his glove and put his hand around it. A pleasant, feminine voice emitted from it. "You are not Dr. Jeanne Kinders. Please summon her. She must be here within the next twenty-one hours and forty-three minutes."

Michaels faced her. "And there you have it. Assuming a one-day timer, it's been waiting for you for two hours and seventeen minutes. That coincides with our report of the thing's appearance."

Her mind whirled. What was it? Where did it come from? And, the bottom line question, what could it—or rather its makers—want with her?

She took in a deep breath and winced. Her lungs still ached from a recent bout with the coronavirus. Ten days in the hospital, six of those on a respirator. Standing where she was, she said aloud, "I am Dr. Jeanne Kinders. What do you want?"

It just hovered there.

Waving her arms at it, she whistled and yelled, "Yoo hoo, over here."

Nothing.

"Maybe you have to touch it." He looked at his hand. "I have. See? No burns or anything."

She frowned. "Yeah, but it isn't asking for you." Jeanne Kinders looked at it again. Nothing about it made sense. She'd not seen anything like this anywhere. "What is it?" more of a sigh than a question.

"Touch it. We might find out."

She reset her stance, getting up enough gumption—like going in to see the parents of one of "those" students. "Well, I guess there is only one way."

She stepped up to the orb and lightly grasped it between her forefinger and thumb. A gentle pressure rippled across her thumb.

The voice said, "Welcome, Dr. Jeanne Kinders. Thank you for coming. Please continue touching this device. This will take but a moment."

In two breaths they were bathed in a very bright flash of light.

Commander Michaels winced hard when the blinding light hit his eyes. Blinking, he asked, "Dr. Kinders, are you all right? Dr. Kinders?"

He stood there alone. No device, no Dr. Kinders. "Damn it!" he said aloud.

*

It took several moments for her eyes to adjust. She shivered. That little ball kicked out one helluva series of sensations, none of which last more than a nanosecond. A quick electrical shock followed by a wash of extreme cold and then a soothing warmth.

Jeanne clenched and stretched the hand she'd used to touch the orb. Looking around, she found herself in a small featureless room. Then it got interesting.

"Welcome, Dr. Jeanne Kinders." It was the same voice. She looked around but failed to see the orb.

It continued. "You are about to enter a sterilization area. You are asked to disrobe and proceed through the shower area until you are thoroughly wet. Please keep your eyes closed as the sanitizer can damage your eyes. Once through, dryers will blow you dry. There is no time limit on this.

"When you are ready, a set of sterile clothes is available. Please put them on when you are dry and join us on the other side of the door. Wave your hand in front of it to open it."

"Where am I?" Jeanne asked.

"All of your questions will be answered when we see you," the voice said.

"I'd really like some answers now, or you can stop whatever it is you are doing to me and let me go home."

No response.

Jeanne looked around, determined to wait this out until she had some answers, but found no chair or bench. She leaned against the wall for a bit. Three hours later, she'd gotten comfortable on the floor.

She slept, still weak from her bout with COVID-19 and recent hospitalization.

She woke up coughing, and sat up. She stretched, achy from the unforgiving floor. "Damn," she said as she realized she was still wherever here was.

"All right, damn it. I've had enough. Let me out!" she screamed.

"You have already been told how to get out," said the voice.

"How did I even get ..."

"Your questions will all ..."

"Yes, I know. I know." Jeanne had reached her limit. In a frustrated flurry, her clothes were dramatically thrown down and stomped into a tangled pile. "Turn off your damn cameras, too, perverts!" She had to wait out a coughing fit before entering the shower area.

Stepping out of the shower, her lips stung a bit. The blow dryers did their work, coming from every direction.

"I feel like my car at the Speedway car wash," she noted to no one.

The clothes were a bland cream color and the seams of the pants and shirt sealed like they were magnetic, but there was nothing metallic to them. In a recess in the wall, she found a brush and worked it through her hair.

Still seething from being abducted, she faced a panel in the wall and waved her arm. It rose up and she walked slowly out into a glass-enclosed confine fashioned into a cozy one-room apartment. Three people beyond the glass were dressed in clinical uniforms and applauding her. It was definitely some kind of laboratory, or another hospital.

She slumped into a stuffed chair and cried.

*

Jeanne watched intently as the older woman wheeled her desk chair in front of Jeanne's window and plugged in a headset. She settled into place and smiled at Jeanne.

"Hi, Jeanne. I'm Nancy Spencer, the project manager here. How are you feeling? Did you sleep well last night?"

Jeanne estimated her age to be somewhere around seventy to seventy-five. She wasn't an ancient seventy, either. She looked very well-maintained with smooth skin and salt and pepper hair. "I'm feeling fine, considering I'm being held against my wishes."

Spencer nodded and gave her a wry smile. "I expected as much from you. You aren't being 'held' as much as you are being rescued."

"From what am I being rescued?" Kinders asked.

"The coronavirus."

"You're too late for that one, honey. I've been hospitalized for that little viral villain."

Spencer nodded again. "I know. It was through your hospital records that we found you."

"Then what the hell are you talking about?" Jeanne Kinders asked. There was a rapidly developing sense of frustration to her voice.

"All right. You need to listen. Be careful not to judge and don't let your science get in the way. I'm technically going to be breaking just about every rule in the book ... I think that's how you say it ... to let you know exactly what is going on up until now. Okay?"

"It's your show. Go ahead."

"Good." Spencer said. "Your exposure to the coronavirus, along with approximately 117 million other people, was a first stage. It lasted for twenty-eight months. By that time a vaccine had been prepared and proved to be effective. About ninety percent of the global population was immunized.

"Slowly, things started going awry. By 2024, the global birth rate dropped rather suddenly to a point below the global death rate. Two years later, it was less than half. For every person born, two and a third people were dying. Turns out that this coronavirus had worked its way into our genetic structure and pretty much prevented conception. By 2028, there were no more births.

"Many of the traditional killers mysteriously went away. Diphtheria, cancers of every kind, measles, typhus, leprosy, malaria, and even Ebola and TB disappeared. Immunologists went crazy working to find out why. Again, the coronavirus was hard at work defending its territory from other kinds of infestations."

"Can I interrupt a second?" Jeanne asked.

"Sure," Nancy said.

"This is, to the best of my knowledge, the year 2020. Where the hell do you come off insulting my intelligence with this bull crap story about the future?"

"It isn't the future. It's the past."

"Wha ...?"

"I'm going to take you for a bit of an eye-opening ride," Nancy said as she stood up.

*

The ship allowed Jeanne to wear what amounted to a space suit to maintain her own sterile atmosphere. She asked why.

"None of us have been exposed to COVID-19," Nancy explained. "Being so would probably kill us rather quickly, I might add. We have to keep ourselves and you uncontaminated."

"I don't get it," Jeanne said.

"I promise, you will. But we have to do first things first. Ready?" Nancy spoke into her mic and Jeanne felt the aircraft wobble a bit, then she was pressed into her chair as the ship leaped skyward.

Through the larger windows, Jeanne saw them rising high above a snow-scaped horizon. They banked left and flew high above an expanse of ocean. Within minutes, a darker mass loomed ahead of them as the western sky faded into a new night.

"South America," Nancy said. "Have you flown before?"

Thoughts of her graduation trip to Australia and New Zealand came to mind. "Yes, I have. So, we've been on Antarctica, eh?"

"Good for you."

"How did I get there?" Jeanne asked.

Nancy patted her leg and said, "I'm very close to being ready to tell you that."

As they flew over the southern tip of Chile, the Earth's shadow dominated. The craft veered north and followed the eastern coastline of Argentina. "Would you please look down and tell me what you see?" Nancy asked.

Jeanne had been watching the far away coastline speed passed. "What do I see? I see darkness. I see nothing. Is this what Patagonia looks like? It should be near here, right?"

"Coming up in a few. See anything yet"

"What am I supposed to be looking for? It's too damn dark down there to see much of anything."

"So you're flying over a major continental coastline and you see only blackness. What's missing?"

Jeanne thought for a second. A thought struck her and she silently whispered an apology to her sixth grade geography teacher. "There are no lights. No cities, no roads. What's going on? Oh, God, Nancy, I'm suddenly very scared."

"I told you everything that had happened from a historical perspective. You even called me on it. For me, it had all happened very long ago. For you, it hasn't happened yet. We took you in 2020. All the lights went out about 2047."

"Humanity has died? We're all dead? So what are we doing? Who are you then?" Jeanne's breathing was rapid and shallow.

Nancy came and sat next to her. Even through the fabric of her suit, Jeanne calmed a bit with the touch of Nancy's hand on her arm. "This is the part that gets hard for you to understand. Please know that you and the others are going to be just fine.

"It was the vaccine. We've found that it was the catalyst that resulted in our own destruction ... something about a latent heterotypic plasmid. I don't pretend to understand it. The original coronavirus did mutate us, everyone who got it, gradually became embedded in our genetic code. But it wasn't until the vaccine's introduction that things ran amuck. It fought back.

*

"Those floating orbs, the transfer devices that you were asked to touch, immobilized you and transferred you, not spatially, but temporally. You were pushed ahead in time so we could retrieve you and bring you to Antarctica.

"Brace yourself. The Earth you are seeing right now would be, in human terms, the year 2518.

*

Sleep eluded her. But then Jeanne expected that after Nancy's revelations. Their flight had crossed the Atlantic and headed south along Africa's western coast, also steeped in a primordial darkness. Myriad nightmares drifted through her consciousness. She couldn't help but imagine zombies rampaging through the ruins of mankind's greatest art museums and libraries. At the realization of the death of so much science and factual knowledge, and of friends and family she'd never had a chance to say goodbye to, tears streaked her cheeks—she made no effort to wipe them away.

One thing yet needed to be explained. She considered different approaches to ask, but was undecided on how to crack open a door to information she wasn't certain she wanted to know.

*

Eighteen in all. Seventeen others now all visible to her in glass-fronted chambers identical to hers. Twelve women and six men. Somehow, the monitor stations had all been removed—lowered probably. Nancy and two other women stood in the middle of the room.

"Good morning to all of you. Thank you so much for your patience and understanding in this horrible situation you are enduring. Let's start with some basic facts. First, all of you were exposed to the original coronavirus infestation. Each of you contracted and survived the disease.

"Secondly, none of you were ever a recipient of any kind of vaccine. It simply didn't exist at the time we intervened. Third, we—meaning myself and my two associates who also happen to be my daughters, Bobbi Bakers and Sue Atkinson—are here for the sole purpose of double checking your physical status and preparing you for your future roles.

"Fourth, we are from your future. Scientific and technological advances have made this possible, even practical for us to safely use. The fact that you are here is proof since you have been brought to this present, 498 years in your future. Each of you has seen the dead Earth you now occupy.

"Fifth, the eighteen of you represent a new beginning, the Adams and Eves of your species. You are going to be given a fresh start, the founders of a new humanity. It is through you that humanity will continue. We are part of that future you will create.

"We know this for a fact because we learned all about you, each of you, in our history studies. Each of us is to some extent related to each of you. Exactly how and to which generation is not our concern. But know we bear that relationship to you with distinction.

"You will learn many more things as you go and we cannot divulge any more of our history as we will not unduly influence you and your choices.

"It is time for you to go. Your health, knowledge, and insights will carry you through. I, for one, know you will make us proud. God's love to you all."

The doors at the back of their chambers opened and they were instructed to take a seat on the ship waiting for them. Ten minutes later, Nancy and her daughters, Bobbi and Sue, watched as the ship, a much larger one this time, rose to a point one hundred miles above the South Pole. It flared just like the apple-sized teleporters. As it did, Nancy smiled at her girls and hugged them.

"What was that for?" Sue asked.

"It worked," Nancy said. "Look at us! We're here, so our past is stable. We've set our world, our very existence into motion."

Bobbi asked, "When do they realize the extent of what's happening to them?"

"I asked your great-grandmother, Jeanne Kinders, that once at a family gathering. She said that they all realized it when they saw that the planet they were suddenly orbiting had two moons. All of the rest with their longer lifespans and, of course, meeting their interplanetary neighbors came later.

"Speaking of that, let's go home."

***

ABOUT THE AUTHORS

Paul K. Metheney

Paul was the featured author for dozens of sports magazine articles, has numerous stories published in various Left Hand Publishers and independent anthologies (*Beautiful Lies, Painful Truths Vol.1, Beautiful Lies, Painful Truths Vol.2, It's About Time, Classics ReMixed Vol. I,* and *Classics ReMixed Vol. II*), and is contracted for two collections of his own short stories, and is working on a much-delayed novel or two.

Paul has nearly three decades working in advertising design, print, and graphic design. For nearly thirty years or so, he has been working in the web design, SEO, PPC, social media, and marketing fields, including writing marketing copy for his clients' blogs and social media.

Paul can be reached at his blog on writing, poker, travel, reviews, and all things politically incorrect at paulmetheney.com, on Twitter at http://Twitter.com/PaulMetheney, and on Facebook at http://facebook.com/Paul.Metheney.

In full disclosure, Left Hand Publishers, besides publishing some of his work, has contracted Paul's company, Metheney Consulting, as one of their book cover design artists and marketing consultants to help assist with authors' branding and marketing.

Paul is happily married to his one-time high school sweetheart, loves riding his Can-Am Spyder motorcycle, occasionally smokes a good cigar, and is an avid poker enthusiast. Paul, his wife, and two dogs are currently living full-time in an RV, traveling the country.

Steve Rouse

He has always loved words. However, crafting them into viable stories that carry the full weight of emotion, action, or scene description to the reader that resided in his brain at the time of its writing is another thing altogether. He whittled away at this craft while teaching middle schoolers to love words and stories, too.

Sharing the end product has been an obstacle, as any writer will attest. Bearing his share of rejection scars, he has realized some success. "The Traveler" is Steve's seventh published short story. "The Gilric" in the

Blue Kingdoms' Mages and Magic, a Walkabout Publishing anthology was in 2010. Then his teaching job kept interrupting his writing. In 2018, "Hodag" appeared in Left Hand Publishers' anthology *Mindscapes Unimagined.* "Sailor's Saga" appeared in the first Left Hand Publishers' *Classics ReMixed Vol. I* anthology. Three other shorts have been on the Haunt Jaunt's website, "When You Buy an Old House" (3/16/2019), "The Note" (3/23/2019), and "Nothing" (4/27/2019).

Now retired from teaching, Steve's wife and he enjoy quiet times at home in Northwestern Wisconsin. She with her recipes, he with his writing. The love of kids, grandkids, pets and an occasional zoo trip fills the void.

Win A Free Kindle!

If you enjoyed any of our books, please register to review one of our books (and sign up for our e-newsletter). In our newsletter, we give you previews of upcoming releases, discounts, as well as free stuff for our fans! But if you review some of our books, you can also win a FREE Kindle.
https://bit.ly/2Fc021g

***

Please Review Our Other Books

If you enjoyed this book, or any of our other books, please feel free to leave reviews. All of our books are available at all major online retailers, including Amazon and Barnes. You can also leave reviews at Goodreads.com.

Beautiful Lies, Painful Truths Vol. I **Amazon:** http://amzn.to/2reSyIe **Goodreads:** http://bit.ly/2BobVCi	**Beautiful Lies, Painful Truths Vol. II** **Amazon:** http://amzn.to/2ngBq0i **Goodreads:** http://bit.ly/2slkBpP
Realities Perceived Amazon: http://amzn.to/2Dbe1ny Goodreads: http://bit.ly/2nU9hvw	**The Demon's Angel** By Maya Shah Amazon: http://amzn.to/2EVjj7V Goodreads: http://bit.ly/2son5E2
Drawing from the Well By Rachel Bollinger **Amazon:** https://amzn.to/2th8WGE **Goodreads:** https://bit.ly/2M8h57h	**Terrors Unimagined** **Amazon:** https://amzn.to/2OsldAT **Goodreads:** https://bit.ly/2LkLO17
Suspense Unimagined **Amazon -** https://amzn.to/2UwG7VI **Goodreads -** https://bit.ly/2VlHN1x	**A World Unimagined** **Amazon:** https://amzn.to/2yvJ4vS **Goodreads:** https://bit.ly/2K7b6zj

Mindscapes Unimagined **Amazon -** https://amzn.to/2FNVkZ4 **Goodreads -** https://bit.ly/2ORO1nq	Classics ReMixed Vol. I **Amazon -** https://amzn.to/2M0qRLx **Goodreads -** https://bit.ly/2LZsIQI
Classics ReMixed Vol. II **Amazon -** https://amzn.to/2M0qRLx **Goodreads -** https://bit.ly/2LZsIQI	

***

More Books from
Left Hand Publishers

BEAUTIFUL LIES,
PAINFUL TRUTHS VOL.I

There's an ironic beauty between humanity's love of Life and fear of Death. Life seemingly brings joy, happiness, hope, and love. Death can end sadness, illness, suffering, and pain. We asked writers to "Let the title and quote take your imagination, your story, wherever it wants to go." Join them now as an international blend of authors, both fresh and seasoned, bring you an exceptional menu of speculative fiction, mystery, realism, horror, and the supernatural. If your palate varies from the macabre to the dramatic, *Beautiful Lies, Painful Truths* provides an assortment of tasty treasures that will chill, delight, and give you food for thought.

Reviews

★★★★★

"An incredibly amazing anthology.
Every author in this anthology should be commended for their work in this collection. Bringing in life and death into a collection of stories, all by different authors, and how their writing varies, but brings to life, this grand collection. I believe there was a lot of thought put into which authors would be contributing their work, and how this work will be displayed."

Amy Shannon, Author. Writer. Poet. Storyteller. Blogger. Book Reviewer.
Author Blog: http://bit.ly/2yLHuFZ
Facebook: http://bit.ly/2ho273i
Review Blog: http://bit.ly/2iPVV4x
Amazon Author Page: http://amzn.to/2ynn2qM

***

"The quality of the stories read are amazing, with intricate plots in a short story form coming off as so perfect in their construction. The scope of the imagination of the writers just boggles the mind in the executions of stories that make you think. What might be considered 'good' isn't. What is seen as dark and painful is honestly the way it should be. Major kudos to these stories.

"Life is good and beautiful and death is dark and bad. Maybe not. This book presents twenty-four approaches with an amazing array of imagination in the depths of human drama, supernatural, humor, and unexpected twists. These stories will challenge everything you thought you knew—think again.

"*Beautiful Lies, Painful Truths* has stories guaranteed to challenge your view of life and death in mind-boggling ways, taking you down unexpected paths of the serious, humorous, pathos, and the twisted turns of fate. The qualities of the stories are good. The writers are to be commended. An excellent book. Kudos!"

Bruce Blanchard, Book Reviewer
http://bit.ly/2yLBq09

***

"It's an impressive read… It may be about death, but the mood isn't always dark. This anthology spans several genres including science fiction, horror, mystery, and even some humor. Well-written and well-edited, this book may be long, but it's hard to put down."

David Watson, Book Reviewer

Beautiful Lies, Painful Truths Vol. I
Amazon - http://amzn.to/2reSyIe
YouTube - https://youtu.be/4m1BR6BIBTM
The Reviews on YouTube - https://youtu.be/tTtdf0LQC7Q
LHP's Web Site - http://bit.ly/2FHXzw9
The Reviews on LHP - http://bit.ly/2FHhMlN
Goodreads - http://bit.ly/2BobVCi

***

REALITIES PERCEIVED

Nothing's more dangerous, or delightful, than invoking a cadre of talented authors to create short stories that defy our perceptions of reality. Do we create our own truth? Or does our view of it shape our world? Neither heroes nor heavens, victims nor villains, may grasp the true nature of our being.

From science fiction, to horror and the supernatural, to dramas about the fabric of our existence, this international fusion of artists will thrill you with an eclectic selection of tales that cross all genres. Sit back and be prepared to have your perception of reality both challenged and distorted.

Reviews

★★★★★

"... it kept me on the edge of my seat and I did not want to put it down even to eat or sleep. You have a great book here."

Lori Kibbey
Book Reviewer

Realities Perceived
Amazon- http://amzn.to/2Dbe1ny
YouTube - https://youtu.be/3SLjzDd9o3Y
LHP's Web Site - http://bit.ly/2Do87SE
Goodreads - http://bit.ly/

***

BEAUTIFUL LIES, PAINFUL TRUTHS VOL.II

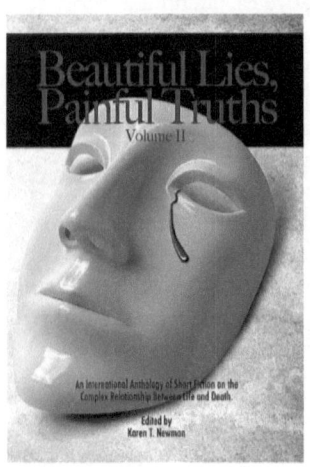

Most believe that Life promises light, bliss, and wonder. Death scares most with its shadow of mortality, darkness, and destruction. But what if those may be, if not lies, just facets of the complicated entities that bookend our existence? Life does not mock Death, but feeds it. Death is not the cessation of Life, but an alteration of existence. What would you do if faced with either truth?

An international galley of authors brings us a second repast of tales featuring the complex relationship between Life, Death, and humanity. From the supernatural to the sublime, these writers, both novitiates and accomplished, serve up a banquet of speculative fiction across a wide spectrum of genres. Beautiful Lies, Painful Truths Volume II will continue to feed your craving for the fantastic.

Reviews

"You have to love an anthology that can give you well-written stories no matter what the genre is and it looks at important issues in addition to death such as love, religion, and redemption."

David Watson, Amazon Book Reviewer

"This collection is a recipe for a lost weekend as I found myself wanting to read 'just one more' until by nearly midnight I had finished all sixteen. I will recommend this to my friends and fellow bibliophiles without reservation."

Natalia Corres
Book Reviewer, Twitter.com/Ncorres

"I read the first volume and was more than excited to read a new collection. Life and death is not just black and white, but all the in-betweens and as the title alludes, both are beautiful, but also full of lies and truths."

Amy Shannon, Author. Writer. Poet. Storyteller. Blogger. Book Reviewer.
Author Blog: http://bit.ly/2yLHuFZ
Review Blog: http://bit.ly/2iPVV4x

Amazon Author Page: http://amzn.to/2ynn2qM

Beautiful Lies, Painful Truths Vol. II
Amazon - http://amzn.to/2ngBq0i
YouTube - https://youtu.be/i8dAMSAbkAM
LHP's Web Site - http://bit.ly/2Dxu9n8
Goodreads: http://bit.ly/2slkBpP

***

THE DEMON'S ANGEL
By Maya Shah

Neha was excited to enter her sophomore year in high school. That was until the boy she went out with sprouted wings, and Lucas, the man who raised her since she was a baby, turned into a demon.

Neha is far from human. She is an angel, the natural enemy of demons. An angel raised by a demon has never been heard of before, which makes some angels see her as a threat. Neha not only has to prove that she does not know anything about demons, she has to prove that she is on the side of the angels.
And she is. So she thinks.
This Young Adult supernatural thriller follows the tribulations of the teenaged Neha as she learns both the truth about her past and herself.

Reviews

★★★★★

'Intensely unique.
The character Neha is something very remarkable, she has depth and grows as a character, especially when she feels she has to prove herself. She thinks she's proving herself a good angel to the other angels, when in fact she's also proving it to herself. Neha is not your typical teenager, nor typical angel."

Amy Shannon, Author. Writer. Poet. Storyteller.
Blogger. Book Reviewer.
Review Blog: http://bit.ly/2iPVV4x

"This flight of fancy with engrossing plot twists tempts anyone ever dumbfounded by a parental deception."
Wendy Landers, Book Reviewer
Author of Just Let Time Pass
www.wendylanders.com

The Demon's Angel by Maya Shah
Amazon - http://amzn.to/2EVjj7V
YouTube - https://youtu.be/FZuvbiGjMcU
Maya Shah's Web Site - http://mayashahbooks.com/
LHP's Web Site - http://bit.ly/2DuXieD
Goodreads - http://bit.ly/2son5E2

***

A WORLD UNIMAGINED

Beyond what is conceivable to what might be is a universe full of the unexpected and the unexplainable. From science fiction to science fantasy, the location of this realm of creation and the mind is...

A World Unimagined.

An international manifest of authors, both new and experienced, crew this voyage to the other side of the unbelievable with stories unique and thought-provoking. This anthology of science fiction short stories transports us to the future, the past, and to cultures and civilizations undreamed of. Set your imaginations to stunned and your minds to light speed.

Reviews

"An eclectic menagerie of *X-Files* material. My favorite was the alien invasion of the Vietnam War's Hanoi Hilton."
Wendy Landers, Book Reviewer
Author of *Just Let Time Pass*
wendylanders.com

"Science Fiction is the great cosmos governed only by the power of What If. It requires minds seeing beyond our world of limitations and creating through imagination different species and stories boggling anything we ever thought. The stories here prove the writers included have done just that. They lay the backdrops of science and provide the fiction of imagination bringing the reader into other worlds and hopefully opening up their minds.

"... for the record, science fiction doesn't usually appeal to me. These stories do ... very nice. If these can turn me on, the book is definitely worth reading."

Bruce Blanchard, Book Reviewer
https://www.facebook.com/bruce.blanchard2

A World Unimagined
YouTube - https://youtu.be/2IO3rl0N_q8
LHP Web Site - https://bit.ly/2IG7Dea
Amazon - https://amzn.to/2yvJ4vS
Goodreads - https://bit.ly/2K7b6zj

***

DRAWING FROM THE WELL
By Rachel Bollinger

A collection of parables, poems, and anecdotes to enhance your spiritual journey. Author, Rachel Bollinger walks you through her personal challenges and triumphs, referencing scripture and entertaining you as she walks closer to God.

Join her as she draws from her well of experience, faith, and victories on a journey of faith and discovery.

Reviews

"We all journey through dark nights of the soul. In this lovely collection, Rachel shares some of her most challenging life experiences and how she coped and grew in grace through the unchanging Word of God. Rachel's memories, in story and verse, are honest, brave, and witty. I came away understanding that the grief I hold in my heart has a permitted place to live."

Susan V. Smith, Amazon Reviewer
https://amzn.to/2JuDfmz

Drawing from the Well by Rachel A. Bollinger
LHP Web Site - https://bit.ly/2LqIzER
Amazon - https://amzn.to/2th8WGE
Goodreads - https://bit.ly/2M8h57h

***

MINDSCAPES UNIMAGINED

Open the door to any genre and you will find places where the unimaginable and the unexplained collide with reality. These stories take you far past that point. From the horrifying to the macabre to the edge of real madness, you will travel to ...

Mindscapes Unimagined.

An international bevy of authors, new and experienced, weave tales both fantastic and exciting. This genre-bending collection of short stories blurs the line between what can be and what can be imagined. No monster, dimension, or mortal villain is off limits. When you are ready to risk sanity and sleep, start on the first page.

Reviews

★★★★★

"*An adventure in reading*

Mindscapes Unimagined is a collection of stories from a grand variety of writers. This collection contains stories stemming from the imagination that blends horror, paranormal and science fiction into one great collection. Most of the authors in this collection, I haven't read before, but I will definitely keep them in mind for future writings. I found the order of the stories very interesting, as one led into another. As Rouse wrote in his story 'Hodag,' 'Did you not just see what joy I brought to these less fortunate? They have broadened their lives, enriched their experiences through my eyes and my story,' it worked perfectly with the concept and collection of the stories. I enjoyed each one, enticing and captivating as the one before it, and yet its own story and imagination of the darkness.

"This collection is definitely a menagerie of stories, from different minds, mixing dark and light, and blending it perfectly. Some are first person, and others are written in third person, and with most stories, it makes a difference and takes a story where it wants to go. I always embrace the anthology that has many different authors, points of views, stories that are shown and not told, and this is no different."

Amy Shannon
Writer. Author. Reviewer.
Amy's Bookshelf Reviews
Facebook: https:// https://bit.ly/2C2YSpS
Blog: https://bit.ly/2mat8sy
Amazon Author Page: https://amzn.to/2ENvyGu
Author Blog: https://bit.ly/2g7KQYn

Mindscapes Unimagined
LHP Web Site - https://bit.ly/2SGN5nf
Amazon - https://amzn.to/2FNVkZ4
Goodreads - https://bit.ly/2ORO1nq

***

SUSPENSE UNIMAGINED

Not all monsters have fangs, fur, or horns. Many times the worst demons are as real as tomorrow's headlines. From criminal suspense to psychological thriller to just plain scary, these short stories of pulse-quickening fear will drive you to ...

Suspense Unimagined

An international fusion of authors, new and experienced, craft tales of terrors unimaginable and thought-provoking. This anthology of suspenseful short stories drags us down paths both inconceivably possible and more horrifying than the supernatural. Unclench your knuckles for a ride to inspire you to think and cringe.

Suspense Unimagined
LHP Web Site - https://bit.ly/2P4mvS4
Amazon - https://amzn.to/2UwG7VI
Goodreads - https://bit.ly/2VlHN1x

***

TERRORS UNIMAGINED

Far beyond what you can imagine lies a dreamscape full of the unexpected and the unexplainable. The supernatural, the paranormal, monsters, demons, magic, witches, and inconceivable horrors reside in a world of...

Terrors Unimagined

An international cadre of authors, both new and experienced, lead you down a path to the other side of the unbelievable with stories unique and thought-provoking. This anthology of supernatural and horror-inspiring short stories drags us screaming into a world of creatures and nightmares undreamed of. Prepare to ponder your nights away.
Sleep is no longer an option.

Terrors Unimagined
YouTube - https://youtu.be/ow4XfWt2q7w
LHP Web Site - https://bit.ly/2MSohot
Amazon - https://amzn.to/2OsldAT
Goodreads - https://bit.ly/2LkLO17

***

CLASSICS REMIXED VOL. I

An anthology of short stories twisting classic stories and your imagination in all new ways.

Alternate versions of stories you know taking you in new directions.

From much-loved fairy fables to time-honored tales, no genre or classic is off-limits. Classics ReMixed Vol. I spins and twists divergent versions of old favorites and stories we all know. Be prepared to have all your...

Classics ReMixed

Classics ReMixed
LHP Web Site - https://bit.ly/2XLgkY9
Amazon - https://amzn.to/2M0qRLx
Goodreads - https://bit.ly/2LZsIQI

***

CLASSICS REMIXED VOL. II

After the success of Classics ReMixed Vol. I, Left Hand Publishers released a second volume of classic tales twisted and spun into alternate versions of stories you know, taking you in new directions.

From much-loved fairy fables to time-honored tales, no genre or classic is off-limits. Be prepared to have all your...

Classics ReMixed Vol. II

Classics ReMixed Vol. II
LHP Web Site - https://bit.ly/2XLgkY9
Amazon - https://amzn.to/2M0qRLx
Goodreads - https://bit.ly/2LZsIQI

***

255

www.ingramcontent.com/pod-product-compliance
Lightning Source LLC
Chambersburg PA
CBHW031942240626
47153CB00003B/833